AFRICA
HEART *and* SOUL

AFRICA
HEART *and* SOUL

– A NOVEL –

MIKE NEIL

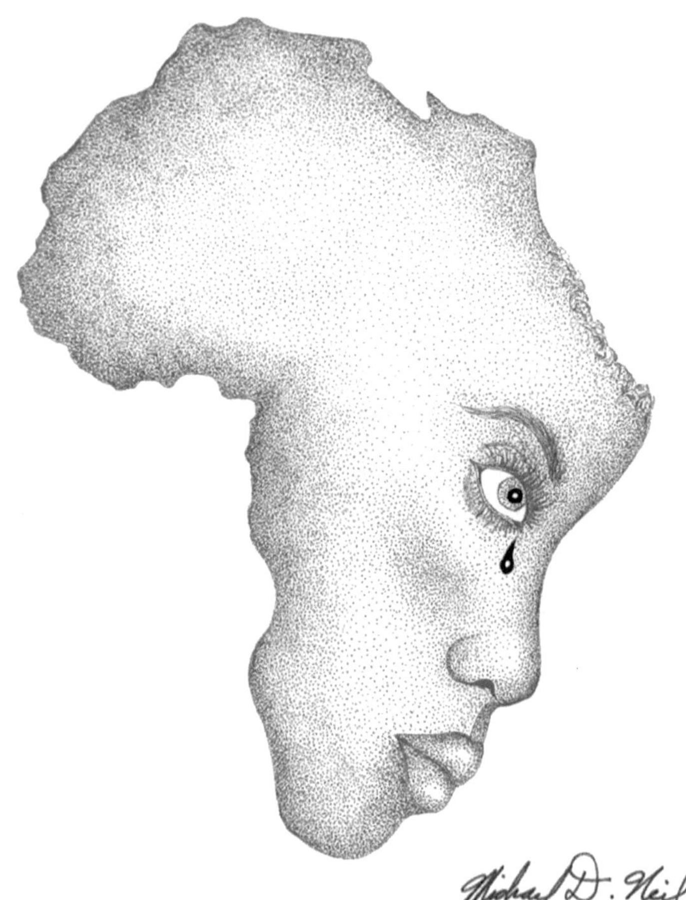

PROLOGUE

My name is Lance Miles, the protagonist of this book. I live in British East Africa with my wife, Esther, an American citizen and a dark-skinned beauty. We found each other here in Africa by chance after she decided to bring the gospel to the African tribes. We grew up together in America, where our parents were friends in the late 1800s. I came to Africa to help my best friend, Johnathan (John) Rivers, with his pursuit of Darwin's missing link.

John is quite the character—flashing, articulate, and adventurous; he draws a crowd when he speaks. Everyone seems to know him and love him. I have the privilege of being his best friend and colleague. I don't know anyone closer to John Rivers except his wife, Betty. She came to Africa in 1912 to prove herself ready and able to take on a safari, which John had much skepticism about. He had been to Africa many times but he'd never felt that Africa was a place for a woman. Betty definitely proved herself worthy as a huntress on an African safari. (I know the word "huntress" might be socially incorrect for some readers, but for me in my context, it is a respectful title.)

John has been an atheist for as long as I have known him. That's what makes the book that comes before this one, *The Miracle of Africa*, such a fascinating story. I have never given God much thought, but I guess I always believed He had to exist, growing up in a church as I did. If God isn't real, then I don't think any of us would exist. When I listened to my wife explain it to me, it all made total sense. (She is quite the Christian evangelist.)

Betty Rivers, while not the main person in that story, in my mind, turned out to be the star of the show. Her strength was particularly on display when she counseled John to be easy on Jason when he wounded a lion on the farm.

When I first met Jason, the young man who came to live with John and Betty in Chicago, my suspicions grew. He seemed too impulsive for my taste. He was too quick to make a decision without consulting people around him who had much more life experience. Jason pulled some real boneheaded, adolescent mistakes along our safari, to the point where I was surprised he made it out alive. But I will be the first to acknowledge that the kid grows on you. Over our time together, I have come to appreciate him very much.

And then, of course, there is Chuck; he is the anchor and voice of reason. It pleased me to see him take Jason under his wing and spend quality time with the boy. Jason will surely benefit from that relationship his whole life.

We knew it would be difficult when Esther and I decided to get married. Somehow, I thought the people in Africa would be more understanding of a mixed marriage. I thought Americans were the only people with prejudiced feelings. Honestly, the pushback caught me by surprise. But I guess that's what makes a truly epic story: the troubles we face and the hardships we have to endure. Suffering always builds character and makes us put down more roots so the winds are less likely to blow us over.

I want to give a shout-out to Mike Neil, our author. He has put so much of himself into our story. With all the research and digging into old books and stories of Africa that he's done, he has made our story come to life. You see, Mike Neil lives in a time when the Africa we all know is long gone. Mike would have been totally lost without the help of authors such as Teddy Roosevelt, Martin and

Osa Johnson, Carl and Mary Jobe Ackley, Ernest Hemmingway, and many more. But seriously, we owe our very lives to this man who created us in his thoughts, almost out of thin air.

I wish I could say that I knew Mike as much as he knows all of us, but that just isn't possible, seeing that we live worlds away. It seems like a "thank you" is so shallow and inadequate for the things he has done for our lives.

God always uses other people to mold and shape our pathway and character. I see how Esther's influence on John Rivers changed him for all eternity. Mike really impacted me personally, and I know our whole team feels the same. I hope you enjoy this sequel to *The Miracle of Africa* as you follow our story. It begins with all of us coming home from the safari. I have to tell you this so you won't be confused about where we have been. I won't tell you any more about that now, though. I will keep it a surprise and let you find out on your own.

With warm appreciation,

Lance Miles

ENGLISH
TEA

CHAPTER 1

OPTIMISM

With great miracles come great tests. The more you know, the more you are attacked. The more you have, the bigger a target you become.

My name is Lance Miles. You may have heard of me because of the miracle that happened to John Rivers, a friend of mine. This story only begins as another great chapter of my life closes. The only truly significant question in the universe is "What now?"—a question that has haunted me since boyhood. I suppose it's a question that will continue to haunt me all the days of my life.

If you missed the story called *The Miracle of Africa*, by Mike Neil, you might want to read it first.

* * *

British East Africa (now Kenya), 1912

"That dot in the trees way down the valley is your farmhouse, isn't it?" said John as he and Betty, Esther, and I sat perched on our horses and overlooking the river valley from a hillside.

"My butt is crying out for home," I replied with a laugh. I glanced back: the number of native porters marching our way had dwindled significantly since we began our journey. We needed fewer and fewer as we progressed, so John had released them one by one. The green hills we had left in the late fall in May had now turned brown.

"You can smell spring in the air," I said.

"That's September," replied Betty. "It's growing season."

"I miss the Big Dipper," said John.

"I just feel like I am living upside down," said Betty.

"It's all very sanguine, though, isn't it? Like spring," I said.

"What does that mean?" she asked.

"Springtime corresponds to the running of blood in your veins—optimistic, hopeful, positive, confident . . . all things I aspire to, and just the sight of home is sanguine to me."

"I suppose all those hours you spent behind a desk weren't wasted," said John. I just smiled and nodded, thinking about the prospect of getting my hands dirty in the coffee fields.

"It will be nice to sleep in my own bed," said Esther, "and be able to cook for myself."

"Cooking has never been my gift," said Betty.

"I think I am most looking forward to sitting on the front porch with you, John," I said. "I'm anxious to have a glass of brandy and puff on one of those Havana cigars." John's eyes lit up at the thought.

I could hear the whine from a Ford echoing through the hills, the sound increasing as it approached. Chuck Crawford, a good friend of John's who he worked with in Chicago at the institute, was riding with Jason. They had fallen behind the rest of us, probably looking for a last-minute adventure before returning to the farm on our last day.

"You should enjoy your kickback time now, I guess," said John. "When the harvest comes at the end of October, you will be busy enough picking the first coffee cherries."

"Let's get going," urged Betty. "There's a lot of work to be done before anybody puts their feet up and sips brandy." She kicked her horse in the ribs and headed down the trail. We fell in line for the final push, which would last no more than an hour.

As I remembered later, those were our last words on safari, that long-awaited adventure for which I had prepared my whole life. I remembered my mother always reading to me at bedtime the stories about African hunting. The page had turned, and the book was about to close. It seemed like the end of the story, but not quite. For my wife Esther and me, our story had only begun.

I had come to British East Africa ten years earlier at twenty-six, looking for a better life. Back in America, I had studied the humoral theory, which was the theory that there were four humors in the body that kept it healthy. The theory originated in ancient Greece, and it taught about the four bodily liquids known as blood, mucus, black bile, and yellow bile, which all needed to be balanced. These essential elements in the body were associated with the four fundamentals in the universe: air, water, earth, and fire. Get any of them out of whack, and a man would be done.

Of course, the humors were also related to the four seasons, during which too much of the corresponding humor could exist in the body and make a person sick. Blood, for example, was associated with spring, and an ill patient needed to be relieved of this excess, especially during this time of year. Tests had proven that bloodletting was vital and could quickly bring a sick patient back into balance.

Having been educated in the finest schools in New York, my plan had always been to become a doctor—until tragedy changed everything. Influenza struck, which both my mother and my father fell ill and died from, as well as my young, beautiful, and pregnant wife, Felicia. My grief was the greatest reason for me to leave that city. I had to move where the air was fresh, the hills were cleansed by the rains, and my mind could be free and uncluttered from the pain and stress of everyday life in a big city.

I grew up in a Christian home and had always believed in the story from as young as I can remember. My dear Felicia said when my parents died that it was God's judgment. Her words still echo in my ears even now. Back then, I watched helplessly as she eventually fell victim to the same fate. My hopes and my dreams died on the day my wife died, and I just wanted to run as far away from the pain as I could. I guessed halfway around the world would be far enough.

I thought of heading to Alaska to search for gold with the rest of the hordes, starting in Seattle and then heading north for Nome. The Klondike had been such a bust for so many, but news of a new gold find in Nome twelve years earlier had sparked new interest—apparently, at that time, they were picking gold nuggets off the beach left and right, and the mere thought of finding money in the street like that caused instant panic . . .

As I said, I almost went to Alaska—until I came to my senses. By chance, I heard a speaker at my college, Professor John Rivers, give a lecture about Africa. That day made such a huge impression that I began planning immediately to move here. It also sparked a lifelong relationship. I was sure Africa was a place where heart and soul would become one, a place where faith could take root, and a place where dreams could come true. I guess I also made an impression on John Rivers, because that day sparked a friendship neither of us could describe.

The movement of my horse beneath me brought my thoughts back to the present, as I had to keep him from breaking out in a full gallop toward home. Coming up over the rise, the farmhouse stood in the distance. My head man, M'Culay, spotted us and came running. I could see him grinning and waving his arms like a wild man.

"Somebody is excited to see us," said Betty.

"Not as excited as I am. I just don't know how to show it like he does," I answered.

"I think he is excited to see you, Lance," said John.

"It's not me," I said. "It's either Esther or you, John. Remember, John, you are his friend. He wanted to die when I told him last spring he had to stay behind and take care of the farm." M'Culay began jumping wildly and whooping like a crazy man.

"Look at him," said John. "I think it's you!"

"Nope," I insisted. "You are his friend; I am his boss."

"Bwana . . . BWANA!" M'Culay shouted. "You are home; you come to me!"

John looked at me with a smile that said, *Told you so.*

"We have so much story to tell, you and me, Bwana. Our trees happy with coffee cherries. They are good . . . you will see. You be very proud of M'Culay."

"When the wagons come in, pull them up to the shop," I said. "Gather all hands. We will need to settle up with our porters and safari staff. They will be eager to be discharged."

Our horse boys took charge of our mounts, and we quickly left our saddles. I rubbed my backside in relief, knowing I probably wouldn't be riding anytime soon just for fun.

"Ah . . . it is wonderful to be home," said Esther as her feet hit the dirt. "Come on, Betty. Let's go get nestled in the house while the boys tend to business." Betty jumped off her horse and handed the reigns over to M'Culay.

Betty was a striking woman who didn't look a day over twenty-nine. Her soft skin showed little signs of her real age. She had long lashes, bright eyes, and delicate features: a small turned-up nose, strong chin, high cheeks, and a rosebud mouth.

My wife, Esther, could have been a model in a magazine. Gentle black curls framed her face like an artist's masterpiece, giving her a youthful appearance much younger than her years. The hairstyle was all the rage among women of our day. Her striking smile often left me with goosebumps. Beautiful, straight white teeth contrasted sharply against her dark skin, making the whites of her eyes seem to pierce a person's soul. Her strong chin and narrow nose completed the package of one beautiful woman.

"We girls are going to take a hot bath," said Betty.

"I have hot water ready, Memsahib," said M'Culay. "I have made it every day for a week now, hoping you might come home since the runner came in to say you are close."

"Then you can come and get the tub ready, but the men are restricted from the farmhouse," said Betty. John caught my glance and rolled his eyes as the ladies headed for the house, excited for their first warm bath in months.

Jason pulled up in the Ford with Chuck at his side. He had a big grin on his face as he maneuvered the Ford between the line of porters. The squawking camels had also realized they were back where they'd started.

"I'm glad to see Chuck let the kid drive," said John.

"M'CULAY!" I shouted.

"Yes, Bwana?" he said.

"Take care of the girls first. Then, I will need you to help organize the final details of our safari. You will need to coordinate with Willie."

M'Culay bowed, acknowledging that he understood, and disappeared through the front door. Jason bounded out of the Ford, ready to go to work. His dog jumped out behind him, shaking like he was trying to rid himself of something.

"Hey, Dad, where is Mom?" he said.

"She is in the house," said John. Jason started for the farmhouse.

"You'll have to wait," I said.

"That's ridiculous . . . I want to see her!" he insisted.

"If you go into that house right now, you are going to see way more of her than you want to," laughed John.

"What do you mean?"

"Because she and Esther are taking baths," I said. The corner of his lips came up to a smile, and his cheeks turned red. We broke out together and had a great laugh at Jason's expense.

Jason's hair was never out of place. His strong chin and narrow, pointed nose gave him the appearance of strong leadership capability His eyes were confident, as if he had purpose in his life.

We had much to do; as the afternoon slipped away, we focused on every detail of closing out our safari. The most challenging part of the day came when we had to say goodbye to our guides, Janga and Tomba. We had no further use for native trackers here on the farm.

Special attention had to be given to our trophies as they were made ready to ship back to Chicago. That evening, after Esther and M'Culay prepared a wonderful meal, John and I sat on the front porch with our feet on the rail, sipping brandy and puffing on the last of his Havana cigars.

"I tried my hand at growing tobacco here in the protectorate, but I found it to be very labor intensive, more trouble than it is worth," I said. "I think I need to stick with coffee for now. Find something you do well, learn everything you can, and become an expert at one thing."

"That's my philosophy," agreed John.

"I feel bad about Janga and Tomba, but they wouldn't be happy working the fields on the farm," I said.

"No, they are hunters and trackers. They'll find work. With all the safaris coming to Africa, they will be fine."

"Are you hurrying to get back to Chicago, John?" I asked.

"The only urgency is to get Jason back to school before he gets too far behind," said John, taking a long puff.

"He's a fine boy," I said. "It's too bad for me that you and Betty snagged him away, but you deserve him. Esther and I will have children—I'm confident."

"How long will you stay, John?"

"We should be ready to go in a week. I'll have to see when we can board a steamer in Mombasa. The people at the train station will know. I think I should like to attend your church before we go."

"That will please Esther. And will you come back again to visit us next year?" I asked.

"You know my heart. I have every intention right now, but we live in a dangerous world. You know that Germany, France, Russia, and Great Britain are all attempting to keep the lid on this simmering cauldron of imperialism and world domination. Who knows how long that will last? This is a powder keg: one spark could ignite the whole thing. If it does, you will be fighting Germans here in Africa."

"Oh, that will never happen, John. An armistice was signed between Germany and England to keep Africa neutral if a war were to break out between the Germans and the Brits."

"Yeah, those agreements will go out the window when hostilities flare up."

"I hope you're wrong, John." Somehow, though, in my heart, I knew the facts. War seemed inevitable. How terrifying, the thought of a war here in Africa. It sent a chill up my spine. But I also wouldn't run from a fight, and I found the prospect of a war strangely exciting.

The week they stayed seemed to go by quickly. Chuck, Esther, and I found ourselves in Nairobi, bidding John, Betty, and Jason a fond farewell at the train station, bound for Mombasa.

"I had the time of my life," said Betty.

"I can't believe our time has come and gone," I said.

"I feel like I have known you my whole life," she answered as she hugged Esther, who had tears streaming down both cheeks.

"I feel like we have been at a party, and the band has just quit playing," wept Esther.

"I hate it when the party is over," said Betty.

"I don't know if I will ever return home to America," said Esther. "You just have to come back—if you don't, the thought of never seeing you again here makes my heart sick."

"If I know John, we'll be back," Betty said, tears welling in her eyes.

"You take care, my friend," said John as he grasped my hand. I wanted to throw my arms around him and hug him like a big brother, but the two of us knew better about such a public display of affection. People were already talking enough about Esther and me in a mixed marriage--a beautiful, black American woman and a white, Anglo-Saxon man. I supposed it was true all over the world, really, that mixed marriages were looked down on, but especially so here in Africa. Too bad they'd never met Esther.

"That was some testimony you gave the other day at church," I told my friend. "I must say, John, you are quite the public speaker."

"I have had a lot of practice," he chuckled.

"We are going to have an uphill battle with this town," I said, shaking my head.

"You will be okay," said John, trying to console me over the comments made by some of the congregants as we'd left the church the previous day. "Esther is a strong woman, and you are an amazing man. It would be the two of you if anyone can win them."

Jason found his opening with Esther, threw his arms around her neck, and kissed her on the cheek.

"You are like my second mom," he said. "I will be back someday; you can count on it." Esther grinned and kissed his forehead.

"This kiss will have to last until we are back together again," she whispered. "I'll never forget what you said about me being a second mom. I am holding you to it. You take care of that dog, Jason. I think I will miss him, too." Isaac knew she had spoken about him, so he wagged his tail and nuzzled her leg.

"John, I just wanted to say it has been a pleasure to hunt with you," said Chuck, taking John's hand. "It has always been a pleasure to serve with you at the institute and now to be with you on safari. Bon voyage, my friend. Good health and Godspeed. And take care of your trophy."

"Which one?" he asked with a twinkle in his eye.

"The only one that counts, my friend—her name is Betty." Chuck's thick, white mustache, gray hair, and wrinkles on his face showed signs of his age and hinted of his wisdom. "You have greatly influenced me as well, my son," he responded. "I am getting up in years and slowing down, and I should be home to America in a few years. I want you to remember the things we talked about."

"How can I ever forget, sir . . . until we meet again," he said, stepping back. "I salute you, sir." Jason brought his right hand to his brow as he stood at attention, then snapped his arm to his side. Betty's eyes brightened and she came running with her arms open wide. Like a little girl, she melted in my arms, and the smell of her sweet perfume filled my nostrils. I thought of her as my big sister. Neither of us said a word, nor did we have to say a word, knowing the depth of the other's affection.

"You take care, Farmer Lance," she whispered in my ear. "You watch over and protect your beautiful wife. She is precious, strong, and yet vulnerable to the wolves. Be strong and courageous—I know you will!"

"I will never forget our time here," I replied, "and the miracle we both witnessed together."

"Wow . . . so right," she whispered. "Take care, my friend, my little brother." She kissed me on the cheek and walked toward the train.

I watched them board and take their seats at open windows. The conductor took up the step, the engine let out a puff of steam, and he yelled at the top of his lungs, "ALL ABOARD!" Signaling the engineer, the coast was clear to fire up the steam horse.

The train lurched forward, and we all waved eagerly. I had to think realistically that this might be the last time we ever laid eyes on each other. I had a lump in my throat, and my heart must have weighed a thousand pounds as the train lumbered off down the track. Jason's head stuck out the window with Isaac, and they faded away in a plume of white smoke from the stack. Esther, Chuck, and I stood silently, not wanting to make a sound or knowing what to say.

"You are right, my dear," I mused to Esther.

"What is that?"

"It seems like the band has quit playing, and the party is over," I said.

"Then we need to find a new party," she quipped. "That is just what we will do."

The three of us strolled back toward the Ford, then headed back to the farm, straining to find a suitable topic to discuss. But for the most part, we were quiet. The word *sanguine* echoed in my head.

The word meant optimistic, hopeful, buoyant, positive, and cheerful, especially in light of difficult situations.

Sanguine, that is what we will be . . . we will have to be. We had no other choice.

CHAPTER 2

PEN PALS

When we returned to the farm, it did seem strange. Jason had even taken his dog with him, to whom I had grown so accustomed to being around. Esther and I sat silently in the house, trying to figure out what to do.

"Do you think I am beginning to look old?" I asked.

"Oh heavens, no," she replied.

"Okay, I just thought . . ."

"Lance, you are a beautiful man. I have always been jealous of your strong chin and narrow nose. I love that you are clean-shaven, and you try to keep it that way. Your thick eye brows and dark eyes mesmerize me. You captured the attention of your first wife Felicia, and I am not saying that I am happy she died early. I would never say that; you know that. But if she hadn't, my life would be very different right now."

I paused, wondering how different my life would be if Felicia were still here on this earth. I quickly changed the subject.

"You know the natives talk about the wild dogs and how they all come out of the dens when the sun comes up?" I found myself saying. "Every dog has to greet every dog in the pack to say good morning. That's how I felt saying goodbye to John, Betty, and Jason."

Do you think they will come back someday?" she asked.

"I suppose it will be sooner than you might think. Heck, you know John. He has never been able to stay away from Africa. I think his heart and soul are here, and when he gets home, he will be chomping at the bit to get back. Just like Dr. David Livingston, who gave instructions to his natives to bury his heart near Lake Bangweulu in Northern Rhodesia. After that, they carried his body a thousand miles, loaded it on a ship, and took it to England."

"That's pretty amazing. I hope you are right," she responded. "Betty's spirit makes me come alive."

"What about me? Does my spirit make you come alive?"

"Oh, darling. I'm sorry; I didn't mean you don't complete me. " Rising to her feet, she wiped her hands on a towel and put her arms around my neck. "You are my everything. My protector, inspiration, best friend, and lover. You are the guy I hitched my wagon to when I was just a little girl. You are the reason I ran away from America. I knew I could never find a guy like you.

"I don't know what I expected to find here in Africa when I arrived. I wasn't sure; I was following God. And now, look at what he has done for me: we found each other. I am so happy to be on this farm, just for the chance to start our new life, to follow my dreams and find my roots. I want to help the natives find Christ. That's why I came. That's what I need to get back to.

"I want to help you run the farm and get my hands in the soil. I am so excited to be with you, darling, in this house. I want to fill it with our children, who can grow up where everyone is accepted, black or white. I know we will make it because you have the character for it. You are my man, the one God picked for me, for better or worse, until death do us part. We will make it, by God."

"We will have an uphill battle with the settlers. You know that, don't you?"

"What . . . you mean bigotry? Heck, that's no big deal to me. I have lived with that my whole life. It's just part of my life. There is no changing this skin color," she laughed.

"All that is just window dressing," I said. "I fell in love with all of you, including your skin, but mostly the person you are."

"I remember when we were little and none of that mattered . . ."

"And the only ones it seems to matter to now are the white settlers. But look at our game warden friend. Blaney Percival never batted an eye when he met you. He fell in love with you the minute he met you. You have that ability to melt hearts. I don't know how you do it, but you do. John Rivers used to be one of the most prejudiced men I knew. I was scared to death the day he and Betty arrived in Africa. I wasn't sure how he would take this whole arrangement between you and me, but look how your life changed him."

"It wasn't my life that changed him. It was God that changed him."

"Oh, I suppose . . . but you were the vessel for God. The Lord worked through you and with you."

"The only thing I know is that this old house is pretty quiet with all of them gone. But I don't intend to mope around here for any length, living like someone died or the party is over," she insisted. "We are going to strike up the band and get living. We are going to get on with it, upward and onward."

"I'm with you, darling. We will start living like the day we met when you stepped off the train in Nairobi."

"My goodness, that has been almost two years now, hasn't it?" she asked. "I am going to make you babies," she abruptly added. She kissed my lips.

"I will make babies with you any day of the week, sweetheart, but hold that thought until tonight. Right now, I need to check in with M'Culay and get a look at the crop he is so proud of."

"I will finish up putting together everything for dinner. You go tend to your business. This is going to be a perfect night. After all these months, we will finally be alone, just you and me. We are going to strike up the band," she said with her beautiful smile.

I jumped off the porch with a little more spring in my step. My heart was soaring with anticipation for our future. Names started to pop in my head as I thought about the children Esther and I would make and fill our home with together: Matthew, Nathaniel, Rachel, and Abigail. How many would we have? How many could she have?

I suspected she would bear strong children. She was a strong person. Still, the thought of having children and the possible complications of it all were terrifying. I had so many friends who had lost their wives to childbirth. It was not a perfect process. In my medical training, years earlier, I remembered learning that one out of eight women died from it.

I recalled professors teaching about "the four horsemen of death" in maternal mortality: fever, hemorrhaging, convulsions, and self-inflicted abortion. *Why does my mind always go to such depressing topics when I am at my highest point?* I asked myself. *I have just been at such a high point in my life, feeling like my heart was about to soar, and then the fear of death comes in and tosses cold water on the newly kindled fire. There must be something wrong with me. I wonder if other people struggle with this same thing, or if it is just me.*

Anyway: Matthew, Nathaniel, Rachel, and Abigail. I could almost see their faces in the visage of my beautiful wife. I could almost hear little Abigail calling me Daddy. I knew she would have me wrapped around her finger. It was the name Felicia and I had picked out together, but only she and I knew that secret. Now, it would be my little secret. I had lost Abigail once, and now I would get a second chance at seeing her face.

* * *

The better part of a year had come and gone and Esther had received a number of letters from Betty Rivers. Betty had come to almost rely on one of Esther's like a cake on a birthday.

"Chuck was in town today, and he brought a letter from Betty," I said to Esther as I stepped through the back door, into the kitchen, handing her the sealed envelope.

"Oh, she is such a faithful friend. I love these letters so much. They are like receiving a fruit pie."

"I could have opened it," I said.

"You could have, but check the address there, mister. It is addressed to me."

"That was the other reason I didn't open it," I chuckled.

"I can hardly believe it has almost been a year since I have seen her." Esther took a knife and slit open the top. "Wow, two full pages this time." Her eyes lit up as she pulled the pages out of the sleeve and sat in the easy chair to consume the words. Then she broke out in laughter.

"What is it? What's so funny?" I asked.

"Okay . . . I can see I will have to read this out loud."

"That would be nice," I responded.

"My dearest Esther, I hope life finds you well and that you have been able to find some peace in that small house with nowhere to escape your husband's advances."

She had a smirk on her face, and I had to laugh to myself. I was the one who came home dead tired every night from working on the farm like a dog. She was the one who wanted to make babies. She smiled at me, knowing what I was thinking, and then looked back at the letter.

"Things are going well with John and me. He has put his nose to the grindstone and has greatly advanced toward becoming a Bible scholar. With the same intensity he pursued Darwinism, he has now tackled the Bible."

What a miracle it is, I thought to myself, *to see a man raised from death to life.* As Esther continued to read, her words became a distant blur as the thoughts of that day on safari with John, a year earlier, filled my head. That great lion had nearly bitten his head off. My skin had goosebumps thinking about it, but what of this miracle? What about John's apparent new life in Christ that made him into some born-again spiritual giant? It was enough to make someone like me feel left behind or left out altogether. I had read the Bible story in the book of John when Jesus spoke to Nicodemus and said, "Except a man be born again, he cannot see the kingdom of God." I had assurance because I believed Christ died on the cross for me. But as for being "born again," I just didn't know. It left me wondering.

"He is studying business at the institute."

"John is studying business?" I asked, refocusing on Esther's words.

"No, *Jason* is studying business, John is studying theology," she corrected. "Haven't you been listening?"

"Oh yeah, I just have a lot on my mind, that's all."

"We can read her letter later if you like."

"Oh no, it's just fine . . . continue," I insisted.

"It's just news from Chicago. But I have some news for you from Africa," she said.

"What is it?" I asked.

Esther stared deep into my eyes. "I missed my cycle!" she said, taking a breath and waiting for my reaction.

I winked. "Oh, that thing; it's been leaning against the barn right where you left it the day you got that flat tire. Do you suppose one of the natives stole it?"

"Not that cycle, silly. I missed my menstrual cycle!"

"You're pregnant?" I jumped up and took her hand, pulling her out of the chair. The letter fell from her hand and fluttered to the floor. I embraced her and started dancing to the music playing in my head. "Abigail!" I cried in glee.

"What if she is a boy?" Esther stopped in her tracks and tilted her head.

"Abby is not going to be a boy. She is going to be Daddy's girl, her father's joy. She will be tough like a boy, but she will be a girl to the core. She will be just like you, darling, and just like me."

"I know one thing for certain," she laughed. "You are going to have to fix the flat tire on my bicycle."

The months continued to roll on as I waited for the baby bump to show. A woman has such a glow when she is with child. Esther was so happy to be pregnant. We were filled with hope and joy as we waited for our child to arrive. I never had any doubts about Abigail's entrance into the world.

Then Esther began to show her pregnancy. It had been well over a year and a half since John and Betty had left Africa. Esther and Betty wrote letters every few weeks to keep up with our lives and theirs. March had landed upon us, and we were headed into the rainy fall season, a great time to be a farmer as long as we didn't get torrents.

"How are the roads?" asked Esther one day as we finished up breakfast in the kitchen of the farmhouse.

"We haven't had any torrents for over a week now. Why, were you planning to go to town?" I responded with suspicion.

"Tomorrow is Sunday, and we haven't been to church in quite some time."

"I like having church here with Chuck and the few natives from the farm who always straggle in," I said, hoping she wouldn't insist on going back to that congregation.

"I think we should go back and try again," she said, folding her arms across her chest and waiting for me to react.

"You know how I feel . . ."

"Yes, I do, but you can't escape my skin color. We have to face this challenge head-on. We can't continue to isolate ourselves on this farm. Those people were your friends before I showed up, and I can't handle being the one who turned you into a hermit."

"You told me it was spiritual," I said, folding my arms. "Remember, you said we could become Christians living a life of secluded prayer, which was biblical."

"That is not the kind of life I want for me or my children. I want them to be well-adjusted and comfortable in their skin, just like I am in mine."

"But how can those people in that church call themselves Christian and yet be so bigoted?" I protested. I recalled my encounter almost a year earlier with people who believed that white skin was somehow a preferred condition by God himself. They thumbed their nose at the mixed community they called the "Basters" in Rehoboth, Namibia. The name *Baster* was derived from the Dutch word for "bastard" or "crossbreed." I had already vowed to myself that Abigail would never hear the term.

"Just because they are Christian doesn't mean they are perfect," she smiled. "I cannot continue to live in seclusion and have my only friend in the world be a pen pal."

"According to the women's encyclopedia, a pregnant woman should avoid undue excitement, such as crowds. What makes you think the church is different?"

"Oh sure, and I suppose that book says a pregnant woman should not be seen in public," she snapped.

"I don't understand you sometimes," I said. "Why would you want to put yourself through the pain of humiliation time and again?"

"I think it is *your* humiliation and not mine. I was born into this and am comfortable with how God made me. When he made me black, the only thing I can figure out is that he called me to greater humility. It's God who lifts us up and not man. Me . . . I just want to love them despite their pride."

"Maybe we should go on Easter Sunday," I said.

"This Sunday is the warm-up for the big day on March 23," she said. "I want to go on Easter Sunday too, but all this week is Holy Week."

"I will take you anywhere you want to go, my dear. I just don't want to see you hurt," I said. Her resolve reminded me of why I had married her: because she was remarkable.

"Walking into a crowd of people like that is what God made me for. I want to go to church tomorrow. Besides, I want to dress up."

"Yeah, like that's going to work," I laughed. "How are you going to fit into your clothes?"

"You think I haven't thought about that?"

"I suppose you have given that a lot of thought."

Early the following morning, Esther got up with the birds as I lay in bed, getting ready to face my friends in town. My marriage to Esther made my heart soar on the wings of an eagle, but my friends just couldn't see it like that. *Whose problem is this anyway? I guess our pride is always our problem*, I had to concede. I'd known the job was dangerous when I took it over two years earlier, when we struggled to find a pastor in Nairobi who would agree to marry us. Reverend Bartson had finally agreed, but warned us profusely about what we were taking on. He even said it would cause problems for him, but he was willing to do it as long as we had sought God for his approval.

Maybe it's time to come to terms with who I am, I thought. *I am the husband of a lovely and intelligent American black woman. Even though I know that in most places in America, they wouldn't just refer to her as a Baster. It would not only be frowned upon as it is here—it would be a felony in many states, and they would throw us in prison. Yeah . . . America, the "land of the free"! At least in our home state of New York, it has never been illegal.*

I crawled out of bed and splashed water on my face from the lukewarm washbasin Esther had prepared for me. *Wow, that will wake you up!* I dried off with a towel and felt my face to decide whether to run a razor over my cheeks again. I found all my church clothes placed out for me, hanging over the back of the chair. I could smell coffee on the stovetop and buttermilk biscuits baking in the oven. I had a pit in my stomach, but the desire to protect Esther from anyone or anything that could hurt her gave me courage.

As I exited the dressing room, she greeted me with joy. Her white dress flowed to the floor, tied with a big red bow above her womb. It hid her condition quite well.

"I saw it pictured in the Sears and Roebuck catalog Betty left behind," she explained. "I had the fabric from last summer and pulled it together."

"Wow . . . all stitched by hand. I'm impressed. You have some talent here. Maybe I'll have to buy you a sewing machine."

"There are many things we need before spending money on a sewing machine."

"I saw that catalog. Their sewing machine sells for seven dollars."

"All well and good, but by the time you get it shipped to British East Africa, it will be about a hundred."

"I don't know how you do it," I said, shaking my head. "You were up with the chickens, you're dressed to kill, and you still had time to make us breakfast."

"I don't want to disappoint anyone, especially you, dear," she answered.

I took a bit of the piping hot biscuit she placed in front of me. "These biscuits are delicious," I said as I took a bite of the warm roll lavished with butter and jam. "Are we going to be late?"

"No, we have plenty of time," she said. "I sent M'Culay out to get the Ford going."

"Are you sure about this?" I asked.

"Sure about what?"

"Facing all those snobbish townspeople," I answered.

"We already discussed this," she said, putting her hands on her hips.

"I know," I muttered, realizing I couldn't turn this stubborn little mule. I could hear the familiar sound of the Ford coming across the yard toward the house as I sipped the hot coffee.

"Are you ready?" she asked, reaching for her white straw hat with the big red bow.

"After you, my dear," I said, opening the front door. M'Culay sat behind the wheel, probably hopeful he could drive the car in for us.

"I can take her from here," I said as I approached the driver's seat.

"M'Culay must drive you, bwana," he insisted. I acquiesed and motioned for him to continue. He held the door while Esther struggled with her tummy. She maneuvered herself into the seat, careful not to allow her long white dress to pick up any dirt. She looked determined and confident, and I knew the thoughts that must be going through her mind. People had been so mean to her the last time we attended church a year earlier, and I had sworn I would never step back in that place. I couldn't believe we were now on our way back.

CHAPTER 3

The Sabbath

The Ford bounced in the chuckholes, and my concern grew for Abigail, wondering how she would take the ride.

"What about the baby?" I asked. "Is she going to be okay?"

"Yes, dear," Esther said, touching my knee. "The baby is fine." I watched every inch of the ride to town, looking for game. It was a convenient pastime that felt so comfortable—and it was a habit impossible to break. *Like the constant routine of pride and assuming you are better than somebody else*, I mused. *Man is in a constant state of either thinking he is better than the other person or of being jealous of another person's status. Pride and envy are the two worst sins in the book.*

I didn't know how to feel about this situation with my wife and the townspeople. It seemed so confusing. I had married an American woman, not a native African. She was strong, intelligent, beautiful, spiritual, and funny. She had more love inside her than the whole bunch of those hypocrites. I couldn't believe how she had chosen to live her life and run headlong into a challenge with her chin up. She had every confidence that she could win over the townsfolk and come out victorious. I wished I had an ounce of her character.

As we entered the town, I could see the steeple of Reverend Bartson's church. M'Culay maneuvered the car past horse-drawn wagons and the pedestrians. Some were wearing their glad rags as they walked toward the church. As we passed the livery stable, a

group of rough-looking men stared at us and I looked away. M'Culay pulled up to the front steps, and the pit in my stomach grew even bigger. I felt like a soldier facing an opposing army. I didn't want to look at the faces, but I could feel their stares and almost hear their thoughts. Esther patted my knee and gave me a motion to keep my chin up as M'Culay opened her door and took her hand. I had to hurry to get out on my side and scurried around the back to greet her.

"Smile!" she whispered with a big grin. "Don't let 'em see you sweat. Are you coming with us, M'Culay?" she asked.

"No, ma'am. I should be waiting with the car."

"That's silly," she insisted. "You will park the car and meet us inside."

"But ma'am, M'Culay's dress is not so good."

"Don't be silly; this is God's house, and he does not care how you dress."

"I think M'Culay would like to watch the auto."

"I won't force you," she said. "I would like you to come, but this is your choice, sir."

M'Culay did an about-face and retreated to the Ford. *Coward*, I thought, chuckling to myself. But at the same time, I secretly wished I could wait with him. Looking up the steps of the Anglican church, I spotted Wayne Pusser with his blonde wife, Celeste, on his arm. He was chatting with Reverend Bartson, who wore a long, white robe. They were standing together at the wide doors at the top of the steps.

I hadn't spoken to Wayne since he and I had discussed my relationship with Esther almost two years earlier. He had been one of the first people to abandon me. John said he had spoken with Wayne when he arrived in Mombasa and had received a cold reception when he mentioned my name. *Why, God? Why do you have to put Wayne Pusser in my path?* My feet must have weighed fifty pounds apiece as I dragged myself up the steps of the church. Wayne made eye contact and struggled to terminate his conversation with the pastor as he tugged on his wife. She made eye contact with Esther and pulled back, stepping in our direction and coming face-to-face.

"What are you doing here?" asked the blonde creature, whose eyes pierced like sharp daggers.

I knew this would happen.

"Celeste, have you met my wife?" I asked, ignoring her pointed question.

"I have not had the pleasure," said Esther, extending her hand with a smile that could have melted an Alaskan glacier. Celeste folded her hands and turned up her nose, leaving Esther's hand empty, but Reverend Bartson reacted quickly and jumped between them, taking Esther's hand.

"How nice it is to see you again, my dear. We have missed you in this church."

Wayne tugged on his wife and pulled her away from the conversation. He looked over his shoulder and rolled his eyes at me as they disappeared through the doors.

"I am so sorry," the Reverend said, glancing over his shoulder and speaking to Esther. "You are a strong woman to come here. You must have the courage of a lion!"

"I can't change who I am, Reverend. But I might be able to change how they think of me!"

"I will pray for you," he said. "Now come in, and I hope you enjoy what I say today. I had no idea you would be coming, but God has prepared his message for this occasion."

I thought about how curious his words were. We stepped through the door, and all eyes were on us. People began to whisper, shielding their mouths with their hands. I found an empty pew in the back and began directing Esther toward the open seats. She would have none of it, just as I suspected, and marched ahead of me to the front of the church, where she took a place in the front row.

Surprisingly, the church was dotted with quite a few black couples—not at all how I remembered the all-white congregation a year ago.

"Did you notice the other Negroes in the church, dear?" I whispered. She nodded her approval.

The organ music began the processional, and the congregation came to their feet. An altar boy led the way carrying the cross, which was followed by another man and our Reverend. All wore long white robes, each taking their place on the altar while the organ music paused. Michael looked over the congregation, gazed at Esther and me, and smiled at us. I had such great respect and love for this man, remembering when Esther and I had walked into this church to ask if he might consider marrying us. It was the third church we had approached. Esther had nearly concluded that we might have to perform the service privately at home. We still did it privately, but it was in this church, at this altar, where we said our vows. No one knew that our local Game Warden, Blaney Percival, had had the courage to be my best man and our witness.

The music began again, and Esther took the hymnal, thumbing the pages to find the song. The place erupted with beautiful noise that raised goosebumps on my body. When she found her place, I reached over, took her hand, and smiled. God had brought us together and blessed our life with little Abigail. As we sang the words to a hymn written in 1597 by Philip Nicolai, from Germany, the song entitled "How Lovely Shines the Morning Star," I began to take heart as I read them off the page:

Thy Son hath made a friend of me,

And when in spirit Him I see,

I joy in tribulation!

I knew Esther was following along and that this was what she lived out: joy in tribulation. That was what she did so miraculously. She faced trouble with joy. I had a lot to learn about life from this gorgeous woman.

The song ended, the Reverend told us to sit, and we eagerly waited for his message to begin.

"This morning is special. I didn't realize just how special it was until it started to unfold," he said as he stood in the center in front of the altar. "I want to take this opportunity to thank you all for coming this morning. As you know, this week is Holy Week. And this is Palm Sunday.

"This morning, my message is on the greatest commandment, which calls us to love God and our neighbor. And who is our neighbor, pray tell? Is it the person who lives next to you? Is it the person who is most like you? Living next door to someone sometimes allows us to see how different we are. It is not easy to love a person who is different. They have different political views than we do and probably have various religious beliefs. They eat different foods, wear different clothes, and might even have a different outward appearance, such as the color of their skin."

People around us began squirming in their seats when he mentioned skin color.

"The Bible," he continued," is very specific in certain places about race. Even God seems to have chosen one race of people over another to be unique and separate. But this is only what you see on the surface of the Scriptures.

"As humans living in this fallen world, we look to the natural and have difficulty understanding what is spiritual. There is a reason God chose Abraham, Isaac, and Jacob as the seed of a chosen people. He picked this ruddy little shepherd boy named David to kill the giant and ultimately become the king of a nation. It was a test, my dearly beloved, a test of humility. David built a nation, and he built up a prideful people who believed that God had given them favor above the whole world. Their world was set in their tradition and a religious system they knew had been given to them by God. And no one, not even God, if he came down from heaven in the flesh, would be allowed to change it.

"Do you see how God tests us? He tests our pride, and he challenges our humility. He continually works on us to help us grow in our faith and righteousness. God desires holiness, and at the same time, God demands humility and the love of our neighbor."

I wondered where Reverend Bartson would go with his sermon, but what happened next left no doubt.

"Jesus challenged the Jewish world of that day with what took place at a well in Samaria. The Jews hated the Samaritans because they were a mixed race. Let me explain.

"The reason they were considered different from the rest of Israel was because they were part of the Northern Kingdom of Israel during the time of King Jeroboam. Samaria was the capital city. There was a long history of fighting between the North and the South. After the division, Jeroboam changed the Israelites' worship, and they no longer traveled to Jerusalem to offer sacrifice. Jeroboam set up idols in the North where they could worship.

"Later, after Israel fell to the Assyrians, they began to intermarry with the Assyrians, and their descendants, the Samaritans, were considered half-breeds. The Jews who had remained in the South, when traveling to the North, always took the long way around Samaria, but Jesus marched right through it, probably with the intent to meet up with this woman at the well.

"Remember also that in Jesus' day, men did not converse with women in public, especially such a woman as this, who had been married five times and was now living with a man out of wedlock. Not only were Jesus' disciples likely indignant that they had to follow Jesus through this region, but they were surprised their master had been talking to this woman.

"But Jesus loved her for who she was and had compassion for her. It wasn't her fault that she had been born in Samaria. God loved her because he had created her, and in her innocence, she had followed the ways of worship instituted by her ancestors. She didn't know she had been born any different. As far as she was concerned, she was just like everyone else. But the Jews would have considered her as a dog, a half-breed—what our own white people in this community might refer to here in our own country as a Baster."

People in their pews began to squirm even more, and one man made a scene when he stood up and escorted his wife and two children out of the church. Reverend Bartson paused, waiting for the commotion to pass. The man slammed the back door as he went out, and it echoed through the sanctuary.

"Dear friends," the Reverend continued, "God made the races different to test the hearts of men. He could have made us all the same, but God intended this life to be difficult. It would have been too easy to love your neighbor if we were all the same—if we all had the same thoughts, married the same people, and had the same children. If we all lived in the same town, ate the same things, and worshipped the same God. God made the world difficult, so we have to take the narrow path. Wide is the path and easy is the road that leads to destruction. But narrow is the path and difficult is the way that leads to salvation.

"Also, easy is the pathway that leads to racial division, but narrow is the way that leads to the love of your neighbor, no matter who your neighbor is. It doesn't matter whether he or she is black, red, yellow, or white. God didn't make one race better than the other; inside, we are just people trying to find a way to live in this world together. We look at the commandments of God, and we know we fall quite short of fulfilling the law. Jesus said that all the law would be fulfilled in this commandment: to love the Lord your God with all your heart and soul, and to love your neighbor as yourself. Who is your neighbor?"

He looked over the congregation, trying to intentionally make eye contact with those who would look up. "I intended to preach this message with a certain couple in mind this morning. Almost two years ago, this couple came to me and asked if I might officiate their wedding. They had a beautiful love story that originated in America when they were children, and God brought them together here in Nairobi. I was given grief by members of this congregation and members of this town as a result of that decision. Heck, it is no secret about who I am talking about. Everyone here knows. So I would like to reintroduce them to you if that would be okay."

Oh brother, I thought, *here we go.* I hated speaking in front of a crowd. Esther eagerly looked to me for approval with a big smile. I saw that same grin on her day after day as she brought joy to my life. I took her hand, and we stepped to the platform, facing the congregation.

"As most of you know, this is Lance and Esther Miles. They are an American couple from New York who are good friends with Professor John Rivers from Chicago, whom so many of you have come to admire over the years. Many of you heard his incredible testimony before departing for Chicago in this very church last year. Now, I would like to introduce to you Esther, who is a gifted evangelist. She could preach in this congregation if we allowed women in the pulpit. Change comes slowly, so we will tackle one thing at a time. For now, I am asking that you try to get to know this couple. They are amazing. Not knowing them and loving them would be a loss for this community. Even though I cannot have her teach or preach to us this morning, I can have her close us in prayer. Please, Esther, will you close us in prayer?"

She had the pregnant glow, and I could feel her joy bubbling up as we took center stage. She stepped ahead of Reverend Bartson to make a slight separation between us as we stood just behind her.

"I can't tell you what this means to me," she began. "This is a gift from God. I came here to Africa because of the racial prejudice I was experiencing in America. I thought that if I came to a place where beautiful white people such as you lived, things would be different. You came to this country with a much greater knowledge of black and white. As you can clearly see, I am carrying my husband's child. For those of you who have children, you will understand my greatest hope is that all our children will be able to live in a world where they are loved and accepted. Let us pray." She paused briefly. I knew she was praying silently; you could have heard a pin drop in the sanctuary.

"Dear God of the universe, God of God, Light of Light, very God of very God, hear my prayer this day as I speak these words, and bless these souls. We praise you that you are a God of difficulty, a God who extends grace only because we have all fallen short. A God who overflows with mercy, not because we deserve it, but because we need it. We thank you for life in abundance, not only for the joyful times, but also for the difficult times. We need you even more because we are left with a rat's nest when the backlash comes.

"The Lord's beloved brother, James, said to consider it pure joy when we face all kinds of trouble. Lord, I have been filled with pure joy my whole life because of all the trouble I have seen growing up in this black skin. Lord, I thank you for allowing me to be born into this world as who I am. The trouble I have faced has made me into the person I have become. It has not made me bitter. It has made me *better*, with more wisdom and understanding, compassion and kindness, resilience and strength, and humility and faith. It has given me a greater capacity to love and depend on you, my God. My suffering, it turns out, is the best thing that could have ever happened to me. The trouble I faced as a single American Negro woman sent me on a journey that allowed me to find the love of my life.

"Lord, as a community of devoted believers, let us not make trouble for one another for the sake of joy. Let us find pure joy from the love we share. There is enough trouble in the world to go all around, so fill us with your blessed Holy Spirit and grant us your peace and joy as we seek you together. Lord, bless this congregation as we grow in faith. Watch over and protect us and our families. Keep us safe from tragedy, sickness, wars, greed, and power. Help us to be better neighbors and to have the capacity for greater love. All this, my dear, beloved friends, I pray in the name of our precious and holy Savior, Jesus Christ our Lord . . . amen."

Esther looked up with her famous smile to the congregation, who were all smiling back. She stepped back, and Reverend Bartson continued.

"That prayer was sort of what I expected from you, my dear. Let us continue our worship with a final hymn from page 513, and I will send you God's blessing so you can finish your Sunday with your families."

I took Esther's hand, and we took our seats. The organ began, the music filled the sanctuary, and Esther found a hymnal and thumbed through the pages again.

Once the song ended, Reverend Bartson blessed the congregation. The organ music began, and the Reverend waited for the altar boy to take the cross and start the procession. He paused as he passed us and said, "Please fall in behind the procession and meet me at the church's front doors." I couldn't believe he was going to try this. I knew he could lose members of this congregation. His attempts at forcing his flock to love us certainly could backfire on him.

Esther took my hand, and we followed the procession down the aisle. Some were smiling, but others wore blank faces. I spotted a woman known to me as Lydia. She had a smile on her face, and she was standing with her husband. I had met Lydia shortly after I arrived in Africa. At the time, she had been looking for a husband and set her eyes on me. For me, it was too soon after my dear Felicia's passing. I could have been with Lydia, but I knew I could have lived without her. Felicia had been my girl, and everyone else would have to measure up to that yardstick for the rest of my life. I needed to find a girl I couldn't live without, and Esther was that girl. Lydia knew it too; she had found the proper man in Dennis Johnson, a tall, good-looking Scotsman and businessman with the general store. Dennis had a bright smile, which enhanced the crows-feet lines on his face, giving away his age—pushing fifty. He had thick, dark hair with greying sideburns.

I had to hand it to her when she came to me explaining how she had found a man and how they had plans to marry. I wanted her to be happy. She would have melted into my arms if I had asked her to be with me and not marry Dennis that day. Dennis had always been the perfect gentleman every time I visited his store. He knew about Lydia and me, but he never seemed threatened, and I liked that about the man.

When we reached the door, the altar boy opened it and Reverend Bartson encouraged us to stand by him. The music ended, and the congregation began to stir as they gathered their things.

"You know what to do, Esther," he said. She nodded and then closed her eyes in silent prayer. I could only imagine what her prayer contained. I knew she had seen Lydia, but I also knew I had never told her anything about that story. At any rate, I could feel another one of Esther's God moments about to take place.

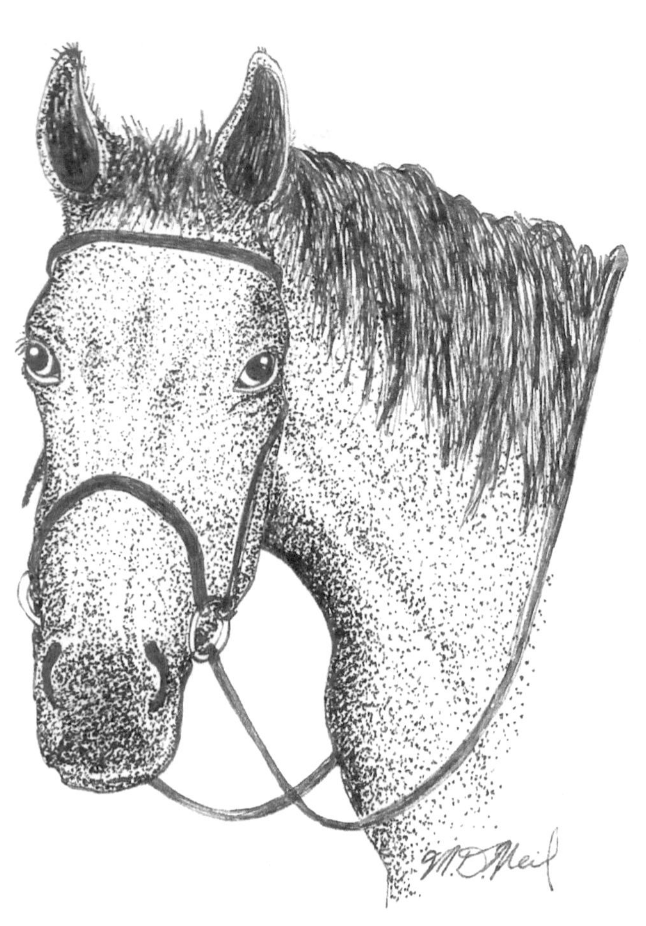

CHAPTER 4

THE CAMPFIRE STORY

My knees began to tremble as I saw the faces of the congregation glancing around. I could only imagine what thoughts were going through their minds. We stood at the door, with the Reverend blocking a swift escape. The people were very polite, and I began to relax as longtime acquaintances I hadn't seen for a year shook my hand and greeted Esther.

As Dennis and Lydia stood in the crowd, I began to pray over the inevitable encounter. A meeting between Lydia and Esther made me nervous. I knew I would have to tell Esther about the nature of my friendship with them, but this moment would not work. I tried not to stare at them but found it challenging to read Lydia's face. Some people skirted around those greeting us and slipped out the doors. It was so sad that they were coming up short and not being blessed by Esther. Her face beamed radiantly. Secretly, I had hoped that Dennis and Lydia would leave without coming face-to-face with us. Dennis had a smirk like a man on a mission. I should have taken him aside and told him everything, but I knew the opportunity for that exchange had passed.

Then they moved up and took center stage in front of us. I opened my mouth, but no words came out. Lydia interrupted my thought and put her hand out to mine.

"Are you going to introduce me?" she said with her sweet smile, which I remembered so well. It had been nearly eight years since we had parted ways.

"These are my friends, Lydia and Dennis Johnson," I announced to Esther. "You remember Dennis; he has a store in town." Esther put her hand out to Lydia.

"Have you picked out a name?" inquired Lydia, catching me off guard for a second.

"Lance insists it is a girl, and he is stuck on the name Abigail."

"You always were a pushover for the girls, weren't you, Lance?" Lydia batted her eyelashes at me in a provocative way.

"I can see we have a lot of people who need to greet you," said Dennis, seeing the line.

"We will let you go, my dear. But we would like to have you out to our home for supper," said Lydia. "We have a lot to catch up on. I have also done a fair number of deliveries here in town as a midwife. Do you have a midwife, Esther?"

"I do not," responded Esther with enthusiasm. "A native woman has offered me help, but she had some strange suggestions."

"Then it is settled. I will be your midwife, and the two of you will come for dinner. Maybe we can come to the farm for an afternoon getaway if Dennis can break away from the store?" she remarked, giving him the eye.

"Anytime! Please stop by the farm. Lance, you can drive me in, and we can have a girls' day."

Lydia took her hand, and Dennis bade us goodbye as he nudged Lydia toward the doors. She looked over her shoulder, and Esther gave a little wave.

"Those two only recently began attending our church," said Reverend Barton.

For the next several minutes, we shook hands. We greeted the rest of the congregation, some of whom were prior acquaintances. I looked for Wayne Pusser as the crowd dwindled, but he must have slipped by without my knowing. Or else he'd left when that man took his family in the middle of the sermon. I couldn't be sure because I didn't dare look.

It certainly is peculiar, I thought, *how you can't seem to change a person's mind about such things as their racial views, politics, or religion.* Wayne disappointed me; the two of us had always been so close. We'd met ten years earlier on a ship from New York bound for England. We had so much in common. He dreamed of becoming a doctor, but his family couldn't afford the cost of medical school. My family could afford it, but my plans were cut short by tragedy. I used every bit of my inheritance to invest in a coffee plantation.

Wayne and I headed to Africa when most Europeans were flocking to America. He wanted to hunt big game, and we talked about becoming professional hunters. I didn't know what I wanted; my grief had me in a fog. At the time, Wayne and I were heading off into the unknown and each needed a friend. I remembered how good we were together and how reassuring it was to have a traveling companion to experience the first time on African soil. I thought we would be friends forever. Silly me.

Then, the line ended, and the last couple greeted us politely and introduced their two young children. They reached out to the pastor and complimented him on his message. Then they took their leave, and the church was empty.

"I don't know if the words 'thank you' are adequate," said Esther, taking the Reverend's hand.

"I am the one who should thank you. I only recently heard what happened to you last year, and I should have come out to your farm."

"Oh, we understand," insisted Esther.

"No, you don't understand. My horse fell ill and died four months ago, and the one I bought had not been buggy-trained. She must have been spooked by a buggy because she just wouldn't pull one—still won't, in fact. I tried to trade her in, but no one wanted her. Guess I need to find a saddle. I have been housebound for four months."

"We have extra horses left over from our safari last year," said Esther.

"I wish I had known," I said. "We have a beautiful horse, and she is just pasturing. Esther is not allowed to ride in her condition. But that horse will pull a buggy."

"Oh, I couldn't . . ." Reverend Bartson responded.

"Yes, you could," insisted Esther. "We will have Willie bring her to town this week. She is a wonderful girl. Her name is Lilly; I named her after a beautiful camel I once knew."

"I would not turn her down, but this is very generous. I spent a hundred American dollars on that feed bag I ended up with. I am sure the one you are offering is worth more than that."

"Consider her a donation to the church," said Esther.

"Well, thank you very much. And who is Willie?" asked the Reverend.

"Willie is our dear friend; he works for us on the farm. He is one of our two assistant managers who take orders from our friend Chuck, from Chicago. Willie led our safari a year ago. He is a hunting guide by trade, but we asked him to stay on with us at the farm and work with M'Culay, who has been such a great help to us over the years."

"Sounds like quite an operation!" the Reverend said. "Did you keep most of your safari staff with you here on the farm?"

"Only a few. We had an amazing cook named Bamira with us in the bush. He loved being a safari cook and has since signed on with a safari company in South Africa. I tried getting him to stay here, but he wouldn't. So M'Culay runs our home, is our chief cook and personal assistant, and runs the house staff. Willie runs the farm, with Chuck overseeing the whole operation."

"How big is your—oh, I'm sorry." Reverend Barton stopped mid-sentence before he could finish his thought. "Asking someone how big their farm is—it's sort of like asking how much money one makes."

"As far as farms here in Africa go, we are modest. Does that give you an idea?"

"A perfect picture," he replied.

I could have told him that our farm consisted of ten thousand acres. Still, only about 5 percent was usable for cultivation. Of those five hundred acres of fertile ground, we had cleared less than a hundred. And of those hundred acres, we had only planted coffee trees on about fifty. And of those fifty acres of coffee trees, only about ten acres of those would be producing coffee cherries in the coming year. It would have been impossible if I had tried to explain everything in one breath. If I had given him the first number, he would have been impressed with a false picture, and if I had given him the last number, he would have felt embarrassed for asking.

"We will have you out for dinner soon," said Esther.

"I will be looking forward to it," he replied. I shook his hand and thanked him for everything. Then Esther threw her arms around him in her best way. The look on his face said everything about his lack of comfort in accepting her affection. Esther didn't care about such things as that. She had a lot of love in her heart, and sometimes, like a cup filled to the brim, it would just spill out.

M'Culay had the Ford running and was waiting at the bottom of the steps when we exited the church.

"How do you think it went?" Esther asked, climbing in the back seat, where I joined her. M'Culay revved the engine, and we were off.

"I think it went splendidly. Don't you?"

"I think it went more than splendidly; it was miraculous—a true God moment in every aspect. You know we almost didn't come, and what a disaster that would have been to have missed the moment. Now, tell me more about Lydia!" She raised her eyebrows. "Old girl-friend, huh?"

"Now, how would you know that?"

"I caught it when she said, 'We have a lot to catch up on.'"

"She is pretty cute, isn't she?"

"Yes, she is adorable; you chose me over her?"

"It's much more complicated than that. We talked a lot about Felicia and how much I had loved her, and you know what it did to me to lose her. I found myself in a dark place after she died. You know I ran away wounded. I wanted you. Heck, I always wanted you. I just never knew it would be possible. Lydia found me, but I knew it would never work, and the more she tried, the more she understood it would never work either. I never told her about you. I never told anybody about you. I'm not sure I even told myself about you."

Esther seemed as if she wanted to speak, but she held back and just listened. Her dark eyes reached my innermost being, just like they always did. They pulled everything out of me—even things I had never admitted to myself.

"I wasn't sure what I wanted back then," I continued. "I guess I wanted my dreams back." As we motored out of town, the streets were empty from the usual weekday bustle. "You were always the love of my life, you know that, but I knew it would never work in America. Heck, we could have been arrested in some states."

"How do you figure Lydia will think about me?" she asked. "I guess I need to know how to think about her. Won't she feel that she got put aside by a guy who traded her for a woman with black skin?"

"I don't think so. Lydia is a beautiful, caring person who always wanted the best for me. When she met Dennis, she was very concerned that I would get hurt. She knew I wasn't ready to be a husband again, and I told her I didn't know if I would ever be ready. I even attended their wedding."

"How come you never told me any of this?"

"How does that come up in a conversation? Maybe it goes something like this . . . 'Oh, by the way—'" I paused for a second, and then we began to laugh together.

"Is that everything?" she said, wiping the smile off her face and looking deep into my eyes.

"I can't think of anything else."

"Were you ever with her in *that* way, if you know what I mean?"

"No, we were never together like that."

"Okay, I . . . I just needed to know," she stammered. "Not that it would make any difference, but it's good to know."

M'Culay motored out of town and started down the long trail leading to the farm. I had traveled a familiar road many times before, like an old pair of socks. I knew every pothole and bump, every tree and hillside. I even named some of the animals I spotted along the way. I could only imagine thoughts about what had happened this morning and how they must have churned in Esther's head. Neither of us spoke a word. I sat quietly as the motor echoed through the trees, the wind blew in our faces, and the sweet smell of blossoms filled my nostrils. I looked over at her, and she smiled back. Oh, and one more thing. The love of a beautiful woman filled with my child lifted my heart on wings that made me want to fly. I could hardly wait to meet Abigail. I could hardly wait to witness her first words, her first steps, and then the day she would call me Daddy.

Chuck stood on the front porch as we turned down the drive toward the house, and he came out to meet us as M'Culay pulled up and parked the Ford.

"How was your morning?"

"Very enlightening," said Esther with her sweet smile.

"It was like a campfire story," I added.

"Wow, sounds like there is a lot to tell!"

"More than one could tell here in the driveway," she laughed.

"Your kitchen staff has lunch ready. Is anyone hungry?" asked Chuck.

"I am starving," I said, bouncing out of the motorcar. I took my sweetie's hand, helping her safely down from the gadget. *It's funny about these automobiles; I don't know if they will ever catch on*, I mused. *A horse-drawn carriage is so much more serene to ride in. Much less noise, and the constant, nauseating smell of the exhaust cannot compare with the infrequent and almost fragrant droppings from a horse. You have to tell this machine how to get back to the farm every inch of the way. In comparison, all the time, a horse knows the way. Besides, you can have a relationship with a horse; it's pretty tough to have a relationship with a bucket of nuts and bolts. These are just a passing trend that will fade with time as people discover there's nothing special about riding in one.*

"I like that motorcar, don't you?" asked Chuck as we stepped on the porch.

"Oh, yeah," I said, secretly thinking the worst. "It beats the Stanford parked in the barn."

"Have you had any luck finding the parts we need to fix her?"

"Nope, not at all! I don't know why the previous owner bought that thing in the first place. It drives like a pig. We might have to move it outside to make space in the barn."

"Do you think we should cover it with a tarp?" asked Chuck.

"Beats digging a hole and burying it," I laughed.

We had lunch together, and then Esther and I sat on the front porch chatting with Chuck for several hours. We relaxed in the sunshine, enjoying the serenity of the Sunday afternoon. We covered many topics, from John and Betty to Jason and his dreams to the tensions rising in Europe, the farm crops, and so on.

"I think I should like to start a revival," said Esther at one point.

"Whom would you revive?" said Chuck, trying not to laugh.

"Anyone who needs it, and I might just start with you," she said with her sweet smile.

"You might just give me a heart attack talking like that. At least if you did, then I would hope you could revive me." I knew Chuck had witnessed all that happened in the bush with John. I knew his heart was too calloused to accept what had happened out there. I didn't know what it would take to get through, but I figured that God knew. Esther knew it, too. She had an incredible knack for being a fisher of men. I didn't dare say a word.

A master fisherwoman will work the currents to get the fish to take the lure as it hides just below a boulder in the current. A novice will only mess things up when trying to cast a worm over their line. It surprised me that she didn't say more, but sometimes, less *is* more.

"Look!" said Esther, breaking the silence and pointing off to the clearing where the road passed through, about a mile down the valley. "There is a horse carriage."

"Looks like two people," I said, not recognizing the carriage or the horse at first, but trying to remember where I might have seen it before.

"Is that Blaney Percival?" asked Chuck, squinting through his spectacles. I knew with his eyesight he had no clue.

"Nope, not Blaney. He rides a paint, and I'm not even sure if he has a carriage. Besides, one of the people in that carriage has a woman's hat on, and Blaney doesn't have a woman," I answered. The carriage disappeared in the trees as it made its way up the road approaching our farm.

"Should I get my field glasses?" asked Chuck.

"If they are coming here, we will know soon enough," I responded.

"I suppose they might be headed up toward the Crocker place," said Esther.

"Maybe they are coming here for the revival?" laughed Chuck.

"Oh, stop it, silly," she said, giving him a shove on his shoulder.

"I have never seen that carriage before," I answered, "and old man Crocker don't take too kindly to visitors. I remember a couple of years ago, I tried to make a neighborly visit, and he shot over my head with his rifle."

"Wow!" said Chuck. "You never told me about that."

"Yeah, well, he don't go to town, and he don't take visitors."

"Look now, they are turning down our drive."

We all sat silently as the carriage slowly moved in our direction. "Now I wish you had gotten those field glasses," I said.

"I think that's Lydia," said Esther. "I recognize the hat." She rose to her feet.

"Okay, I *did* see that carriage before," I said, remembering it parked behind the Johnson store one day a couple of months ago. I didn't shop at Johnsons' market much because I didn't like running into Lydia. But my regular market had had no more flour, and they sent me down the street.

"I'm going in to straighten up," Esther said.

"They will be here in just a minute," I said.

"It will only take me a minute, but I wasn't expecting company. Try to hold them off till I come out on the porch."

Esther disappeared through the front door, and Chuck and I got ready to greet Dennis and Lydia.

CHAPTER 5

The Visit

Chuck brushed the front of his breeches off, trying to make himself look presentable. I brushed my hair with my hands, then grabbed my hat off the hook. I could hear a squeak from a back axle on Dennis's carriage.

"Good afternoon!" I shouted. "Welcome!" Lydia had a grin on her face like the Cheshire cat from 1865. It's funny when you hang around someone and admire them so much that you think like they do—John Rivers always spoke in such descriptive terms, and he always had a metaphor. Now, he had me doing the same thing.

"Thought we would just take you up on your offer right away, Lance," responded Dennis.

"I'm glad to see you," I said. Esther came scurrying off the porch and joined us as the horse let go with a loud whinny.

"That is a beautiful animal," said Esther.

"I think she was saying hello," laughed Lydia.

"Well, hello to you, my dear," said Esther. "I'm so thrilled that you came."

"We got home from church, and all our chores were done. Dennis asked me if I would like to take a Sunday afternoon ride, and this is where we ended up."

Willie shouted across the farm as he approached some of his workers to take care of the guests' horse.

"Can you stay for a while?" I asked. "Can I have my staff start dinner?"

"We didn't mean to impose," insisted Lydia.

"Oh, it is no imposition. Please, we have a cured ham in the meat house waiting for such an occasion as this," said Esther.

Lydia removed her hat and took a long sniff of the air. "This is such a beautiful setting for a farm," she said.

"I can't believe I've been here in Nairobi so long and have never been on this farm," said Dennis.

"Should I feed her?" said Willie as he led their horse away.

"Not a lot, just give her a little snack, but make sure she gets plenty of water," said Dennis. He turned to me and spoke under his breath. "That horse doesn't get much exercise, and she eats all day. I noticed she was getting a little fat, so I'm trying to cut her back."

"What did you say, honey?" said Lydia, crossing her arms and making a frown.

"I was talking about Lolly."

"Who is Lolly?" asked Esther.

"Lolly is the mare," he responded. Lydia rolled her eyes.

"Come in and see our home," said Esther. "I will have them put on a pot of tea."

"I just can't get over this farm," said Lydia as we made our way to the house.

"Hey, Chuck," I said, "can you have Willie take a look at the back wheel? I think it needs a little grease." As he nodded and made his way to the carriage, I found myself remembering the first day our friends, John and Betty, came to the farm. *Why, it was nearly two years ago that they arrived in Nairobi. I had been so worried about everything that day. Would they accept Esther? Would Betty find our home acceptable after what I knew about her home in Chicago? They were such humble living quarters for anyone, let alone her. I needn't have been anxious. And now here I am, worried about what Lydia might think, knowing they live in such a fine home in Nairobi. I know she must be very thankful that she married Dennis and not me, no matter what she says about this setting.*

"How do you keep your lawns manicured?" asked Lydia, drawing me out of my thoughts.

"We have sheep," I answered. "Our keepers scoop every afternoon, and of course, we keep the sheep in a pen at night to prevent the lions from getting them. But nothing is wasted; we use the scoopings for fertilizer."

"Come and sit," encouraged Esther as our kitchen server, Kianjahe, set out the tea service on the coffee table.

"This is Kianjahe," I said. "His name means 'mountain of beans.'" Kianjahe beamed as he realized we were speaking about him. He spoke very little English, and most of our conversations were in Swahili.

"Utakuwa kuandaa ham kwa sisi usiku wa leo?" I asked, inquiring about the ham dinner.

"Ndiyo bwana, sisi ni kuwa ham na viazi dhana," he answered.

"What did he say?" said Lydia as Kianjahe disappeared into the kitchen.

"He said we are having ham with fancy potatoes," I explained.

"Mountain of beans," laughed Dennis.

"Yeah . . . Kikuyu names always have a meaning, don't they?" I said.

Lydia continued gushing over the house, telling Esther how beautiful she found it. I watched as Lydia and Esther began to bond like old friends who hadn't seen each other in years. Lydia's gorgeous blond curls, slender nose, and big, round, blue eyes were captivating.

I remembered our days when we were much younger; she hadn't aged a day. Except maybe she had put on a few pounds. I heard the girls talking about children.

"You have never had any children?" I asked, talking to Dennis in a low tone to avoid interrupting the girls' enthusiastic conversation.

"We are still trying, but so far, no children," he whispered. "I know it's a cause of some pain for Lydia."

"What are you boys whispering about over there?" said Lydia. Esther raised her eyebrows in curiosity.

Chuck came through the front door and removed his hat. "Willie has your mare all settled in the corral," he said. "And he is going to look into that squeak in your axle. That is a fine animal. She is so gentle. Where on earth did you find her?"

"Quite a girl, that Lolly, hey?" said Dennis. "She is like a family member, except we can't take her in the house. But if you could, I am sure she would curl up on the end of your bed."

"She is so affectionate and so gentle," said Chuck.

"She is one in a million," agreed Lydia. "She has been like that since we got her as a two-year-old."

"How old is she now?" asked Chuck.

"We've had her almost three years," said Lydia.

"We would love to show you the farm," I said. "It is such a beautiful day; we shouldn't be sitting in the house."

"I'm ready!" said Lydia, jumping from her chair.

"M'Culay!" I called, summoning him from the kitchen. "Can you have someone make the Ford ready?" He nodded and disappeared out the back door. "I thought we should take a little drive."

"I have only ridden in an automobile once," said Lydia, bouncing excitedly and clapping her hands.

"Everyone in town has heard the story about how John Rivers left you his motorcar," said Dennis. "And, of course, everyone saw Stewart driving that motor lorry with his nose in the air, thinking he was something special. Enough folks have them now that yours is just another pretty face."

"I, for one, am excited about taking a drive," said Lydia.

"Excuse me while I get my rifle," I said.

"Your rifle? Do you really need it?" asked Dennis.

"I don't go anywhere without one; do you?" I asked. Dennis opened his jacket with a smile, and I saw what looked like a .44 Colt strapped to his belt.

"Okay then, I understand what you mean," I laughed, taking the Winchester .30-06 from the rack and pulling the bolt open just enough to reveal the shiny brass from the round in the chamber.

"You keep them loaded in the house?" asked Lydia.

"They are no good empty," I responded. "Besides, my philosophy is that guns should be always loaded, all the time."

"That might change when you have kids," she said.

"For now, I have a pack of wild dogs hanging around; it's just a matter of time before they get one of my sheep."

"I would love to talk to you sometime about your faith," quipped Lydia as we stepped off the porch.

M'Culay set the brake and slid out of the front seat, standing beside the car as I approached. Double-checking the safety, I reached in and placed the rifle in the front seat with the barrel pointed to the floor. Dennis helped Lydia into the back, and I quickly ran around, taking Esther's hand. "Let me help you sweetheart," I said, as I carefully hoisted her up into the seat.

"Where are you taking us?" asked Lydia.

"Thought you would be interested in seeing the plantation, maybe the village where our workers live. I thought you might like to ride down by the river crossing." I revved the motor and began to let out the clutch.

"Have a nice time!" called Chuck, waving from the porch. "See you after a bit."

"Did you hear that, Dennis? He calls her *sweetheart*," whispered Lydia. Dennis just smiled. "Are those the coffee plants?"

"Actually, they are coffee *trees*," corrected Esther.

"Can we stop and see them? I have never seen them on a tree, only in a sack."

"Then you'll be surprised. There is a lot of labor to get them from cherry to the bean." I pulled up to the line of trees and set the brake. "I hate starting this thing, so I'm just going to leave her running. Come, let's take a walk."

Esther began to get out of the Ford, but I said, "Darling, in your condition, do you think it is a good idea to climb in and out of the auto?"

She smiled and then settled back into the seat.

"Watch the rifle," I said. Lydia and Dennis followed me to the line of trees. "These trees are about ten years old; that's why they're fifteen feet high. Normally, we would have workers picking cherries, but they don't work on Sundays. See, here they are." I pointed to the clusters of cherries hanging on the branches. They ranged in color from dark green to red. "This is why it is so labor intensive. They ripen in stages, and the workers must keep picking only the ripe ones."

"Wow," said Lydia, "they look like grapes, not cherries. I thought they would be beans."

"Some people call them berries, and others call them cherries. The beans are in a pit, and we lay them on a large brick pad to dry in the sun. After about three weeks of raking them over, the pulp is dry, and the seeds fall out. Then we have a roaster roast 'em and sack 'em."

"Can you eat one like a fruit?" asked Dennis.

"You can! Here, try one," I said, picking two dark, red cherries from the limb and handing one to each of them. Lydia popped hers into her mouth.

"Careful, eat it like a cherry," I cautioned. Dennis sniffed his first and tried to take a small bite of the skin.

"Oh, that's good," she said. "Sort of tastes like watermelon."

"I think it tastes like water with rose petals," I said.

"Can't say I ever had that before," said Dennis.

"Do the birds eat them?" asked Lydia, taking the coffee bean out of her mouth.

"Originally, we thought the warblers were eating them. Heck, old man Stewart had me out here trying to shoot them. But the more we watched them, the more I discovered the birds were eating this little black beetle that leaves a worm in the fruit and ruins the bean. So, I convinced him the warblers were actually providing us with a service. We still shoot the crows, but I don't think birds have as big an impact as the beetle."

"Are you ready?" called Esther from the Ford over the motor hum.

"Coming!" I said, motioning our friends toward the Ford. "The queen has spoken," I whispered. "We don't want to get our heads chopped off." Lydia giggled, and we returned to the automobile and jumped into our seats. Esther looked at me, suspicious that I had made some snide remark to make Lydia laugh. I could tell she wanted to ask me by the look on her face, but she changed the subject.

"So, do you know everything there is to know about growing coffee?" she asked, turning around to her backseat audience.

"All very interesting," said Dennis.

"I never knew any of this before, but I like to drink coffee. I don't know why; it must be something in the drink, because the coffee takes a little getting used to," said Lydia.

"It's the caffeine, which is a stimulant. It makes you feel good," I said.

"Yeah, it grows on you, doesn't it?" said Dennis. "Sort of can't start your day unless you have a cup first." The Ford hummed, and the tires bounced from cart ruts in the road and the chuckholes left from the rainy season. We drove past the plantation and through the dense underbrush, coming out into an area forested by flat-topped acacia trees and wide-open grasslands. Everything looked so green and lush, and the air smelled fresh as it blew across our faces. We passed a line of native women carrying water casks on their heads, making their way back to the village. They wore long traditional native skirts, their breasts uncovered and their necks and ears adorned with beaded jewelry.

"I don't make a big deal of it, but part of the reason I came to Africa was to help fight against female genital mutilation," said Esther.

"I have heard of such a practice," said Lydia. "Why do you think they do that?"

"It's total ignorance," said Esther. "They've been told they will bear more children, and the women believe they will give birth to dogs without it."

"I think it is a way for the male population to control the females," said Lydia. "It's a terrible thought, and it gives me the chills. I don't like to think about it, and I certainly feel uncomfortable even talking about it."

"I have heard that many of the missionaries have started a movement to try to stop the practice," said Esther. "And that would suit me just fine."

"There's the village," I said, pointing down the valley to the round huts with smoke plumes rising above the trees from their cooking fires. We could see children chasing each other, and their dogs came out to greet us, barking at the Ford.

"That's a long walk to get water," said Lydia. "You would think the men would do the heavy work."

"That's not how it works," explained Esther. "It is considered a disgrace for a man to do manual work, and it would be a total humiliation for a woman to allow her husband to do such a thing."

"How strange it is for different cultures and their belief systems," said Dennis.

"They must look at us and think we are crazy," said Lydia.

"I'm sure they do," said Esther. "Shall we stop for a visit?"

"Eh . . . probably not," I said, looking at the grubby little kids and the mangy dogs.

"Our workers will be offended if we don't," she said. "It's Sunday."

"Okay, but just for a second," I replied.

I recognized some of our women pickers who came out to greet us as we approached. Then, I saw the village leader emerge from his tent, and the crowd began to build.

"Such peculiar huts," said Lydia. "I have seen hundreds of them, and they still amaze me every time."

"They are always happy to see us. Old man Stewart was very kind to them, and we intend to keep that tradition," said Esther.

"Some of the farmers have moved the villages off their property, haven't they?" asked Dennis.

"Not this farm," I said. "We intend to honor them as being here first, even though we rightfully own the land." I pulled up and set the brake, then shut down the motor.

"I thought you liked to keep her running," remarked Dennis.

"Well, in this case, I am hoping not to disturb any more of them from their huts. If we aren't careful, we will end up with a whole mob."

"Can I get out this time?" asked Esther.

"Come on, let me help you," I said, coming around the Ford and lending my hand.

Immediately, one of the young girls, who might have been twelve or thirteen, approached Esther with a broad grin, reached out, and touched her tummy.

"Hii itakuwa nzuri mtoto wa kike hata kama wewe ni mjamzito na nyeupe."

"What did she say?" asked Lydia.

"She said it will be a fine baby girl, even though I am pregnant by a white man," laughed Esther.

"She got both things right," I said proudly. "We *will* have a girl, and you *are* pregnant by this man in white skin who loves you more than anything in this whole wide world."

"Oh, Lance, you are such a romantic. I think you spent way too much time with John Rivers."

An elderly woman stepped in, slapped the young girl on the hand, and scolded her in Banta. Then, she grabbed her arm and pulled her away.

"What is going on?" asked Lydia.

"It's considered bad luck to speak openly about the coming birth of a child. This woman is teaching her daughter some manners," I explained.

"Is that Swahili?" asked Dennis.

"Well, they speak to us in Swahili and each other in Banta."

Then, the tribal leader entered the crowd and greeted us.

"Ni siku nzuri sana, bwana," he said. *"Kuangalia kwa simba kama unakusudia kuendesha hadi bonde."*

I looked at Lydia, knowing she couldn't wait to ask me what he was saying. We made eye contact, and then I explained the situation.

"He said it's a very fine day, but we should watch for the lions if we intend to drive up the valley." Lydia looked at Dennis and wrinkled her nose.

The children broke the mood and came running toward us with bright eyes and warm smiles.

"Esther, did you bring that sack of candy?" I asked.

"I'm way ahead of you, darling. I have it right here," she said, holding a bag. She opened it and offered it to Lydia and Dennis.

"No wonder they are so happy to see you," said Lydia, placing the small pieces of pulled taffy wrapped in waxed paper into the children's hot little hands. "Are they dangerous?"

"No, these kids are harmless. Look at their faces," said Esther.

"No . . . not these," she laughed. "I mean the lions!" Everyone laughed at Lydia as her cheeks turned red.

"Not so much when you are in a motorcar," I said, trying to control my laughter. The kids began to disperse as the last one took the candy and disappeared into the village.

"Shall we go?" asked Dennis. "I would love to see if we can find those lions!" Esther and I bade the tribal leader a good afternoon, and Dennis and Lydia got back in the Ford. I could hear them talking under their breath as I helped Esther back in her seat.

"Give me a hand there, Dennis, and we'll crank this thing up and get going," I said. He jumped out of the Ford, and I sat behind the wheel to set the timing stalk and adjust the throttle. "Do you know how to do it?" I asked.

"Yeah, always use your left hand to hold the crank. If she kicks back, the left arm is less likely to get broken. Give it a vigorous half-crank, and the engine should start, right?" said Dennis.

"Sounds like you have done this before," I replied.

"I've had instruction from the best and have had to start many of these things after customers are done shopping in my store."

"Okay, give her a crank!"

Dennis gave a sharp jerk, as if he knew what he was doing, and the motor hummed. He came around the front and got back into his seat next to his wife.

"Lydia is afraid we are going to get eaten by a lion," said Dennis with a smile. I revved the motor, eased off the clutch, and turned back up to the way we came in.

"We'll be just fine in this automobile," I said. "They might recognize a horse as something they can eat when it is pulling a buggy. I heard it once, but I don't remember the details. You ever heard of it, Dennis?"

"Obviously, here in Africa, there have been plenty of livestock killed by lions, including horses. But I can't recall anything where a lion killed a horse pulling a cart."

"We know they will attack a man on a horse," said Esther. "But even that is an infrequent occasion."

"Yep, I guess we all know that. Everybody has heard the story about the lion who attacked the horse team pulling a mail cart in Britain about a hundred years ago. But that was a captive lion that escaped from a traveling menagerie. I don't think lions associate people with automobiles. They never seem to give it much notice."

"Yeah . . . well, it hasn't happened *yet*, anyway," warned Lydia. "I just don't want to be the first to make the history books." Dennis reached over and patted her knee.

"Do you know the story about Lydia in the Bible?" asked Esther.

"No, can't say as I do," Lydia answered as I crested the hill and turned back toward the valley.

"Lydia was a woman of God," said Esther. "She sold purple clothing and was likely a well-off widow. In those days, purple was seen as a sign of royalty. Lydia lived in Philippi, but her name means 'woman from Lydia,' which was in Asia Minor and a province of the Persian Empire. That would have made her a Greek, a Gentile. Her heart opened up when Paul was teaching about Christ, and she became Paul's first convert in that place. She became a deaconess in the Philippian church. She was known to be the apostle Paul's first convert in Philippi and thus the first convert to Christianity in Europe."

"Wow . . . that makes me feel special. I guess our English names do have meaning, don't they?"

"There's the pride," I said, pointing up the valley to a band of lions. They appeared to be working on the remains of a zebra kill.

"Don't get too close, Lance," said Esther. "Lydia is afraid."

"Oh . . . I'm okay," said Lydia. "I'm just afraid for you and the baby. Oh my goodness, they are so beautiful."

"I won't get too close," I said, pointing the Ford in their direction and pulling up within a hundred yards.

"That's close enough, Lance," warned Esther. The male lion had his eyes on us and stepped away from the kill. He trotted about fifteen yards toward us and opened his mouth, exposing his fangs and wrinkling his face.

"Give 'em some space, Lance," encouraged Dennis.

"Should I take him?" I asked.

"You're not going to shoot that beautiful thing, are you?" asked Lydia.

"We shoot them all the time; they are a nuisance," I explained.

"You didn't tell me we were going on safari when we left the house," said Esther. "If you shoot that lion, we will have our hands full."

"We'll just have the natives deal with it; we won't have to," I responded.

"This isn't good for the baby, Lance," warned Lydia. "Esther shouldn't be in this situation. She needs to be calm and quiet, not eat too much—and she shouldn't be looking at animals."

"Animals?" I asked.

"That's right, they say a pregnant woman's child can take on the characteristics of the animals if they spend too much time looking at them."

"I, for one, wouldn't be disappointed if she had the heart of a lion," I said.

"That would be okay; she would have courage," said Lydia. "But you don't want her coming out with fangs."

"What else do they say?"

"Hmm . . . let's see. They say never to throw a cherry at a pregnant woman. I suppose that would include coffee cherries, too. It will leave birthmarks on the baby. Oh, and, ah . . . never eat the head of a hare or leap over one. That can result in a child having a split lip. Never eat fish heads: that can produce a child with a trout mouth."

"You are full of good knowledge," I said.

"You have to be to be a good midwife," she answered. "And one more thing, Esther: have you been cutting your hair?"

"I have to keep the curls under control somehow."

"Don't do it anymore until after you have this child. Your hair is your life force. Your child needs that energy from the mother to be strong. And just like a little athlete, he is preparing for the most dangerous struggle of his life."

"This was supposed to be a nice little afternoon outing," said Esther, changing the subject. "Lance, let's just leave that lion be and drive down by the river. Besides, you could wound him, and then what?"

"Yeah, and we don't want to miss out on that ham dinner," said Lydia. "But if he charges, let him have it." Esther looked over her shoulder with a smile, and Lydia giggled.

"Esther, you always have the best advice," I said, putting the Ford in reverse gear. Two lionesses, preoccupied with us, slipped in behind the male and pounced on the kill. As I slowly put space between us, the lion looked over his shoulder, then turned around and charged the lionesses. The whole scene erupted into a colossal catfight. Roaring and screaming, the fangs were bared and the claws came out. Then, the lionesses fled to a safe distance, and the lion went back to his lunch. I set the rifle down, put the Ford in first gear, and turned away from the pride. Driving back across the prairie, we found the road again. It wasn't really much of a road at all; it was more like a trail. But at least I knew it would lead us to the river crossing.

"That was unbelievable!" said Lydia. "I have been here this long and have never seen something like that. That left me with a lump in my throat!"

"Dennis, you need to get her out more," I said.

"We're not going to cross the river, are we?" asked Esther.

"Not this time of year," I answered. "The river is swelled up from the rains, and if we tried it, they might never find us again."

"Lydia, going back to childbirth: I have had many discussions with natives since I have learned their language," said Esther. "You can't believe the things I have learned about their customs."

"What is that?" asked Lydia.

"About their marriage practices and bearing children," she explained. "They have ghost wives whose husbands have died, so they become the wife of a ghost. A father can even buy a wife for his dead son so his family line will live on. Any children that a woman conceives will become his property. They have the practice of giving excess infants away to childless mothers. Women can marry women and then have kids with any man they choose. There is a lot more, too. If a woman conceives before marriage and has a boy, that boy is considered bad luck and will likely be killed before he reaches the age of five by the family. And the witch doctor is the most powerful man in the tribe. He can put a curse on anyone for the right price, and that curse usually comes true. That is why it is so hard to get them to convert—because they are afraid of the witch doctor."

We drove to the river and then headed back to the farm in the afternoon sunshine. The sunshine was a welcome break from the almost non-stop rain over the previous several weeks.

CHAPTER 6

Bad Apples

When we got back to the farm, dinner time had arrived. Chuck came out to greet us as I pulled up in the Ford.

"That was a nice little drive; you were gone two hours," he said, taking his pocket watch from his shirt.

"Did you miss me?" I laughed as Chuck rolled his eyes and gave me a smile.

"Dinner is about ready," he said.

"Come on, Lydia," said Esther. "I am sure you will want to freshen up." My wife eased out of the seat without any help.

"I never asked you how many weeks along you are," said Lydia.

"Is there a way to calculate it?" asked Esther, waiting for Dennis to help his wife out of the Ford. "I just thought it went by the month, and my best guess is I am almost in my eighth month."

"Okay," she said, taking Esther's hand. "It's forty weeks from the first day of your last menstrual."

"I guess we would have to think about that," said Esther, shaking her head. "I guess I should have marked the day on the calendar. I just figured when the baby was ready, it would tell me."

"*She*," I corrected. "The baby is not an it; her name is Abigail."

"Time will tell. I just don't want you to be disappointed with me if I have a boy."

"A son? Do you really think I would be disappointed with a son?" I said.

"We just have to make sure you have an easy delivery and a healthy baby," said Lydia. "Let's work on that first. You know I will have to come and stay with you when the time gets close."

"The thought crossed my mind," said Esther, "I was going to ask you about that."

"Then it's settled; we'll have a look at your calendar and then make plans."

"After dinner," said Chuck. "I am starved. Can I tell them to get the fixin's ready to serve?"

"Wow," giggled Lydia. "I don't think I have ever had *fixin's* before. Are they fresh from the garden?"

"Now, that's funny . . . ever thought about vaudeville?" I asked. Lydia's cheeks flushed. The girls took hands, and Esther led her up the steps.

"I'm starved, too," said Dennis. "Thanks for inviting us to stay for dinner. We'll have to get scooting after we eat so we can make it back to town before dark."

"You might have to stay the night," I said. "Take a look at that storm cloud coming. Do you have a good top on that carriage?"

"Oh . . . that looks bad," he responded. "We could get up early and leave at daylight."

"The roads will be pretty bad. You'd better stay the night, and I can drive you in the Ford first thing. Besides, this will give the girls a little more time together after dinner."

"What about Lolly?" he asked.

"She will be just fine here. We'll put her up in the barn tonight to get her out of the rainstorm. We can bring your cart in this week. I need to make a trip to town anyway, and Chuck can take the buggy.

I am sure Esther wants to attend some of the events for Holy Week. Furthermore, I have a new store to shop at now to get my supplies."

"That would be nice. I think the only thing you ever bought from me was a sack of flour," said Dennis, putting his hand on my shoulder as we walked up the steps to the front porch.

"Okay, but you know what that's all about, right?" I asked.

"I know," he smiled, then patted me like his best buddy. *It would be nice to have a friend again, someone more my age, I thought. Chuck is old enough to be my father, and much of the time, he treats me like a kid. I feel comfortable with Dennis, and it makes me feel good to know Lydia has such a good man to take care of her.*

"I'll need to fetch our contingent bag from the buggy," he said, turning and heading back down the steps. "I'll be right there."

The smell of ham dinner filled my nostrils as I entered the room. The dining table had five places set with fine china and crystal goblets, a clean white tablecloth, and fresh flowers arranged as a centerpiece. I watched as Kianjahe popped open a wine bottle. M'Culay came out of the kitchen with a wine glass and held it for Kianjahe.

"Having wine, are you, M'Culay?" I asked in surprise. I didn't remember that he even drank.

"No, bwana, is for you," he said, handing me the stemmed crystal.

"We saw lions up past the village," I said, tipping the glass away and holding it to the white background of the wall to look for clarity in the dark burgundy color.

"Did you get crack at one?" he asked. I swirled the wine in the glass and then sniffed it. The smells of oak, berry, flowers, and light citrus lingered.

"I almost pulled the trigger, but the girls stopped me!"

"The girls, bwana? I thought you in charge," he said, shaking his head. "Never listen to woman." I almost laughed out loud, knowing exactly how the Kikuyu men treated their women like dogs.

"Once, I had a wine connoisseur explain all the stages of fine wine tasting. To me, it was all mumbo jumbo," I said, taking a sip that tasted like wine and not vinegar or paint thinner. "You may pour the wine."

"Maamajomboo?" exclaimed M'Culay. "You know Maamajomboo? He is wine, what you say?"

"No, it is a figure of speech, M'Culay; I heard it said once to describe confusion."

"Maamajomboo is no confusion. He is a controller of women for the Mandinka," he explained.

"Tell me," I encouraged.

"Unruly wife is stripped, tied to post, and punished by the masked Maamajomboo while the rest of the village cheers," he continued. "He is West African god of women. He come at the night to discipline while the man's other wives watch. This to spare husband from such pain and his harem will keep in order."

"We can only marry one woman," I said.

"You are lucky, bwana."

"No, it is actually illegal here for us to marry more than one wife," I said.

"What is punishment?" he asked with wide eyes. "I think a man punished enough for more than one." I laughed to myself.

"Do you have more than one, my friend?"

"Yes, bwana, I have three wives and sixteen children," he said.

"But you never see them," I said.

"I don't need to see them; they know who I am. I send my money to help them."

"When was the last time you went home?" I asked with my hands on my hips.

"Just there six month back."

"You haven't seen your family in six months?"

"I have three wives, bwana, and take two-hour walk from here."

"Two hours . . . that is nothing!" I said. "Don't they miss you?"

"No, bwana, it is not like that. Kikuyu man not enjoy his women. They are my possessions and my children, too. If I go home, my wives will want to make more children, and sixteen plenty. After two hours walking, M'Culay very tired." I laughed, thinking about how silly different cultures were. I lifted the wine glass to my lips and took another sip.

"I will have to compliment our vintner," I said.

"Vintner, bwana?" he asked.

"Winemaker," I said. "It is either the grapes he picked at the right time or his skill as a winemaker. Or both."

"Wow, smell that ham!' said Chuck as he and Dennis came through the front door.

"Here, Chuck, have a glass of wine," I said, taking one of the glasses off the table. "You cleaned up. Are those your Sunday clothes?"

"Where should I put this bag?" asked Dennis just as the girls came out of the main bedroom, all pretty and fresh for a Sunday dinner.

"Oh . . . come here with that, dear," said Lydia. "That has my night clothes."

"You will need to wash up, Lance," said Esther. "The pitcher in our room has fresh hot water in it."

I slipped away to our room, where I saw Esther had laid out a new shirt on the bed and a clean pair of breeches. After I washed up and changed, everyone gathered around the table.

"Now, Lydia," said Esther. "You sit here next to me. Dennis, you can sit across from her so you won't miss a minute of her beauty. Chuck, you sit here next to Dennis." She turned and smiled, knowing I always sat in the same place at the head of the table. I took the back of Esther's chair and pulled it away from the table, and Dennis scurried around to do the same for his wife. M'Culay looked on with a smirk, and I could only imagine the thoughts running around in his head. Chuck pulled out his chair, waiting for the women to sit. Then, at the appropriate time, he lowered himself into the chair next to mine with a sigh and slid it across the hard wooden floor as he bellied up to the table. I took my place at the head, and Dennis sat beside Chuck. I looked at M'Culay and gave him a nod. Immediately, he nodded back and headed for the kitchen.

"Shall we toast?" I asked, raising my wine glass. Everyone else raised their glasses. "To good friends, old friendships, and our life together here with all the hopes and dreams for the future. May you be healthy and prosperous, may the Lord shine on your circumstances and bless the work of your hands, and may he watch over and protect you in all that you do."

"Amen," said Dennis, tipping the wine glass to his lips. Everyone followed suit. Just then, M'Culay appeared, leading his line of servers, and stepped aside as Kianjahe carried the nearly twenty-pound bronze glazed ham on a silver platter to the center of the table. Lydia's eyes were as big as saucers, and her mouth dropped at the sight. The three other staff members followed up with a large bowl of scalloped potatoes, fresh-cut apples, and steamed green peas.

Everyone set their wine glasses back on the table and waited for them to set out the rest of the food.

"Now, we should have a proper blessing," said Esther.

"Would you like to say it for us, dear?" I asked.

"You are the king of this castle. I would love to pray, but you should do the honors."

"Let's bow our heads," I began. Pausing just a second to look out the corner of my eye, I noticed Chuck with his head bowed. "Dear Lord, thank you for this day and bringing us together here on this farm. Thank you for the courage of these dear people to befriend us and to give us encouragement in our love. Thank you for helping us stand firm against the bigots who might want to destroy us. Lord, we pray that peace will continue here in our country despite the rumors of war in Europe. Lord, bless this farm, our love, and friendship together, and bless the meal we are about to partake in and the hands that prepared it. This we pray in the name of Jesus our Lord. Oh . . . and bless Abigail. Amen."

Esther looked up from the prayer and gave me a little look that said, *You can only hope.* Then she reached for her wine glass and put it to her lips.

"Do you think it is a good idea to be drinking that wine?" asked Lydia.

"Why?" replied Esther. "We are not teetotalers. Even though we do not have hard spirits here on the farm, I believe that wine and beer are just fine in moderation."

M'Culay handed me the carving knife, and I cut the end piece off the ham in keeping with our usual custom of allowing me to make the first cut. I handed him back the knife, and he began to carve. I took Esther's plate, the queen's plate, and held it out for M'Culay to put the first piece of meat on it. I had to laugh, thinking that Betty had always been treated like a queen and that now Esther had taken her place.

"But in your condition, the extra calories are not good for a pregnant woman," Lydia explained.

"In medical school, my professor taught that a little alcohol is good for the unborn child," I said.

Suddenly, the sky opened and the rain began to drum on the roof. The wind howled under the eaves of the farmhouse, and the rain blew against the windowpanes.

"Wow, that's quite a storm out there," said Chuck. "Good thing you folks decided to stay."

"This will all blow over by morning," said Esther.

I reached for Lydia's plate, and M'Culay placed a thick-cut piece of ham on it. She glanced at Dennis, who had a wrinkled lip.

"Can you find me a smaller piece?" she asked as M'Culay removed the ham and replaced it with a thinner cut. "Thank you, that one will be fine. What about the temperance movement? I thought Christians weren't supposed to drink?"

Kianjahe began dishing potatoes with a serving spoon.

"That's the extreme left infiltrating the church." said Esther. "A movement from the communists."

"Didn't Jesus make wine out of water at a wedding?" asked Chuck, holding his plate out for a slice of ham. I encouraged Dennis to go first, who held his plate for M'Culay.

"I suppose if a person has had a drinking problem, then it would not be good for a Christian to drink in front of them," said Esther. "I would never want to cause another person to stumble."

"Are either of you reformed alcoholics?" asked Chuck, putting his plate out for a serving.

"Not so as anyone would know," laughed Dennis, taking some fresh sliced apples while Kianjahe began dishing out cooked peas.

"Do you drink hard liquor, Dennis?" I asked.

"I have been known to have a shot with the gents at the men's club now and again. But I'm pretty busy with the store to spend much time there."

"Is that the one on Main Street?" I asked.

"That is the one," said Dennis. "Just two blocks from my store."

"I have been in that place," I said. "The smoke is pretty thick, and the men pretty stuffy."

"You just go there to schmooze your clients," said Lydia as Kianjahe gave her a scoop of peas.

"That's why my father's store is still in business," he said.

"Have these peas been whirled?" asked Lydia with a little smirk.

"Memsahib?" asked M'Culay, wrinkling his nose.

"I long for whirled peas. Get it? *World peace*," she giggled. "Unlike what is going on in Europe right now with the threat of a world war." Everyone had a good chuckle, but the prospect of a world war was not a laughing matter.

"The war is a reality, you know," I said.

"I didn't mean to make light of it," she insisted.

"We all know that colonialism here in Africa was the best thing that could have happened," said Esther, "because it ended the Arab slave trade."

"I think I am happy here under the British protectorate," said Dennis, taking a sip of wine.

"The Brits are very powerful for such a small country," said Chuck. "They certainly had their hands full in North America in the late 1700s and into the 1800s. The old Star-Spangled Banner showed 'em a thing or two about British expansion."

"Spoken like a true American," said Dennis.

"I am glad to be an African American!" I said, wondering if that name would ever stick as a white person from America living in Africa.

"The day is Juneteenth—the 19th of June. That was the day in 1865 when Union troops landed at Galveston to inform Texans that the Emancipation Proclamation would be in full force. The last battle of the Civil War was fought in Texas. But it's that day that will go down in history for all Negroes in America."

"I suppose befriending us will cost you money. Aren't you worried about the threat of being shunned?" asked Esther as she cut a bite of ham.

"Time will tell, but the price I pay will be worth it to us," Dennis replied.

"You saw the folks at the church," said Lydia, careful not to speak with her mouth full of food. "Only just a few of them had ill feelings toward you."

"It only takes a couple of bad apples in a barrel," I warned.

"We might even pick up a few extra customers," said Dennis. *If you looked up the definition of wishful thinking, you might find this under the explanation*, I mused. I caught Lydia's eye, and she smiled back. I didn't remember her being such a comedian when I knew her all those years ago. I could see the gears in her little head working and always trying for a laugh. Then I glanced at Esther, prim and proper but devilish in her own right, always trying to pull some practical joke on me. She would try to tickle me when I wasn't expecting it or put her cold feet on me in bed. I think that was her favorite thing to do. Those were our special times—after a long day on the farm and dinner together, we'd go to bed laughing and talking in the dark before we fell asleep. *If you looked up the word "love" in the dictionary, I know you would see our names there.*

"Did you girls figure out when the baby is due?" I asked.

"Yes, we have it all figured out," said Esther with a beautiful grin. "I remembered the day I told you was the same day you picked up Betty's letter in town."

"Okay . . . that's right," I said.

"I found the letter, and from the postmark, we pinpointed the day it arrived. Besides, it was a Saturday after you received the letter that you fixed the tire on the bicycle."

"I'm anxious to know how many weeks you figured," I said.

"According to the calendar, she is thirty-six weeks along," said Lydia. "I will have to be here when the baby comes. We are planning for me to return in two weeks, and I am prepared to stay with her here on the farm until after the baby is born."

"What do you think about that, Dennis?" I asked.

"I will finally have some peace and quiet," he said, giving Lydia a gentle nudge on the shoulder and laughing.

"Sure thing, mister," she laughed. "I will remember that."

"When she comes to stay, I will be staying in the guesthouse with Chuck, and the girls can have the main house all to themselves," I offered. No one said a word. They didn't have to; it made perfect sense not to stay in the main house while another man's wife slept in the guest room. The more I thought about it, the better it seemed, especially when that other man's wife happened to be an old girlfriend.

We sat around and made small talk after dinner, until we all decided to turn in early, since Dennis had to be back first thing to open his store. We could hear the storm raging from the howling wind and pounding rain, and finally, I fell asleep.

CHAPTER 7

A Hole in a Hand

I awoke in the early-morning darkness, and all I could hear was the dead silence of the complete calm after the storm. Esther never liked the early mornings and threatened to kill me if I tried to wake her. Eight months of pregnancy had only increased her desire for rest.

I got up quietly and dressed in the dark. I found a match in my pocket and struck it to get some light. The flame lingered as I lit the kerosene lamp in the living room. I knew it would be light soon, so I opened my watch to see the hands read five o'clock. The kitchen door was closed, but I could hear the kitchen boys working quietly, and the smell of bacon seemed intoxicating. I listened to a stir from the guest room, and Dennis appeared in the dimly lit hallway.

"Shall we rustle up some coffee?" I whispered.

"Lydia is getting dressed," he said glancing down the hallway where I could see the flickering light from under the bedroom door.

"I heard M'Culay in the kitchen," I said. "It's only a thirty-minute drive to town in the Ford; we'll get you there before the crows are up."

"Took me two hours in the buggy," he replied.

"I asked Chuck last night if he would follow us this morning with your buggy. I have business in town, and by the time I am done, he'll have Lolly put up at the livery stable."

I opened the kitchen door, and the smell of smoked bacon hit me in the nose.

"Coffee?" asked M'Culay, grabbing a cup and pouring from the percolator that he picked off the stove with an oven mitt. "Are you ready for breakfast, bwana?" I took the cup by the handle and passed it to Dennis as M'Culay poured another cup.

As we entered the living room, Lydia stood in the hallway wearing a different dress from the previous day. "You brought a change of clothes?" I asked.

"Just a different dress," she said. "I always come prepared. "Besides, I keep the white dress for Sunday best."

"You look ready to work the store," I said.

"When we get home, we'll have to go right to work," said Dennis.

"Besides, our horse could have fallen ill, or the buggy could have broken down," she said. "I didn't want to be stuck in my Sunday clothes without a change."

"Would you like some coffee or tea?" I asked.

"I would love a cup of tea," she answered. Just then, M'Culay broke out of the kitchen with fried eggs and a big plate of bacon. Kianjahe followed him with a plate of freshly baked bagels.

"Do you eat like this all the time?" asked Lydia. "A girl could put on a few extra pounds if this is what it's like."

"Madam Lydia would like a cup of tea," I said. M'Culay barked orders in Swahili to one of his men standing at the kitchen door.

"Please, sit," I said, pulling out Lydia's chair in the kitchen. We took up the topics we hadn't sufficiently resolved from the night before. Just as we finished the meal, Esther came creeping down the hall, trying to tie the cotton robe around her bulging waistline.

"Oh . . . you didn't need to get up to see us off," said Lydia.

"What kind of hostess would I be if I let you go without saying goodbye?" she said. "And I wanted to tell you how grateful I am for your friendship."

"Oh . . . it is we who are grateful," said Lydia. "I have never met anyone like you, Esther—so warm, real, and ready to love us. It is our pleasure, indeed!"

"I will see you this week at church," said Esther.

"Oh no, you don't!" insisted Lydia. "You can't travel in your condition anymore until the baby comes. No excitement and no bouncing around in that Tin Lizzie!"

"I have to attend Easter services next Sunday!"

"I wouldn't advise it! As your midwife, you must take my advice," said Lydia. "It's for your own good and for that child. Having a baby is a serious business, and there are a lot of potential complications."

"But—"

"There are no buts about it, my dear. You have to stay home now until the baby comes. You could lose the child or go into labor in the Ford. Please, don't chance it."

"It is time," said Dennis. "We should probably be flying out the door to catch the early birds at the store."

"We'll come out to the farm next Sunday after church to check on you," said Lydia. "And we can make a plan for me to come and stay."

"M'Culay, fetch the Ford," I called. "Maybe we'll stick with the original plan to bring Lolly and the buggy later this week. I haven't seen hide nor hair of Chuck all morning."

"I'm sure he is sawing logs over there in the bunkhouse," said Esther.

"Oh no," I said. "I forgot about his snoring when I agreed to sleep in the bunkhouse while the baby is born."

"You'll have to put cotton in your ears," laughed Esther. "Just don't expect me to pick it out." I looked at Dennis with a frown as he began to laugh.

"I don't think she was trying to be funny," said Lydia. Dennis sobered up and looked toward Esther for a clue. Then Esther broke out laughing, and we all joined in. Dennis slid his chair away from the table and looked out the window to see the activity as the sun began to nudge away the morning darkness.

"Well, look here," he said. "They have Lolly all hitched and ready to go." We heard Chuck's footsteps at the front door, and he poked his head in.

"Wow," he said. "Smells like you had breakfast!"

"I can have them find you some," I suggested.

"Oh no . . . I had some jerky and coffee. I might take one of those bagels for the road. The buggy is hitched, so I will get a head start." Esther pointed to the bagels, and Kianjahe handed one to her. "I will see you on the road," he said, taking the bagel from Esther and disappearing out the doorway.

"I will grab our things," said Dennis, disappearing down the hall.

"We will see you in two weeks," said Lydia.

"I don't think I will try to come to town again until after the baby," said Esther.

"I am so excited to come," she said under her breath. "I am looking forward to the girl time."

Out the front window, I saw Chuck get into the buggy, and he gave the reins a little jerk. Esther smiled and looked over her shoulder to see if I had heard her, as if they had kept some secret from me. Girls had the gift of babble; they seemed to be able to talk the hind legs off a donkey. I had to laugh to myself, thinking about a woman speaking to a donkey until it relinquished its posture, sitting like a dog unable to cope with all the words thrown at it.

Then, I saw Chuck leading Lolly down the driveway.

Dennis came down the hall carrying the overnight bag with Lydia's white dress hanging out and dragging on the floor. He stopped and took his hat off the hook.

"Let me help you, dear; my dress is dragging," said Lydia, taking the bag and gently pushing the fabric safely inside. "Where is my hat?"

"Oh, your hat! Sorry, it's in the guest room," he said, returning down the hall.

"If you go into labor early," said Lydia to Esther, "send Chuck in the Ford. I can be here in less than an hour."

"That's comforting," said Esther. "And if you don't arrive on time, I must rely on my husband. I can only imagine how comforting that will be." She grimaced slightly then winked at me. "I still wish I could come visit you in town, Lydia," she added. "And God knows how disappointed I am to miss the Easter service."

"You will have plenty of Easters ahead of you," said Lydia. Dennis came down the hall with Lydia's Sunday hat in hand. "I'll take that," she insisted, treating it with much more reverence than Dennis had and glaring at him.

"If you can find someone to mind the store during the week while Lydia is here at the farm, you might like to come out. We can hunt that lion up the valley," I said. "Have you ever killed one before?"

"I am almost embarrassed to say I have not," he answered.

"What do you do for fun?" I asked.

"Golf," he said, puffing his chest. "I belong to the Royal Nairobi Golf Club."

"Golf?" I answered, shaking my head and chuckling to myself. "Such a strange game for you Scotts and Brits. You hit the ball and then spend all your time looking for it. Then, when you find it, you hit it again and do it all over again. I could never figure out why anyone would want to spend so much time trying to lose something they've already found."

"You're kidding . . . right?" he asked, squinting his eyes at me.

"And the other thing is that when you get really good at the game, you must be handicapped to play it. Does that mean they will break your arm?" Dennis began laughing, knowing I was pulling at his leg.

"The only handicap I have," said Dennis with a smile, "is that I stand too close to the ball . . . after I hit it!" Esther and Lydia joined in the laughter as I held my stomach.

"I think golf is something you should do during the calving season when they suggest you should not hunt big game," I said.

"I remember once leaving my sand wedge on the eighth-hole sand trap and telling the groundsman I needed to go out and retrieve it. He said he didn't want people packing a lunch during the game because it holds up the players. Esther looked at Lydia with a grimace and shrugged her shoulders. "Sand wedge, don't you get it?" he said. "He thought I meant *sandwich*. He thought we were stopping to eat lunch during the game."

"Are you ready to go?" asked Lydia. "If we leave now, we will just get there by seven. I have a few things to get ready before we open."

"Come here, my darling," said Esther, holding her arms out for Lydia. "I will miss you every day."

"I have had such a good time with you, Esther," said Lydia, melting into Esther's embrace.

"I can't thank you enough for coming out yesterday," said Esther.

The two women hugged, and I turned to shake Dennis's hand. Dennis had a firm grip. *I like that in a man. It says he respects you and enjoys your company*, I thought. *He is glad to see you, and until we meet again, he will uphold your honor. All this is said in a handshake, and men don't have to say a word to each other. Heaven forbid a man would ever embrace another man; that would be dishonorable.*

Looking out the window, we saw that the sun had begun to poke over the horizon. M'Culay moved the Ford up to the front steps.

"Looks like the automobile is ready for us," I said as the girls separated and held hands, facing off to gaze at each other for a second or two. I reached for my forty-four hanging on the hook and strapped it around my waist.

"You are like the sister I never had," said Lydia.

"Well, if we are sisters, then somebody was hiding in the woodpile," laughed Esther.

"That was going to be *my* line," laughed Lydia, embracing her all over again just for good measure. Dennis stepped toward the door and grabbed the handle.

"Not so fast, mister," said Esther, embracing him. I looked at Lydia, and the two of us hesitated, and then she held her hand out for me. I took her hand between my palms and whispered under my breath so that Dennis and Esther, who were talking loudly, would not hear.

"I think a handshake is good enough for now, don't you think?" Lydia smiled and batted her eyelashes at me as I remembered the passionate kisses we had shared years ago. Dennis opened the front door and led us to the Ford, purring like a kitten waiting to be scratched. We piled in, and away we went. I looked behind, and Esther waved from the porch. I worried about leaving her alone on the farm in her condition and wondered what would happen if she went into labor. But we had plenty of house staff here, and Willie knew how to defend the farm from almost anything.

* * *

I knew we would catch up to Chuck shortly as I turned toward town on the road. The rain had left the road slippery with mud. I had gone almost two miles when, up ahead, I finally saw Chuck perched under the canopy of the buggy being pulled along by Lolly in a hurried gait.

"Why is he pushing her?" I asked.

"I told him last night to give her some exercise when he brought her back," said Dennis.

"Oh . . . then he's okay," I said. "I just thought we would have run into him before now." As I pulled alongside, I yelled over to Chuck. "Watch that switchback! It can get a little muddy after a good rain." Chuck touched the brim of his hat, and I sped on to make the incline. I could see one man leading a horse and another man sitting on a second horse. The first had a rifle in his hand; the other man on the horse had a rifle butt sticking out of the scabbard. I stopped short with a bad feeling. The men were trespassing deep on my ranch property. Their demeanor spoke evil to me.

"Good afternoon," I said, pulling up to a stop. "Whatcha hunting?" The man on horseback pulled his rifle from the scabbard and laid it across his lap.

"Hunting?" queried the elderly man. He had a wrinkled face and gray hair poking out of his hat, with a dark sweat mark across his forehead.

"He thinks we're hunting," laughed the other younger man, who had a front tooth missing. He was wearing a tattered and dirty red cotton shirt.

"Can I help you?" I asked. "You're on my land."

"Yeah, you can. As a matter of fact, we are hunting a nigger lover!" laughed the older man with a devil's grin. A chill went up my spine. I glanced down at the rifle pointed at the floor. I started to reach for my forty-four, but Dennis put his hand on mine to stop me.

"Good morning, Hank," said Dennis to the older man. "You boys out for a ride?"

"We came looking for trouble," said the kid with a bad complexion, ruffled hair and the rotten tooth. "Looks like we found what we were looking for."

"Shut up, kid," said the man I knew now as Hank. He had a large nose with a black mustache, and piercing dark eyes. "I'll handle this. Didn't expect to find you, Dennis, nor you, madam." Lydia reached up from the back seat and touched my shoulder.

"Don't try it, Lance," whispered Lydia. "We know him, and he is dangerous!"

"Well, I guess I am the nigger lover you are looking for," I said. The toothless kid leveled his rifle barrel toward me with a broad grin.

"Looks like we might just have to kill you, then!" said the kid as Hank started to bring his rifle up from his lap. A rifle shot broke the silence and a bullet struck the boy in the hand, which started spraying blood. Birds flew from the trees, and the shot echoed down the valley. I knew the bullet had come from Chuck.

The kid fumbled with the rifle, and it tumbled to the ground at his feet. Hank recoiled at the shot; his horse flinched, and he grabbed the saddle horn with his trigger hand, taking his eye off me and looking at the kid. Immediately, I drew my forty-four, pulling the hammer back with my thumb as I came on target. *Click-click* went the revolver as I took a steady bead square at old Hank's nose. He eased the rifle below eye level, realizing I had the drop on him. *You have to have nerves of steel in a situation like this*, I reminded myself. *It's not unlike standing firm before a charging lion, waiting until the last second so you don't miss the kill shot—so he drops dead in the dirt.* I had been in that situation several times before, and it prepared me for this time.

"Drop the rifle!" shouted Chuck from behind a tree just off to our right. Dennis drew his revolver and held it on the kid, who was holding his hand under his arm.

"Lift that rifle, and you are a dead man!" I said. "I have killed lions with this thing, and I will kill you just the same if you so much as move a muscle." Hank raised his right hand, fingers spread, and held the rifle by the forearm with his left hand. "Now drop it!" I yelled as the gun fell from his hand and plowed into the mud at the feet of his horse.

"I got 'em, Dennis," I said. "See if they have any more guns on them." Dennis eased out of the Ford, approached the kid, holding his hogleg on them, and checked his waistband. The boy pulled his hand from under his arm to check the damage.

"He shot my trigger finger off, Hank!" he exclaimed in a pitiful moan.

"Now, down off that horse . . . nice and easy!" I said to Hank. "This forty-four has a darn light trigger, and a twitch can set her off by mistake." Chuck came out from behind cover and approached as Hank swung his leg over the black mare and stepped off the stirrup. "Keep 'em high," I shouted, feeling the tension in my voice, not knowing if they had partners hiding in the bush. Dennis patted Hank's coat at his waist, looking for a revolver, then looked back at me and shook his head. "Kick that rifle out of there."

"Where are the rest of your buddies?" asked Dennis. Hank tilted his head and pursed his lips.

"Just what were you thinking?" I asked. Hank didn't respond, squinting at me in hate. "Has life dealt you such a poor hand that you must make everyone else miserable just to make yourself feel better?"

"What are we going to do with them?" asked Dennis, reaching down and picking up Hank's rifle from the mud. Dennis handed it to Chuck, who tucked his rifle under his arm, then opened the action on the second one, letting a .45-70 round fall to the ground.

"Looks like he meant business with this thing," said Chuck.

"We are going to take 'em to town and let Blaney deal with them," I said.

"You will take me to Constable Lancaster!" demanded Hank.

"Your cousin?" laughed Dennis. "Not on your life. I think you have the right idea, Lance. We'll take them to Blaney Percival."

"Tie 'em up, Chuck," I said. "The rope is in the tool crib." Chuck set both rifles in the front seat of the Ford and went to the back to get the rope. He returned with a length of stiff hemp and began binding Hank's hands behind his back. Chuck took his knife off his belt, cut the excess rope, and then checked the knot. Lydia stepped out of the back of the Ford and grabbed her overnight bag, which was lying at Chuck's feet.

"Let me see your knife, Chuck," she said, pulling her white dress from the satchel and cutting a strip of cloth. "Let's get a dressing on that wound!" She took the boy's hand and wrapped it in the fabric.

"How about that finger?" said Chuck, reaching down and picking up the kid's trigger finger from the mud next to his rifle. He held it up for us all to see. The kid pursed his lips and gritted his teeth. "You are lucky I didn't blow your brains out. I had a bead on your noggin and only dropped my rifle to shoot your hand just a split second before I pulled the trigger. Here, kid, you can keep this for a souvenir." Chuck stuffed the finger into the kid's shirt pocket. "What's your name?" he asked as the young man stood there defiantly and refused to open his mouth. "I didn't shoot your tongue off, too, did I?"

"His name is Butch," said Dennis. "And Blaney will be glad to get his hands on both boys. They are some of his main poaching culprits. I haven't seen you guys around town for a while. Where is the rest of your crew?"

I killed the engine and eased out from behind the wheel of the Ford, all the while keeping my forty-four trained on Hank.

"How did you hear about me?" I asked.

"Everyone knows about you and that Negro wife of yours," said Butch with a hateful stare.

"Yeah . . . well, everybody who knows her falls in love with her, and if you met her, you would know what I am talking about. If she were here, she would be praying for you. Chuck . . . take Lydia back to the farm and make sure all the guns are loaded and ready. If you see anyone suspicious coming around, don't take any chances. We'll take these boys to town, make a full report, and turn them over to Blaney. I'll let him deal with the town constable."

"I'll have your friend there arrested for attempted murder," spouted Hank.

"We'll see who they believe," I said. "Tie the kid up, too!"

"Can't you see he's hurt?" protested Hank.

"Don't take me for a fool. Just 'cause he's injured don't mean he ain't dangerous. Tie him up, Chuck . . . snug behind his back, both hands."

"Put yer hands behind your back, kid. This is gonna hurt," warned Chuck. "He's bleeding pretty good, Lance."

"He ain't going to bleed to death from his finger. Tie him tight." I waited for just a second, covering the situation, until Chuck looked up and gave me a nod.

"I'm going to check something," I said, looking at the ground to examine their tracks. "Give me just a minute." I walked down the road about fifty yards just to make sure the footprints matched what we had in tow. As I returned to the Ford, Hank was chipping away at Chuck about how he would be sorry.

"Don't give us any more of this," I warned. "I'm not in the mood for it!" Hank looked at my face to see if I meant business. "Load 'em up, Dennis, and keep your pistol ready. Chuck, you and Lydia return to the farm and stay with Esther. I'll be back just as soon as I can."

"What shall we do with their horses?" asked Chuck.

"Take 'em back to the farm, and we will deal with them later," I said.

"I'll get the buggy," said Chuck, heading over the hill. Through the trees, I could see Lolly standing with the carriage on the lower road. *That's what he did*, I thought to myself. Chuck must have heard the commotion and snuck through the trees and got the drop on them. Chuck was always watching my back. It was such a comfort to know I had friends like that.

We stood there in the early-morning silence as the birds flitted in the branches and made their warning calls at us for invading their space. The boys were not in a talking mood to give us more information. Chuck made a clicking noise with his mouth, and I watched as the horse began to move the buggy up the road. I was surprised that his horse had heard the sound Chuck had made and responded from that distance.

"Get in the back seat!" I demanded as the two men struggled to load up in the Ford with their hands tied behind their backs. The dressing on the kid's hand had begun to soak through the wrap. "And don't go getting your blood on my seat!" The kid glared at me and worked his way up in the Ford.

"Keep 'em covered, Dennis," I said. Against my better judgment, I uncocked my handgun, holding my thumb on the hammer and pulling the trigger, letting it go back gently, then slipping it back into my holster. I felt uneasy about not keeping my gun hand filled. Taking the black mare by the reins, I led her to the rear of the Ford. "Here, you can hold her, Lydia." I handed her the reins and retrieved the other horse, which was eating at a patch of grass.

The poor thing was ill-kept: the ribs were showing, and it hadn't been brushed in some time. I took the reins and gave her a firm tug to pull her away from her breakfast. I wanted to take my anger out on the horses, but I couldn't do it, knowing they were completely innocent of all the trouble they had brought. Chuck took the black mare from Lydia while Lolly brought the buggy. Looking over my shoulder, I glanced at Dennis, who stood watch over the men sitting in the back seat of the Ford. I dropped the reins and helped Lydia climb into the buggy. The bottom of her dress had picked up mud from the road, and her black shoes were now brown.

"I'm surprised at you, Chuck," said Lydia with her little smile, and I knew she was going to try to lighten the mood with her wit. Chuck looked at her in curiosity about what she might say next. "Is that the first time you ever gave someone the finger?" I tried to hold back my guttural laugh by putting my hand over my mouth. Chuck gritted his teeth, and we made eye contact and fought to hold back our laughter. I took their horses around and tied them to the back of the buggy.

"There's a wide spot right down there to turn the cart," I said, pointing down the road. Chuck made the click with his mouth, and

Lolly continued past the Ford. Chuck shook his head, and Lydia grinned broadly. I waited for Chuck to turn around and then for him to draw near.

"Hey, Chuck, can you give me a hand to get this going?" Chuck nodded, took Lolly and the other two horses well past the Ford, and handed off the reins to Lydia. I set the throttle and the spark, and Chuck came around the front of the Ford.

"Tell me when you're ready," he said.

"Okay, go ahead!" Chuck reefed on the crank; the motor spit, then purred. "Don't try anything funny, I'm not in the mood for that either."

I made sure Chuck was safely on his way down the road toward the farm. Then, I revved the motor and let out the clutch as the Tin Lizzie eased slowly down the road. I didn't want to get stuck in the mud. I had to get these men to town and get them locked up safe. We would have to get some medical attention to Butch. *See,* I thought to myself, *I do have some compassion left inside of me even though I am so spitting mad I want to rip their heads off with my bare hands.*

Bare hands? I chuckled to myself. *No, these are the hands of a bear.*

CHAPTER 8

Making Hay

I could tell both Hank and Butch were getting a little restless as we got closer to town. I kept watching Dennis because he kept taking his eye off them and watching the road. Finally, I couldn't handle it anymore and had to say something.

"You better keep your eye on them," I said. "Here is how it works: the closer we get to town, the more relaxed we feel because this is almost over. But for those guys, it ain't over till it's over. They are more dangerous now than when we loaded them into the Ford."

"How do you know that?" said Hank in a growl.

"Yeah, you don't know nuttin' about us!" said Butch.

"I know enough about you that Blaney is going to be real happy to see you," I said.

"And when your cousin finds out that you have assaulted and threatened John River's best friend, he is going to be fuming," said Dennis.

"He don't know John Rivers," snapped Hank sarcastically.

"By the way, yes, I do," I said, looking over my shoulder. "You might know that John Rivers is friends with Teddy Roosevelt and men like Frederick Selous and the former governor of the protectorate, Percy Girouard." Hank's face sobered up, and Butch looked over at him with a wrinkled nose.

"Sounds like you boys have us, then," said Hank, as I put my attention back on the road to get us there safely. "Look, why don't we just call the whole thing off?" he continued. "We'll take our lumps. We'll walk the rest of the way to town and tell them we had a hunting accident. What do you say?"

"Nice try. We are going to finish this thing out. You started it, and we will finish it," I said firmly. In the distance, I could see the first buildings on the edge of town. The streets were quiet as I made my way. I noticed Richard Ackerley getting ready to shoe a horse as we passed the livery stable. He frowned when he saw Dennis holding a gun on the men in the back seat.

"I know you are friends with Ackerley," said Dennis, "but don't try anything funny." We approached the game office two blocks down, which looked deserted, and my heart sank.

"He usually has his paint tied to the post when he is here," said Dennis. I said nothing; I pulled the Ford to the boardwalk and hit the kill switch. The front door opened, and there stood Blaney, a sight for sore eyes dressed in his bush coat and khaki breeches. At age forty-eight, Blaney's dry and wrinkled face had lost its youthful appearance and was showing the years of wrinkling beneath the scorching sun on the plains of the Masai Mara. His nose had begun to reveal signs of heavy drinking, obvious by the red tone from the underlying veins.

"If'n you're looking for permits, we don't open till nine!" he said.

"Blaney, we got trouble," I said.

"Lance, what are you doin' here, and who do you have with you?"

"Brought in a couple of friends of yours, Blaney. They assaulted us on the road . . . something about wanting to kill a nigger lover."

"Is that so? How is it going, Hank?" said Blaney. "Seems I have a warrant for you boys. Both you and that Butch kid. Haven't seen you around town for a while." I knew Blaney would be glad to see these boys; poaching was about to become the least of their troubles.

"You get that Constable Lancaster down here right now!" insisted Hank.

"Just as soon as we get this sorted out," he said. "Besides, Lancaster has no authority; he's just a volunteer. And he don't have any business over what happens outside of this town. I'm turning you over to the government. Kapur Singh is the inspector of police. Bring 'em in, boys, and we'll put 'em in my cell for now."

I knew I would feel much better when we had them behind bars. I set the brake, came around the side, and grabbed Hank by the arm to help him out of the Ford so he wouldn't fall on his nose in the dirt. He leaped, and his right arm came free; the rope fell limp behind his back. He came around with his fist and caught me with a haymaker on the left cheek. I felt like I had just been hit by a baseball bat. I blocked the second punch with my forearm, trying to protect my face. My knees felt weak as clouds in my head made everything fuzzy. I attempted to fend him off as he reached for the sidearm holstered on my belt. The last thing I saw as I began to fall to the ground was Blaney hitting Hank over the head with his billy club from behind. Then I felt the street call my name as my head bounced on the dirt. I lost all train of thought and felt euphoric, as if I were floating on a cloud.

* * *

"Hey Lance," shouted my old friend John. "Are you in there?"

In where? I thought. *Where am I?* Through the fog, Betty stood behind him with a curious smile. How comforting to be with them again. Betty looked so beautiful. John took hold of my shoulder and shook me.

"What's the matter, John?" I said, trying to mumble the words, but I could feel them coming out of my mouth like warm mush.

"No, Lance, it's me, Blaney! You are okay; wake up, man."

I opened my eyes, and the street was spinning like I had been on a two-day drunk.

"Everything is okay now; we got 'em locked up." I closed my mouth. My teeth gritted together, and then I began spitting out a big mouthful of dirt that tasted like it contained a fair share of horse manure.

"What the hell is going on?" demanded Richard Ackerley in a gruff voice as he crossed the street, decked out in his leather black-smith apron.

"None of your business, Dick," barked Blaney.

"Where's Hank?" he demanded.

"Hank is inside," he answered. "He's talkin' to the storekeeper."

"What are you doing on the ground, Lance?"

"I tripped over a pile of manure," I answered.

"Looks like you got some on your face," he said with a smile. I sank to my knees, wiped my face with my sleeve, and spit out more dirt.

"Hank!" shouted Ackerley.

"In here, Dick!" Hank answered from Blaney's makeshift cell.

"You okay in there?" Just then, Dennis appeared at the front door and swung it closed, standing with his gun hand on his side-arm. We could hear yelling inside the game office, but we couldn't make out the words.

"I have a right to know just what in the hell is going on here!" shouted Ackerley.

"This is none of your minds, Dick. Don't go sticking your nose in where it don't belong," said Blaney. "Just go back to your business, and let me take care of mine."

Ackerly gritted his teeth and made fists with his hands. He shook his head, turned without another word, and walked up the street toward the police station.

"We're gonna have company here in short order," said Blaney to Dennis and me. "You better tell me what happened."

Dennis and I filled Blaney in on the whole affair. How they threatened to kill me, how they had leveled their guns at us, and how if Chuck had not gotten the drop on them, the outcome would undoubtedly have been different. When Dennis told him what they had said about Esther, Blaney frowned, and his face turned red.

"You boys are lucky; I know this Hank character. He killed a man last year in cold blood who cheated him at cards. He claimed the murder was self-defense. The only two witnesses swore the other man drew first, and they never proved anything different. Everybody knew the truth: that the guy never got his gun out of his holster until he was dead on the ground. It was Hank who pulled the gun out of his belt and put it there in his cold, dead hand before the police arrived. Except now I have witnesses who will state that these two killed an elephant on the Tsavo last spring and sold the ivory in Mombasa."

We saw Ackerley returning down the street at a brisk pace with a tall man dressed in a white uniform and a pith helmet. "Is that Lancaster?" I asked.

"That's him," said Dennis. "Stand by; he has quite an inflated opinion of himself."

"You let me handle him," said Blaney as we waited silently, all three of us trying to assess the situation.

"What's the trouble here, Blaney?" said the volunteer constable.

"This is an active investigation," said Blaney. "I have just arrested two men on poaching warrants signed by Colonel Patterson himself."

"You will let me see Hank immediately," he barked, pointing his finger at Blaney

"I will let you speak with him, but he will be turned over to Inspector Singh. And if you want to keep that finger, you will keep it in your pocket!" Blaney stepped to the front door and let Lancaster through. As Ackerly tried to follow, Blaney stopped him. "Go back to your horseshoeing, Dick, before you get in over your head." I saw Ackerley tighten his jaw. "I mean it, Dick; go on, get out of here before I arrest you!"

"Try it, Blaney, and you'll be in over your head," he said in a stern warning.

"They shot the kid's finger off!" said Hank. "They had no call; we didn't do nothin' for it!"

"It was self-defense," I said. Blaney looked over and shook his head slightly for me to please shut up.

"Self-defense?" asked Hank. "That asshole didn't shoot the kid. It was the old man, his buddy, and it weren't no self-defense."

"If this is true, it ain't self-defense," said Lancaster. "I know you, mister. Aren't you the fella that went on safari last year with John Rivers?"

"That would be me," I said.

"And that ranger hit me with his billy club. Look at this bump!" said Hank, touching the back of his head.

"At least he hit you in the head where it ain't gonna hurt you," said Lancaster. "I know John Rivers."

Sure, everybody knows John Rivers, I thought.

"This is going to get us nowhere," said Blaney. "He said, she said—we're going to wait for the inspector. And for now, these boys are gonna stay locked up 'cause I got 'em on warrants."

"What about my hand?" asked Butch. "I need a doctor!"

"You can do me a favor, Lancaster," said Blaney. "You find the inspector, then we'll sort this thing out proper, and we'll find somebody to take care of the kid's hand."

Lancaster turned and came out of the game office, not saying anything to us.

"Go on back to the livery, Dick," insisted the constable. The men stepped off the boardwalk, and Lancaster whispered something to him. The two men parted, each going their separate ways.

"What about this Inspector . . . Kapur Singh? Is he a fair man?" I asked.

"He's a good man. He's an Indian. Tough, smart, and fair-minded," said Blaney. "I got confidence he'll call it the way we see it. You stay here with the prisoners. I'm gonna follow Lancaster and make sure he finds the inspector." Blaney stepped onto the street, and Lancaster glanced over his shoulder to see Blaney following him.

"We didn't have much choice in this outcome," I whispered to Dennis. "If they had killed me, maybe I would be happier right now; I don't know." Dennis gave me a smirk, then shook his head. "I would prefer to meet Abigail before I meet my maker."

"What's the defense?" whispered Dennis. "I don't think it is self-defense if someone else is doing the shooting."

"I don't know . . . I ain't no lawyer. But Blaney thinks Chuck did the right thing in taking the shot. Besides, he could have shot the kid's head off, and he didn't do that."

"They can't charge him with murder or attempted murder 'cause he only shot off the kid's finger," whispered Dennis.

"That's my take. It don't seem like someone has to pull a trigger to assault you. Heck, if the kid had pulled the trigger, I wouldn't be alive right now to say anything. Knowing these boys, they probably would have killed both you and Lydia too, just to shut you up, then tried to cover their tracks."

"I'm still concerned there are more men with them," said Dennis. "And Chuck could have his hands full if they show up on the farm."

"You never saw Esther with a rifle before; she can handle herself," I said confidently, knowing I had taught her how to shoot. We looked down the street. Blaney and Lancaster were talking with a man in uniform wearing a white turban. Blaney always spoke with his hands and appeared to be putting them to good use as he pleaded his case. After several minutes, Lancaster parted from the men, and Blaney came strolling back toward us with the man we assumed was Inspector Singh.

"I'm turning them over to the inspector," said Blaney.

"These men are dangerous and have given plenty of trouble in this town," said Inspector Singh, who was soft-spoken and had a steady disposition, slender nose, and well-trimmed facial hair. "I will see that the boy gets medical care. You men are free to go home to be with your women, if that is what you want. I will visit the farm later today to take a full statement from you and this man named Chuck."

"What about Chuck's defense?" I asked. "I know it's not self-defense."

"If this circumstance is found true," explained the inspector, "then your friend has the right to protect you just the same as you have the right to protect yourself. This legal term is known as *defense of another.*"

"I'm going with them," said Blaney. "Just so there is no further funny business from their ruffian friends."

"It's a good idea, sir," he said.

"Before we go," said Dennis, "let me put a sign on my store for my customers. I'll be right back.

* * *

Once again, I could feel the knot in my stomach as we drew close to the farm, especially when we went past the spot where we had been accosted. I pulled up and showed Blaney the layout and where Chuck got the drop on them. I was relieved that Chuck had not blown the brains out of that kid, Butch. Death is such a messy affair, and no matter how angry a person gets, I never wanted to see anyone killed. I had a vision of the boy with his eyes open in a blank stare with a bullet-torn skull, and the knot in my stomach turned to a sick feeling.

I drove the Tin Lizzie hard and we arrived in record time. The roads were much better now. Turning down the driveway, the car slid sideways in the dirt, and I leaned on the throttle to straighten her up. I could see Chuck stepping off the porch as we pulled up, skidded into place, and shut the engine down.

"THE BABY IS COMING!" shouted Chuck. "Come quick!" As I scurried into the house, I nearly leaped from the Ford to the front door. I could hear moaning from our bedroom, and Lydia met me in the hallway.

"She has started labor," she said, grabbing my arm. "It's a month early, Lance." Pulling away from her grasp, I burst into the bedroom. Esther looked up with relief as she lay flat on the bed and held her hand to me.

"She is going to be okay; I just know it," I said.

"God knows what He is doing here," Esther said. "Everything is designed so that we will rely on Him. Even if the worst thing should happen, God can turn a bad thing into the best thing."

"But I have a plan, and most of the time, I think He must have it wrong," I said, knowing that would get a chuckle out of her.

"I would laugh," she said, "but as you can see, I'm not in a laughing mood." Her face grimaced in pain as another contraction overtook her.

"Take deep, slow breaths," I said. Esther looked at me like I was the responsible party. This little person inside of her was fighting to be born. I had longed for months to take that child by the hand and walk in the garden on a Sunday afternoon. The visions had flooded my head of teaching her how to ride a bicycle, take care of a horse, and eventually shoot a rifle. I couldn't wait to hear her call me Daddy. But now, the reality of what was about to happen terrified me. I had experienced the death of a spouse once and the loss of a child I never had the pleasure of meeting. *I don't know if I can handle this for a second time in my life*, I prayed. *Please, Lord, be with Abigail and give her strength, and be with Esther. And if this little one is to come into the world today, let there be no complications that would compromise her health.*

"I know you want to comfort her right now, but you have to let me take over," said Lydia. "I have done this before, and everything is going to be fine. We had quite the excitement here, and I think that's what started her labor. Chuck will fill you in."

"What sort of excitement, Lydia?"

"Talk to Chuck!" she insisted, frowning at me with her back to Esther so that she could not see her face. I left the women alone to take care of their business. I could see the men talking on the front lawn. There again, Blaney's hands were a big part of the discussion. I stepped out on the porch, entering the middle of the conversation. The men looked up, and the talk went silent.

"What happened?" I asked.

"Chuck killed a man. The other one got away," said Blaney.

Oh no, I thought to myself. *We are in for it now!* "Who'd ya kill?"

"Ever heard the name Blackwood?" asked Dennis.

"Enough to know he's a bad seed," I answered.

"He ain't much of a seed no more," said Blaney. "He's lying out there in the field dead as a mackerel, and this here is his rifle."

"Thirty-thirty lever-action Winchester," I said. "And the one that got away, who was that?"

"Don't know, Lance," said Chuck. "I never seen him before, but M'Culay got a good look at him."

"I know these boys well," said Blaney. "I got a pretty good idea who he is."

"Come on, Lance, I'll show you the body," offered Chuck. We headed out in the field, and M'Culay and Willie stayed behind. I looked back, and Willie motioned for me to go ahead. Chuck grabbed my arm and let some space go between us and Dennis and Blaney.

"It was Esther who shot him," Chuck whispered once the men were far enough ahead of us. "He got the drop on me, but I will swear it was my bullet that killed him." My eyes darted forward, but Blaney was still busy talking with Dennis.

"Anybody else know?" I whispered. Chuck shook his head, looking up at the backside of Dennis and Blaney walking ahead. "We can sort this out later, but thanks!"

That is what pushed her over the edge into labor, I thought. *All that excitement. I should have known something like this would happen.* I saw the toes of the man's boots sticking above the grass as I approached, and then I saw his death stare and open mouth. The blood pooled and dripped out the corner and across the side of his cheek. Blaney reached down and closed Blackwood's eyelids with his hand.

"Yeah," I said, "I've seen this guy before—saw him in town last month. He gave me the evil eye then, and it gave me the creeps."

His shirt had a blood-soaked bullet hole in his chest. "This is where you got him, Chuck; it looks like a heart shot." Chuck looked at me, giving me a confirming nod that said: *We have a secret.*

"This fight ain't over," warned Blaney. "Those boys have lots of friends and they are all negro haters. Let's get in the house. Everybody take a window and keep your eyes peeled." We hurried back to the house; Willie and M'Culay followed. "What'd he look like?" asked Blaney, directing his question to M'Culay.

"I say him man in late forties—curly blond, chubby, flat nose, and cowboy's hat," explained M'Culay.

"A cowboy hat?" said Dennis. "That's Frank Ridley!"

"Yep . . . to a tee," said Blaney. "Just like I figured. Got any extra ammunition for my .30-30?"

"Nope, but we got plenty of guns and ammo," I responded. I could hear Lydia comforting Esther in the other room as she groaned from the labor pains. "I have an aught-six; here, Dennis." I took the Springfield off the rack and opened the bolt.

"Do you mind if I take this Winchester 1895 lever-action rifle?" asked Blaney. "It's a lot of rifle for a manhunt, but I have one just like it." I grabbed it off the rack and handed it to him, along with a box of cartridges from the shelf.

"Okay, it shoots one inch high at a hundred yards," I said. "Here are some extras for good measure. I'll use the .30-40 Kraig. I used it on safari, and I take it with me almost every day. It's what I feel most comfortable with."

"How about this one?" asked Dennis. "Where do I aim?"

"Same deal," I responded. "We shoot them all the time, and they're all sighted dead on. Just shoot for center mass at two hundred, and you can't miss. Here, Dennis." I tossed him a box of .44 magnum pistol ammo. "You might want these for a backup."

M'Culay looked forlorn, because both he and Willie were being left out of the party.

"Want a rifle?" I asked.

"Yes, bwana, You know M'Culay can handle a rifle!" he answered as Blaney raised his eyebrows.

"They know how to shoot, Blaney," I confirmed.

"They may know how to kill an elephant or a lion, but shooting a white man is entirely different," Blaney said.

I ignored the comment. With a broad grin, I pulled the Springfield .275 off the rack and handed it to M'Culay. "This is Esther's rifle," I said. M'Culay took it in his hands like I had just given him a scepter from the queen herself.

"Here, take my .30-30 Winchester," said Blaney, handing his rifle to Willie. "Somehow, I went off without any extra shells, but we'll use the rounds left in Blackwood's gun for a backup. It's full up and shoots dead on at a hundred." Blaney jacked four rounds out of Blackwood's rifle, and Willie picked them off the floor and stuck them in his pockets.

"I don't have to tell you to be careful with that thing," I said. "You know how to use it." Blaney and Dennis disappeared down the hallway, and I pointed Willie to be with the house staff, huddled in the kitchen. "You take the back of the house, Chuck." As I stepped to the front window, I saw the broken pane and the shattered glass spilled out across the floor. The wind blew softly across the farm in my face.

For the next three hours, we sat watching on high alert as Esther groaned at frequent intervals from the bedroom. The time ticked away as our baby got closer to coming into the world. I hoped that having a premature birth would not cause any complications, but in my medical training, I knew the realities of it. But then . . . seriously, my medical education? I think they spent about thirty minutes one afternoon talking about giving birth, and that was about ten years ago. I had learned much more about farming in my time here in Africa than I had remembered in that short discussion all those years ago about birthing.

Finally, I couldn't take it any longer, sitting by the window while listening to my wife in agony. I wanted to do something; I never felt more helpless than I did right then.

"Keep your eyes peeled, M'Culay!" I said, getting up from my post.

"Eye peeled, bwana?" he said, wrinkling his brow.

"Keep watch; I'm going to check in on Esther."

"Yes, bwana, I keep my eye peeled like an orange," he said with a grin.

Esther was in between the excruciating episodes that were causing her so much pain. I had begun to get the picture of why they call it labor. *Even hard labor breaking rocks in a chain gang isn't this hard.* How ironic that we were keeping watch right now, rifles loaded, standing like a bunch of prison guards watching just one prisoner in hard labor. As I entered the room, Esther seemed peaceful, and Lydia rose from her chair next to the bed.

"She is progressing just fine," she whispered. "She has dilated to the point where I will soon be able to help her deliver."

"Oh, Lydia, I can't tell you how relieved I am that you are here. I would have been in way over my head."

"She is an angel sent from heaven," said Esther.

"Are we getting close?" I asked.

"Won't be long now," answered Lydia, "I don't think a woman wants her husband in the room to help her deliver a baby."

"A wife indeed wants her husband with her while going through the most significant event of her life," I said.

"Yeah," said Esther, "so she can get her hands around his neck." Esther's smile turned sour as she began to groan as the contraction overtook her.

"We need to keep her hydrated. Here, fill this pitcher for me," she said, taking it off a table in the corner. Lydia squeezed Esther's hand as Esther gritted her teeth for another go around.

So many of us men think we are tough, I thought. *We imagine we can take a punch and get up swinging. If men had to experience childbirth, then we would see just how tough we were.*

M'Culay saw me with the empty pitcher, leaned his rifle against the window, and reached out to take it. We didn't have to speak; I knew his heart to serve me, especially her. He treated Esther like a queen. Sometimes, I wished I had more of what he had—a heart for service. I handed him the container, and he disappeared into the kitchen. I took my post, watching along the edge of the field and the tree line. If anyone tried to move on us, it would be from there, out toward the main road. I double-checked the rifle to make sure the safety was still set.

Esther's groans had become more extreme; it seemed like her labor had grown more intense. M'Culay came out of the kitchen and handed me the water.

"She is ready to deliver now, Lance," said Lydia from the archway in the hall. I set my rifle against the sill, telling M'Culay to stay put. "I am glad she is going to deliver in the daylight," said Lydia. "Glad that she has been making hay while the sun shines, so to speak." I began to approach the bedroom, and Lydia stopped me. "Very few women in this world have killed a man the same day they brought a new life into the world. You have quite a woman here."

"But I thought you needed my help," I said as she cut me off from coming into the room."

"If I need your help I will let you know. It's time to let me deliver this baby," she said, taking the pitcher. "I'll need some hot water and clean towels now." I went to the kitchen and directed the staff to bring what we needed. Hustling back to the bedroom doorway, M'Culay kept his vigil at the parlor window.

"It's time, Esther," explained Lydia. "It's time to push."

I focused back on the window, and stepped away from the bedroom door, gazing out on the field and crouching down to hide. I thought I saw movement along the fence line and kept my attention directed while Lydia was busy with Esther. Then I heard Esther give out a loud groan. I jumped back to the bedroom doorway.

"She's a girl!" shouted Esther.

What I saw was sort of a rough-looking little thing, all blue and covered with slime. Lydia took her by the feet, held her upside down, and cracked her on the backside. Then Abigail opened her mouth and began to scream.

Lydia cleaned the baby with warm water and a damp towel, then wrapped the child in a blanket.

"I didn't let you down, Lance," said Esther. "God has given us a beautiful, healthy daughter."

"She's a little small, but remember she came early. You still have work to do to pass the afterbirth, my dear," she said. "I wish it were over for you, but it's not." She placed the baby in Esther's arms and helped her finish the birthing process.

Monday, March 17, would be a day to remember for the rest of my life. And the story that we would have to tell this little girl would be something that would shape her life.

Esther purred like a kitten, cradling the child in her arms and caressing her nose with her fingers. "She has a nose like yours,

Lance." She lay still, looking up with her gorgeous grin. "And we will call her Abigail Harriet Miles."

"Harriet?" I asked. "Is that someone in your family I should know?"

"I might be related; I don't know," she said. "But the middle name is in honor of Harriet Tubman."

"Who's that?" I asked.

"I can explain all this to you later; it's a long story," she said with a tired look.

The declaration that Lydia had made continued to ring in my ears. In one day, I had witnessed both the joy of life and the terrifying reality of death. *The truth is that this is God's specialty*, I realized. *The God of joy and happiness in times of elation and victory and the God of comfort and peace in times of terrible tragedy.* I took just a moment to think about all that had happened that day and all that could happen yet. We were not out of the woods by any means. I remembered back to Sunday morning when Esther and I had passed the livery stable, and now I wished I had paid closer attention to those men who were giving us the evil eye. I looked at the angelic little face of my dear daughter, Abigail, and wondered what kind of a life she would have. I knew I had just created something I would worry about for the rest of my life.

The mood shifted as Blaney began shouting from the back room. I burst out into the hall, and saw M'Culay still at his post. He looked over and shrugged his shoulders.

"Drop it, or I'll let you have it!" shouted Blaney. I stepped to the front window, grabbed my rifle as the glass crystals crunched under my boots, and scanned the scene for movement. *At times like these, I really miss John. Man, I wish he were here right now.*

"Stay low!" I said. "I'm going to go help Blaney." M'Culay slithered out of the chair and got to his knees, guarding the house.

"Come out of the house, Blaney; we're gonna torch it," yelled a devilish voice from outside *POW!* went the report of a rifle shot echoing through the valley, and I crouched next to M'Culay, taking cover. *POW, POW, CRASH!* I heard the glass spray across the floor in the back room from a shattering pane. *POW . . . POW,* as two more reports filled the farmhouse, followed by a third and a fourth. Then, silence, a dead silence that gave me a chill.

"Stay here, M'Culay, and get ready to kill somebody. Just make sure it's not one of us," I whispered. I did a low crawl on my elbows to the back room, holding the rifle off the floor. Sort of like putting a stalk on dangerous game, my rifle at the ready. I peered into the back room. Blaney and Dennis were crouched at the window with their rifles ready. What a relief to find them still alive! I let out the breath I had been holding. Chuck looked up from his post at the door and shrugged his shoulders.

"I got one," said Dennis.

"Yeah, I did, too," said Blaney. "It was Frank Ridley. I have known him a long time and he is a bad seed. He wanted to burn the farmhouse."

"How about the man I shot? Who was that?" asked Dennis. We crouched in silence, but Blaney didn't answer. I heard one of the injured men groan something.

"I'm not sure," answered Blaney.

"Did you see any more?" I asked. Dennis looked up and saw me hunkered down behind him in the doorway.

"We didn't see any more," said Dennis.

"Wait here!" demanded Blaney, looking back at me and then crawling on his belly toward me. "Cover me! Stay down and keep your eye on 'em. I'm going out there." Blaney disappeared down the hallway, and I heard him exit the front door.

"We watched 'em come across through the coffee rows," whispered Dennis. "They tied their horses to the tree line about a thousand yards away. Ridley had an unlit torch."

"How's this gonna sit with the town?" I asked.

"This bunch has caused so much trouble in town, most people will be relieved," said Dennis. Blaney appeared in the grass, packing his rifle in his right hand, and hunkered down as he approached the two men. He checked Ridley with the barrel of his rifle, then went quickly to the other, dropping to one knee. We could see them talking.

"Who is that guy?" I whispered as Dennis shook his head and shrugged his shoulders. We both sat vigilantly as Blaney's hands trembled, and he dropped his head, putting his hand on the man's forehead. He looked around and made a sign to us that he was coming back to the house. We heard his footsteps up the porch and the hinges creek on the front door. Blaney came into the room and didn't say a word as if in deep thought. The urge to ask him about the situation crossed my mind, but wisdom prevailed, looking at his face. I had never killed a man before. I could only imagine what might be going through the minds of my friends right now, and, with Esther and Abigail, everything had to be compounded.

"BWANA!" shouted M'Culay from the front of the house. "COME QUICK!"

"Stay here," said Blaney, putting his hand on Dennis's shoulder, crouching low, and urging me to follow him back toward the front parlor.

"Horsemen, bwana!" said M'Culay, pointing down the driveway with his rifle trained on the three men trotting in. "Should I shoot, bwana?"

"Don't shoot, that's Kapur and his men," barked Blaney, taking the rifle away from M'Culay. Could this thing be finally over, or was it just beginning? At least for the moment, I felt like the cavalry had arrived. They were at a full gallop, and Blaney took the front door and jerked it open. The horses approached the front porch—nostrils flaring, blowing wind, soaked in sweat, and eyes wide. The men, all three in uniforms, jumped off their mounts and settled them.

"We heard rifle shots; where's the trouble?" said the inspector as he drew his pistol from his holster. The other two men had their rifles ready and scanned the farm for additional threats.

"It's over for now, Kapur," said Blaney. "They're all dead."

"How many is 'all'?" he asked.

"Three of 'em. Monroe Blackwood, Frank Ridley . . ." Blaney paused momentarily as if he struggled to get the words out. "And Lester Williams."

"If you have Blackwood and Ridley dead out here, this town will be much grateful," Kapur said.

"Their horses are still tied to the tree line out there," said Dennis, pointing to the prairie's edge. Blaney made a motion to Kapur, and the two of them stepped away from us, having a private conversation under their breath. I tried with everything I had to hear what they were saying, or to get a clue from their faces. The two men came back in earshot and Blaney pointed to the place where Blackwood lay.

"That's Blackwood over there in the grass," said Blaney. "The other two are around the side."

"Let's have a look at the other two," said the inspector. His men stayed with the horses and stood at the ready with rifles across their chests. Blaney led the inspector while Dennis, Chuck, and I followed behind.

"This here is Ridley," said Blaney. "See here, I got him right above the eyebrow." He held the side of his head with his boot and pointed to the bullet hole with the barrel of his rifle. It was a gruesome scene, one not worth describing. "This here is the torch he had," said Blaney, picking up the stick with the rag wrapped around the end. He held it to his nose and then dropped it in the grass. "Yep . . . it's soaked in petroleum, all right. He went down like a rag doll, and his rifle is right here where he dropped it."

"Let's look at this one," said Dennis. His eyes were opened and he had a blue-tinted face. Neither man said a word and just looked at each other in silence.

"This man is no troublemaker," said the inspector.

"I know," said Blaney with a pale stare as if all the blood had gone out of his face. "He's been avoiding me."

"Looks like he should have picked this day to avoid you, too," said the inspector. "I will need the whole story; is there a place to talk?"

"How about the house?" asked Blaney.

"Listen, my wife just gave birth during this whole commotion," I explained. "Can we gather in my shop? My wife is resting. In fact, I should go check on her right now."

"Come on," said Chuck. "Follow me." I turned and headed for the house, and Lydia met me on the porch as the other men followed Chuck.

"Is everything okay?" I asked.

"Everything is fine. She is resting comfortably, and the baby has started nursing."

"Does she need me right now?"

"No . . . no, everything is fine, except you might want to think about doing something about boarding up those windows before the night chill sets in."

"I'll get Willie on it. I would like to sit in on the briefing with Inspector Singh to get the details of what's happening."

"You go," she insisted. "We are just fine." I stepped off the porch and saw one of Kapur's men guarding the corner of the house. *The other one must be around the back*, I thought. As I hustled to the shop, Willie greeted me at the doorway.

"We are going to have to board up the windows in the house," I said. "You can use the fence boards we cut out in the barn last week. Heck, I don't have to tell you what to do."

Willie shouted across the yard to some of his men and then headed toward the barn.

"Make sure the insepector's—and his men's—horses are watered!" I added.

As I stepped into the office, Chuck was explaining how he had brought Lydia back to the farm in the buggy to be with Esther.

"After we got settled in, Esther noticed something out of the corner of her eye and stepped to the window. Just then, the window-pane burst and threw shattered glass over all of us, and we heard the gunshot echo across the valley. I grabbed a rifle off the rack—I think it was the Kraig—and I got ready to defend the house. I yelled at the women to take cover in the other room. Lydia disappeared, but Esther took her safari rifle off the rack and crouched behind the door. I spotted two of them, and they both had rifles. They were hunched down behind the outhouse. I rose up to get a shot at them, but a bullet hit the windowsill, nearly hitting me. I saw one of them run across the yard, and I took a running shot that missed him."

Chuck paused, and I scrutinized the faces of Kapur Singh and Blaney to evaluate their reactions. This was not their first rodeo; neither gave away anything about what they might be thinking.

"That same guy," Chuck continued. "You say he is Blackwood, the dead one right out there—well, he came running for the porch, and I backed away from the window and shot him through the door. When you go up there, you will see the bullet hole."

"I thought you said Esther was crouching at the door?" said the inspector. Chuck paused, and he began to stammer for his words. I cringed, knowing that Chuck had tripped himself up over a stick in the pathway and was getting fumbled up in his story.

"That's right . . . ah . . . you're right, I mean," stammered Chuck.

"What do you mean, sir?" said Inspector Singh. "Just give me the straight story!"

"That is it," said Chuck. "He was shot through the door!"

"But how could you have taken that shot if she were standing by the door?" said Blaney, rubbing his chin and trying to look into Chuck's eyes. Chuck struggled to find words and looked at the floor.

"Look me in my eyes when you talk," demanded Kapur.

"It was Esther who killed the man!" said Lydia, standing behind as we all jerked our heads to look at her. "She sent me over here to tell you that she shot the man. She said Chuck told her not to say anything, but she will not have anything but the truth here. She said she wanted me to tell you she had no choice in the matter."

"Why the funny business, Chuck?" asked Kapur.

"After she shot him, she started into labor with that child. The man stumbled off the porch, ran about sixty yards, and fell face-first in the grass. His partner turned tail and I never did get a good look at him. But M'Culay was using the outhouse at the time—he was indisposed, but he got a good look at him through the crack in the sideboard. Heck, Esther was in such pain I just couldn't bear to put her through any more agony, so I figured I would just say I did it, if that was what it took. She and I have grown on each other, and she is like a daughter to me now. You have to understand that I would do anything to protect her."

"You might be in trouble for lying to the inspector," warned Blaney.

"Not under this circumstance," said Kapur, looking back at Lydia. "Any man might do it; it is chivalry."

"Guess if I was going to lie," said Chuck, "I should have known you men would see right through it."

"I don't know, Chuck; you had me convinced," said Dennis.

"Tell me the real story," said Kapur with his calming voice. "Make it straight." Chuck paused and cleared his throat, then looked back at Lydia.

"Okay," he began, looking at Kapur square in the eye. "This is God's honest truth. Blackwood came on the porch and got the drop on me. He was standing behind the door for cover. I dropped my rifle and put my hands up, hoping he wouldn't kill an unarmed man. He said he was going to kill me because I had shot his friend's finger off. Esther could hear his voice just on the other side of the door, and she stood up, took a step back, then leveled her rifle and pulled the trigger. The bullet struck him square in the chest, and he stumbled back with his eyes wide as bagels. Esther jacked another round in her rifle and moved to her left, still training her rifle on the door."

Bagels! I thought. *Why bagels?* I fought to erase the imagery in my head.

"I saw the bullet hole in his shirt with the smoke coming from it. He stood there just for a second in shock, and the blood began to soak through. He let go of the rifle with his trigger hand and clutched his chest. As he was running off the porch, Esther stepped to the window, and I yelled for her to take cover, which she did. Then, like I said before, he jumped off the porch, and all the rest of the story is true. I heard him yell to his partner that he was hit."

"I'm going back to the house," said Lydia. I could hear hammer pounding coming from the house.

"I think that's all of them, isn't it, Kapur?" asked Blaney.

"They have more friends like Richard Ackerley, but he is an outsider, not part of this," said Kapur. "They have relatives; one of my men is a distant relative. Hank claims he is a cousin, but he is much distant than that." As Kapur spoke, he had a soothing and quiet way about himself; self-assured and confident, tough but compassionate. He deserved respect, and he earned mine. He was a calm listener, meticulously gathering each word Chuck said and careful not to raise his voice in any way that might escalate the situation.

"I have all I need," said Kapur. "No need for me to stay here any further. When I get to town, I will send the undertaker to retrieve the bodies. You shouldn't have any more trouble since the other men are locked up."

"I will stay behind," insisted Blaney. "For now, you have my information that will change the charges to conspiracy to commit murder for the other two men. I will be in this week, and we will ask them about some other poaching they are suspected of. But right now, that is the least of their problems. Wire Colonel Patterson, if you please; he will want to know what has happened here."

"I believe he is in Mombasa," said Kapur.

"You are correct," said Blaney.

"We will take our leave, then," Kapur said, getting out of his chair and going to the door. I wanted to shake his hand but waited for him to make the first move. He looked me in the eye, likely realizing my desire. This man was all business and showed no emotion. I couldn't remember ever having met such a man like this, who commanded your respect by his strict stature yet made you feel at ease by his humble nature. Kapur pressed his palms together and continued to look me in the eyes.

"Some Europeans are offended that we Indians do not have their custom of shaking hands," he explained. "I can respect your customs if you can respect mine. The folding of the hands I am now doing is to show you respect and remind you that we share a oneness in our souls. Hopefully, you will take this as a compliment of my respect for you."

I folded my hands together and followed his lead, returning the gesture. I expected to see a smile from him, but his words were good enough. He left the shop, called to his men, then turned to me as he got to his horse. "My best wishes to your wife," he continued, "and to you for becoming a father. I have heard of you and her many times, and people speak highly of you. I have a son named Satbachan, and I hope one day he will follow in my footsteps. This boy is just thirteen, but I am stern with him so that he will learn to become a great man."

He put his foot in the stirrup and swung his leg over, sitting high on his horse. *Not on his high horse, but high on his horse,* I chuckled to myself, knowing the difference. The leather squeaked as he moved to settle in. "Did she give you a son?" he asked.

"No," I responded, "a daughter." I expected him to respond enthusiastically, but he turned to Blaney.

"Will you stay here until the undertaker arrives?" he asked.

"Yes, I will, and I may stay another day before I head to town just to ensure there's no more trouble." The other two men mounted up, and, without another word, all three horses trotted off down the driveway, leaving me with a sense that maybe we could relax just a bit.

CHAPTER 9

RESPONSIBILITY

Late afternoon settled in on us as we waited for the undertaker's wagon to show up. We were still reeling from the day—a day I would never forget as long as I lived. Even though I had wanted to kick back for the last two hours, we were busy supervising the men boarding our windows and watching for further threats.

Blaney had taken Dennis out to the tree line to fetch the horses left tied out there and brought them into the corral to unsaddle them. I watched at the fence with a piece of dried grass in my teeth as Blaney pulled the heavy saddle and scabbard off the back of the white-faced mare. She sat so patiently, seemingly relieved to have her burdens removed. I wondered if she would miss her master and if he had treated her well.

"Whose horse is this one?" I asked as Blaney tossed the saddle on the top of the fence rail. "She seems like a great animal."

"Lester Williams," he snapped. I could see Blaney wanted nothing to do with a conversation right now. He looked in the saddle bag, then turned and unbuckled the throat lash under the horse's chin. He removed the bridle and bit from her mouth. I knew something had to be bothering him, but then why not? We still had three bodies lying in the grass who had to get removed from the farm before the sun went down. I could only imagine how it must have felt to kill a man. If this weighed so heavily on a man like Blaney, I wondered how it might affect Esther.

"Need any help with anything?" I asked. Blaney looked up and wrinkled his brow as if I were bothering him. "I'm going in to check on Esther."

To return to the front porch, I would have had to walk right past Blackwood again, so I walked in a wide circle around, giving him his space. The farm seemed different, with three dead men here still with their boots on. It gave me an eerie feeling, and I wished the undertaker would get here in short order. Dennis and Chuck were sitting in my favorite chairs on the porch; Chuck puffed on a cigar as I walked up the front steps. Both men had their rifles across their laps.

"Taking a break?" I asked.

"Just kickin' back," said Chuck.

"What's eatin' Blaney?"

"Don't you think killing a man is weighing heavy?" asked Chuck. I looked at Dennis, but he sat silent.

"I don't know," I answered. "This ain't Blaney's first time for that. I suppose he'll come around; I'll give him some space." I came through the front door and ran face-to-face into Lydia.

"Are you coming in here?" asked Lydia, standing between me and the bedroom door.

"Planning on it," I answered.

"Not until you wash up first! If I know you, the first thing you will do is get your hands on your daughter. You are filthy, for heaven's sake."

"Okay . . . okay," I said, hustling into the kitchen and getting M'Culay to help me with the hot water, soap, and a towel. When I returned to the living room, Lydia met me with a clean shirt.

"I'll give you some privacy," she said, ducking back into the bedroom with Esther. I pulled the dirty one off and nearly jumped into the other. I tossed the dirty shirt in the corner.

Esther and Abigail looked so beautiful together, snuggled in the bed as I entered the room.

"Do you want to hold your daughter?" asked Esther, looking up with a smile as her eyes met mine.

"It's like a dream come true," I responded as Lydia reached down and took the baby, handing her to my waiting arms. I didn't know how to feel at that very moment. My hands trembled as I took the child into my arms. The whole thing seemed surreal, like a dream that wasn't happening, and someone could wake me at any moment. "Abigail Miles," I said. Lydia stood there momentarily and then put her hand on my shoulder.

"I'm going to give you two some alone time," she said, turning and taking her leave.

"Abigail *Harriet* Miles," said Esther once the door was shut.

"Okay then, but you must tell me, who is this Harriet? Is it Harriet Beecher Stowe?"

"Tubman, Harriet Tubman," she explained. "She was a Negro abolitionist and a Union spy during the Civil War years. She escaped slavery and then worked in the Underground Railroad."

"They had a railroad that went underground?" I said, knowing that would get her a rise. She hesitated before responding, knowing I was pulling her leg to get her goat. Everyone had heard of the Underground Railroad.

"Do you want to hear her story, or are you just going to tease me?"

"Oh no . . . I want to hear. Please go ahead," I coaxed, looking down at the angelic face of my newborn.

"She was in her forties when she escaped from slavery in Maryland across the border into Pennsylvania. It's hard for me to imagine slavery because I never had to experience it. My family always lived in New York, and slaves have been free there since 1827. Both my momma and my daddy had stories about my grandparents. But Harriet made some twenty missions rescuing more than three hundred slaves. She also helped John Brown recruit men for the raid on Harpers Ferry. Her life has always inspired me greatly, and it is right and proper that I give my daughter her name. She is in her nineties; the last I heard, she was still living. As a young girl, I always wanted to meet her, but she is much too famous."

"What about Harriet Beecher Stowe? They say when Abraham Lincoln met her, he said, 'So you are the little woman who wrote the book that started this great war?' Do you think Harriet Tubman was named after Harriet Beecher Stowe?"

"No, not hardly," said Esther. "When Harriet Tubman was born, Harriet Beecher Stowe was only ten. She wasn't famous until 1851, when she wrote *Uncle Tom's Cabin*. Whether it is either of the Harriets, it doesn't matter. One was a Negro, and one was a white lady. I think it is a fitting middle name for our daughter. Why were you so stuck on the name Abigail?"

"I like the story of King David in the Bible."

"I knew that was the Abigail," she said. "You are such a sap for a good story."

"I can just imagine what a beautiful woman she was," I said. "When I think of her, I think of you."

"Nice recovery," she laughed. "Do you even know what the name Abigail means?"

"No, I just liked the name," I said.

"Get ready for this: I looked it up, and it means 'a father's joy.'"

"You have got to be kidding me!" I laughed. "You mean I just pick that name out of a hat, and that is what I get? A father's joy! How about that? How does something like that happen?"

"I just figured you must have known all along," said Esther.

"A father's joy," I said. "That's like a premonition or something."

"You're pulling my leg again, right?" she asked with a curious look, trying to get me to fess up.

"No, I swear, it was because the Bible describes her as beautiful and wise. That's why I liked her. I liked what she did helping David and his men, and I liked her name."

"If that is true," continued Esther. "Then God himself has named our baby girl."

"And just like the two Harriets, she will be famous," I said.

"No, Lance," said Esther. "She will be strong in character and a woman of God. Her strength and faith might make her famous, but fame isn't worth a plug nickel without faith."

"You are much too famous for me," I said as she grinned and batted her eyelashes.

"You just figured that out?" she chuckled. "Yeah, I'm famous, all right, for marrying a white man."

"Are you okay?" I asked.

"Oh, you mean from all the work I did this morning?"

"Right," I said, knowing there was much more to the story than just giving birth to our daughter.

"I will be glad to get some rest," she answered.

"But are you really okay?" I repeated.

"Oh, I see what you are asking," she said, closing her eyes and taking a deep breath. "My whole mission in life has been to save souls. You know my heart; I am as gentle as a lamb. But I am a student of the Bible, and I live my life by it. I pray constantly, and I am confident that I am in the will of God because I walk with Him. I am not a person who takes matters into my own hands.

"I went on that safari with you and our friends and never even shot one animal. I am not a killer, but I will tell you right now, when it comes to defending myself and the lives of my friends and my family, I will. When the chips are down, I will not hesitate to do what I have to do. I killed a man today, and my dear husband, it is weighing heavy on my soul right now. I did not shoot him out of vengeance, because vengeance belongs to God himself. But I did pull the trigger out of a sense of justice. We are all given the right to defend ourselves in the face of such a thing as murder.

"I am glad I will never have to look at his face as I know you did. I prayed before I pulled that trigger, and I prayed after I let the shot go. I knew I would hit him; I heard him breathing on the other side of the door. I stepped back, and I leveled my rifle where I knew I would get him. Then I shut my eyes, and I shot. I took cover when I heard him groan and stumble off the porch. My ears were ringing so loud that I never heard anything else. Right then is when the baby started coming."

"Strange things, life and death," I said, still clutching to my little bundle of father's joy, wrapped tightly in her warm blanket. I thought about Blackwood as he had been shot through the heart and what must have gone through his mind in those last few minutes of life as he ran off the porch. I wonder if he had been able to make peace with God in those final moments of life as he stumbled through the grass.

"The whole thing is strange when you think of it," she agreed. "Life and death, night and day, joy and sadness, rich and poor, faith and fear. We serve a sovereign God we can trust to do what is right and good in our lives, but we are not puppets on a string. We have free will to make our own choices. But in His infinite knowledge,

He knows everything. Jesus said, 'Not even one small sparrow falls to the ground apart from the will of my Father.'"

"So how do we reconcile life?" I asked. "Is it all God, or do we have a part in it? Why did you have to shoot that man? Why didn't you just pray for God's protection? Then maybe those men would have laid their guns down and gone home."

"First off, God didn't send those men out here to kill us. They came on their own accord. Whether that was demons tormenting their thoughts or Satan himself, only God knows. It would have been nice just to pray and make them disappear, but it's much more complicated than that. We make our own choices, but God already knows the choices we are going to make. Time and space do not bind God. All this happened so that we would become stronger. God always prepares you for the next thing and allows bad things to happen for good purposes. When you teach someone a good lesson, it usually involves discipline."

"But I heard it said that God will never give you more than you can handle, right?"

"That's not true, Lance!" explained Esther. "If that were true, then why would we need him? That's like saying that God helps those who help themselves. Lots of folks think that's in the Bible, too."

"It's not?" I said. "I thought that was right out of the Bible."

"Not so much. But I will tell you what is in the Bible regarding suffering. Paul said in his first letter to the Corinthian church, in just the first few lines, that they were under great pressure in Asia. He said it was far beyond their ability to handle it, and they despaired of life itself, feeling like they had received a death sentence. He said this happened to them so they would not rely on themselves but on God. I think the events on this farm came along, so we wouldn't try to rely on ourselves. We will rely on Him even more to find peace in our soul." Her words were like chocolate candy; you could put it in your mouth and taste the sugar as it melted on your tongue. Every time I listened to her, my love for her grew more profound because of her incredible wisdom.

"I wish I could have talked to them and told them about God's love," she continued. "I am in the business of helping people find life. I don't think anyone has the corner on salvation. You know it's plain when a person accepts Christ and is born again. That's easy, but what about the thief on the cross? He wasn't born again, and he didn't accept Christ as his savior. All he said was, 'Remember me when you come into your kingdom.' I guess that confession of faith was enough. But look what he missed by not finding Jesus earlier, a life filled with hope, love, and joy walking with the God of the universe in peace. That's what I wish I could have told those men. Now, we have to forgive them for trying to kill us. Unforgiveness will rot you from the inside out. It's like drinking poison, expecting the other person to get sick."

"Wagon coming," said Lydia from the front parlor. I handed Abigail gently back to her mother as if I were holding a priceless crystal vase. I turned to leave, then paused for just a second to look back and take in the feelings of seeing my two best girls together.

"Where is she going to sleep tonight?" I asked.

"Sleep," said Lydia with a grin, standing in the bedroom doorway. "You don't know much about babies." she laughed.

"Remember that crib you said you were going to make?" said Esther.

"I know; I just figured I had plenty of time," I answered. "I started it, and it's coming along."

"For tonight, she is going to sleep in that dresser drawer until you have a proper crib," said Lydia.

"Where am I going to sleep?" I asked.

"Depends on if you want to put up with Chuck's snoring or Abigail's crying," laughed Lydia.

"Hmm, I might take my chances with Chuck in the guest house," I answered. "What about you, Lydia? Will you and Dennis stay with us for a few days?"

"No, not Dennis. He will return to town, likely following the undertaker's wagon. He's going to have to open the store tomorrow. I will stay for at least a week or two to help my friend care for Abby."

Abby . . . just the sound of that name lifted my heartstrings. I had never heard it said like that before, and I liked it.

I slipped out of the bedroom, leaving the girls to take care of more girl stuff, and then cracked the front door. As I did, I noticed the bullet hole, chest high, right in the center of it. I saw the black flatbed carriage with three coffins roped down, pulled by a two-horse team and two men sitting high in the seat. One man held the reins while the other had a shotgun across his lap. Blaney and Chuck stood in the driveway while Dennis went from the barn to join them. I stepped off the porch, and Blaney glanced back and then trained his attention toward the approaching wagon. I paused to look at the blood-spattered walk boards. *I can probably fix that by having my boys flip them over.* The afternoon sun hung low in the sky perched among the puffy clouds, and a gentle breeze came across the farm. I felt a total sense of relief knowing we would soon be clearing these dead men off my property.

"Thanks for coming out, John," said Blaney, greeting the men. "Thanks for coming, Phil."

"Looks like you had a little trouble here, Blaney," said Phil, the guy with the shotgun, who stepped off the wagon first, carefully pointing his weapon in a safe direction. Phil wore a pith helmut and had a wide handle bar mustache. His face was wrinkled showing his age, and he had a round belly likely from his desire for ale. "Are you okay, Dennis?" he said, putting his hand out to greet him as his foot touched the grass.

"We are going to be okay," said Dennis, firmly taking the man's hand. "This here is Lance Miles," he said, turning to me. "This is a good friend of mine, Phil Tremper." I reached out and shook his hand, trying to size him up as he did the same to me.

It's a man thing, I thought. Two men greeting each other for the first time, trying to gain a sense of perspective from one to the other. Funny how you never get a second chance to make a good first impression. With a man, what they see is what they get, and very little changes a man's opinion of another once they meet. The whole process starts much earlier than usual. Men always talk about this one or that. They are worse than a bunch of old women. That imprint about what one man says about another stiffens up like a corpse and is not likely to change just because they have a pleasant meeting. It always helps to have somebody else do the introduction because otherwise, neither man has a frame of reference. But a man puts much more credence in what he hears about you than in what he can learn about you face-to-face.

"Are you the undertaker?" I asked.

"Nope, I'm just here backing him up," he said, putting the shotgun over his shoulder. I looked out at Blaney, and he and the fellow they called George were standing over the body of Blackwood. George had a slender build and was clean-shaven. I estimated him to be in his mid-thirties. He spoke with a heavy English accent and wore western boots and a white western hat.

"Nice shotgun," I said, admiring the LC Smith.

"Thanks," he answered. "They dropped the price twenty-five bucks last year to one twenwty-five, so I snapped it up."

"Ten-gauge, huh?" said Dennis. "That'll do it!"

"With double-aught buck," he said with a grin.

"Can I see the engraving?" I asked. Tremper held the shotgun out in both hands, barrel up, for me to examine the receiver. "That's beautiful," I said, eyeing the fine detail of the pointing English setter etched in the black steel of the lock plate in an oval just above the double triggers. He beamed pridefully at his wise choice to select such a fine piece of workmanship and power.

"What sort of work do you do?" I asked.

"I figured you would know. I'm a deputy for Blaney," he said. "Who'd ya kill, Dennis?"

"You know Monroe Blackwood?" asked Dennis.

"He is one mean one," said Tremper. "I saw him in a fight a couple years ago down in Mombasa, and he bit this fella's ear off. He jumped to his feet while the guy was still on the ground, holding the place where his ear had been, and he spit the darn thing right in his face. Folks around here give him plenty of space." He paused for just a few seconds in thought. "What about them other two?"

"Frank Ridley and Lester Williams," I said.

"Lester?" he said with wide eyes, putting the palm of his hand on his cheek and pulling his fingers across the stubble on his chin.

"What about Lester?" I asked.

"You'll have to ask Blaney about that one."

"Who's Lester?" I demanded as Phil just looked at me as if he knew more.

"Like I said, you have to ask him," he said.

"Give a hand out here!" yelled the undertaker, whom I had not met yet. The four of us moved quickly across the yard and then made our way out in the shin-tall grass by the outhouse across from the barn. "Give us a hand with the body," the undertaker repeated as we approached.

"This is the farm's owner, Lance Miles," said Blaney as I put my hand out to greet him.

"Hi," he said politely, not extending his hand toward mine, and I dropped my hand quickly to my side, trying to recover my esteem. I knew what this was about; I didn't have to make any further inquiries. Blaney shook his head in disgust and caught my eye in acknowledgment of a silent apology.

"Grab a limb!" he said in a rough tone. I looked away from Blackwood's face as I grabbed his pant leg. I had gotten a good enough look at him before, and I knew I would never forget that death stare for as long as I lived; I didn't need any more of it.

We dragged Blackwood's body across the field toward the wagon lying in the grass, creating a drag mark as we pulled him along. I kept my eye on the wagon, imagining Blackwood's head bumping along behind as we hauled him. George began to untie the coffins that were lashed down to the flatbed wagon. Blaney helped him take the wooden box down, setting it on the ground, and George removed the lid.

"Okay, let's get him put away," said George. I felt uneasy about George, even though Blaney seemed to have a relationship with him. Even Dennis thanked him for coming out and gave him an enthusiastic handshake as if they were old friends, too. I thought I should be praying about this, but I just couldn't do it right now, and I hoped God would understand. Unceremoniously, we plopped Blackwood in the box, and Blaney covered him with the lid. He had already begun to stiffen up with rigor mortis. I remembered the term from my schooling days. It was Latin: *rigor* meant "stiffness," and *mortis* meant "of death." I felt relief, knowing I wouldn't ever have to see his face again. I had no feelings of hate for the man, even though I could still feel the evil in the air lingering from the spirit of hate in his soul.

Okay, Lord, I do pray for his soul, I found myself thinking. *Forgive him, Lord, for what he tried to do here today. Lord, cleanse this farm from these demons and fill this place with your Holy Spirit. And the other two men as well, Lord, I pray for them as you meet them in the air. Give them your grace and your mercy in the name of Jesus. Amen.*

"Can I move the wagon up closer so we don't have to drag them?" asked George, directing his attention to Blaney. *Wow*, I thought, *This guy is something else. You would think he would at least have the courtesy to direct his questions toward the man who owns the property.* Blaney took hold of a horse by the reins up close to the horse's chin and began to lead them across the yard to the side of the house. I didn't say a word, but the hoof tracks broke through the lawn, and the wagon tracks sunk into the soft turf, leaving ruts. But at that very moment, I wanted the bodies cleared away so badly that it really didn't matter to me.

As we approached the other two men, I told myself not to look, but my eyes locked onto the face of Frank Ridley. Like I said before, the top of his head had been blown off, a sight not worth describing. I began to feel warm beads of sweat break out on my forehead. I had seen a lot of things in my day, but this one topped them all. My head began to spin, and I felt light-headed.

"Oh man," said George. "Ridley never knew what hit him." Then my stomach began to churn, and I could feel what little breakfast I had down there knocking at the door of my esophagus. I tried to swallow to hold back the inevitable. If I did this here now, at this time, these men were going to belittle me, and my self-esteem might be wounded to a point of no return.

"I'm going to go check on my wife," I whispered to Blaney as he looked in my face, likely wondering why I had to do this right now when they needed my help.

"Are you getting sick?" he asked.

"I don't know; I just know I have to go to the house." As I turned to take my leave, George piped up.

"Where's he going?"

"His wife just gave birth today. He's going in to check on her," said Chuck. I didn't dare look back as a bubble in my belly began working its way up, and I let go of the sour burp from my lips.

"He looks a little green," laughed George, "like a sixteen-year-old kid with his first cigar. Come on, let's get 'em boxed up."

I reached the front porch, stumbled up the steps, and sat in my chair. I looked at the horizon and let the gentle breeze blow in my face, trying to clear my head. I had felt like this before, standing at the rail of a boat in a rough sea, attempting to focus on the horizon. The queasy feeling in my stomach began to subside, and I sat back, still taking deep breaths. I could hear that George fellow around the side of the house. laughing as the men finished their work. I thought, *That guy is an undertaker? He sure doesn't seem to have the temperament for it. How can I ever hope to help a dying man if this is how I react to the signs of blood and gore?*

But then, maybe God was preparing me for a greater purpose, and, having seen what I did, didn't necessarily mean that I would react the same way next time. It just said that I had come through my first actual traumatic event, and every one after this might just get a little easier. I took a deep breath of fresh air, letting it out slowly. My head began to clear, and my nausea started to subside.

Just then, Dennis came round the side of the house pale-faced and looking like he was ready to faint. He stopped as he saw me on the porch. "I'm going to follow George back to town," he said, bounding up the steps and pausing at the front door. "Are you okay? It looks like you need some of your color back."

"I'm going to be okay. I just got a little queasy, that's all."

"I've seen a bunch of dead guys, but that was a bad one. Even George said it was. I'm gonna say goodbye to my wife," he said, walking in the front door. I could hear the wheels on the wagon squeaking as they turned around to get it back in the driveway. Then I saw the horses coming to the front, pulling up next to the closed coffin lying in the grass. Willie came running across the yard to meet the men, pausing to converse. He called to a group of his workers, who quickly responded, and they lifted the coffin and stacked it on the other two on the flatbed. George tossed ropes over the boxes, and he and Blaney began securing the load.

I heard the front door hinges squeak; I needed to get Willie on them with some oil. They were starting to annoy me, even though it seemed like a good alarm system.

"I wish you didn't have to go," said Lydia as I turned and saw Dennis with his arms around her. I got up from my chair. My knees quivered slightly, but my head felt clear.

"Darn good thing you decided to come out for a visit yesterday," I said. "We would have had our hands full."

"Turned out like God had it planned," insisted Lydia. "What will you do for dinner? It will be too late for Murugi to fix you dinner when you get home."

"I won't bother her with that. I'll go across the street to the hotel and get a T-bone steak," he said. "And a tall glass of cold beer."

"Yeah," she answered. "You are going to need a beer after this day." I looked toward the barn, and Willie's men were finishing the hitching on Dennis's buggy. None of us had eaten since breakfast, and, of course, no one had even thought about food.

"Before you leave, I need to know about Lester Williams. Who is he?" I asked.

"Don't ask me again. You will have to hear it from Blaney," Dennis responded. "I'm not sure what happened, but I know Blaney is hurting right now." I could see in Dennis's eyes that carrying this topic any further was useless. "Sorry, but I'm going to have to go. George is in a big hurry to get back to town, and I don't think I want to go alone on the road back. I'll feel safe with Phil and his ten-gauge."

"You're right," I said, putting my hand out for his. He took my hand in a firm grip and put his left hand on my shoulder. That was as close as two men dared to come together in an embrace unless they were under the age of eight years old. Even then, elders discouraged two boys from showing affection toward one another. The handshake was a male expression of love for one another, and it gave me a warm feeling. *So much for warm feelings*, I laughed to myself. *I have had enough of those warm feelings today to last a lifetime.*

"You be safe," I said. "We will be praying for you." He let go of my hand, turned to Lydia, and kissed her forehead. Then he headed off the porch, putting his hand on his pistol under his coat, probably just to reassure himself.

"So, how well did Blaney know Williams?" I whispered as Dennis walked up the drive toward the buggy. Lydia just shook her head, shrugged her shoulders, and then turned to go back to the house. Then she stopped short and twisted toward me.

"Dennis told me not to say," she whispered. "I want to, but I guess you will have to ask Blaney."

Why all the mystery? How ridiculous this all seems now. I don't want to have this conversation with Blaney; I just want to be in the loop. I looked out at Chuck and wondered if he had any idea. Or he might have been content to not get into anything like this. I knew this had to be weighing heavy on Dennis if it were true because Dennis had fired the shot that killed the man. I wondered what kind of conversation Blaney had had with Williams, which none of us were privy to. There was so much drama for one day; the whole thing made me sick—all of it but Abby and Esther, of course!

The wagons pulled away from the farm, and I watched as Chuck and Blaney stood in the driveway and talked back and forth. I was torn between going down and confronting Blaney and going in to check on my girls. I turned and slipped in the front door, taking the easy way out. Curious, yes, but unwilling to deal with what I knew would be very painful at that moment.

CHAPTER 10

Angelics

Making my way inside, I heard low voices coming from the bedroom. *What now?* I thought. *Haven't we had enough calamities for one day?* I poked my head through the doorway and found myself in the middle of Esther's prayer with Lydia.

"And Lord," Esther continued, "please watch over and protect those men as they travel the distance of the roadway to town. We know, Father, that You are the great protector. Send Your angels to surround them. Give strength to their horses, and allow them safety by Your mercy. And Lord, put a hedge around this farm and give us peace as the news hits the town about this great tragedy that happened here today. May You give wisdom and understanding to all who hear, and may Your favor and grace rest on us. Fill this farm with Your Holy Spirit, and by Your Spirit, please drive off the demons that might try to linger."

Esther looked up from her prayer and saw me standing in the doorway and smiled. "And Lord, be with all those who have had to make a choice to take a life. Be with Blaney as he has been struck with the news that a friend of his has died here today. Give us Your comfort as only Your love can give. Grant us Your peace, as only Your eternal perspective can deliver. Guard us with Your protection, as only Your Spirit can shield us. And finally, Lord, we pray for Abigail, that You would strengthen her and give her a hunger for survival. Watch over and protect her all the days of her life. And this we pray in the name of Jesus. Amen."

I paused momentarily and then spit out the words waiting behind my teeth: "So Lester Williams must have been a friend of Blaney's?"

"Yep," said Lydia. "I know Dennis will be upset with me for telling you this. But the cat is already out of the bag because I told Esther." Lydia seemed so eager to be the one to tell the story. "Now, you mustn't tell Dennis I said this, or he will kill me. Lester Williams has been quite a good friend for a long time. I had told your wife before Dennis told me not to say anything."

"How good?" I asked.

"He was one of his deputies," explained Lydia. "He was up in Tsavo for many years. Until a couple of years ago—seems it might have been about the time Esther showed up here in town."

"Me?" asked Esther. "Hope I didn't have something to do with this."

"Oh no," said Lydia. "You didn't have anything to do with it. He and Blaney had a falling out as I heard the story, and Blaney fired him. I don't know any of the details. Blaney would have to tell you that."

"Blaney was the first person I ever met here in the protectorate," said Esther.

"I thought I was the first?" I said.

"Nope, it was Blaney. He looked approachable, so I asked him where I would find a hotel when I got off the train. He was so accommodating and friendly. Heck, I had no clue he might be the game warden. I thought he looked like just a nice gent waiting for the train. He gave me directions to the hotel and told me that if I ever needed anything, I should come see him at his office. That is when I found out his position. When I headed across the yard to find my luggage, that's when I found you."

"I never knew any of this," I said.

"He has always been like an older brother to me. You remember what he said to me the day he stood up for us at our wedding?"

"How could I forget?" I said. "He vowed always to support and protect us at all costs. Boy, oh boy, the price has certainly gone up for him."

"For Dennis, too," said Lydia. "He is the one who pulled the trigger on Williams. Dennis is hurting right now. He knew Williams too—not as much as Blaney, but we all knew him."

"Well, I'm sorry, but I do feel responsible," said Esther, wiping a tear off her cheek. "Lance, I'm afraid our love has caused this!"

"Our love has produced Abigail," I said, "and not this tragedy. Their hate has caused this disaster, and we have to refuse to take responsibility for their hate."

"This whole thing makes me sick," said Esther. "Not only heartsick, but sick to my stomach. Do you think we will ever recover?"

"Me too," I agreed. "I almost fainted out there. I had to take a seat on the porch to catch my breath. What can we do for Blaney?"

"You let me talk to him," said Esther. "He knows how much I love him, and I have been praying for him for a long time since we met. I've been waiting for a moment like this when he might be open to what I have to say. I know he's dying to see Abigail; just give us some time alone."

"I don't know if you are strong enough today," said Lydia. "You need to get some rest before you go trying to evangelize."

"I will get some rest," said Esther. "Can we put Abigail down and see if she will sleep? Then maybe I can get some sleep." Lydia reached out, took her from Esther, and laid Abigail in the dresser drawer packed with blankets.

"She is already asleep," said Lydia. "Let's just see how long it lasts." I backed out of the room, and Esther lay back on her pillow and snuggled in to get some rest. Lydia tiptoed out behind me and pulled the door shut.

"Wow, one of Blaney's deputies, huh?" I whispered.

"Not anymore," she answered. *Yeah, not anymore,* I thought. "Do you want to check on M'Culay and see his dinner plans?"

"I can do that," she said.

"Lydia . . . thank you, my dear. I can't tell you what this means to me. Did you ever figure we would end up like this?"

"No, not hardly," she answered, smiling back.

I jumped off the porch and walked toward Blaney, who was standing by the corral with one of our horse boys, brushing the white-faced mare. Blaney looked back and turned to face me as I approached.

"Look," he said, "I have calmed down now. You just need to know I need space when I get like that. I hope you didn't take offense to this old bear."

"Get like what?" I asked. Blaney squinted his eyes and put his hand out for me to shake. I put my hand out and took his in a firm grip.

"I was pretty rude to you this morning," he said.

"I know you were upset; I think you have a right to be."

"You don't know the whole story," he said. "I was angry with that damn Williams." Blaney bit his lip, and his face flushed.

"You knew him, didn't you?"

"I don't know what got into him."

"What did he say to you out there as he breathed his last, Blaney?" I wanted to take the words back as soon as they left my lips. I felt as if I were stepping over the line.

"Let's just leave it where it is. He was a friend of mine once. Even though we'd had a falling out, I never thought it would come to this.

I'm just thankful that everything turned out well for Esther and the baby. When can I see them?"

"They're resting now," I said. "We're going to have dinner, and then you should be able to see them."

"You have quite a woman there, you know," he said.

"I have known that for a long time," I answered. "I just never saw the realities of it until she showed up here in Nairobi."

"I took a shine to her that day, too," continued Blaney. "I knew she was something special the minute I saw her. She has been like a daughter to me, the one I never had."

"Yeah, except you are only twelve years older than her."

"Age? Heck, that's just a number," he said. "I've done more living in this old bag of bones than most people have done in ten lifetimes. Just know this: if anyone ever tries to harm her or that child of yours, I will take their head off with my bare hands." We both sat silently as the image of that soaked in our minds. This conversation gave me an insight into Blaney's world, an insight I would never forget.

"Where's Chuck?" I asked.

"He was goin' out to catch an afternoon nap before dinner," said Blaney as he shook his head.

"I ain't never been able to do that."

"Yeah, me either," I said.

"Heck, I wake up like I have been on a three-day drunk," he laughed.

"What's going to happen to these horses?" I asked.

"You want 'em?" he said. "Of course you want 'em."

"I don't know if I want them. What will I do with them? Everybody in town will know the story, and they know Ridley and Williams and their horses, too."

"Neither one of 'em got any family; the only one friend Williams ever had was me. Ridley, he's just a bad seed, always goin' to or comin' from stirrin' up some sorta trouble."

"Well, he stood a little close to the fire this time when he stirred the pot," I said.

"He got burned all right," said Blaney. "He never knew what hit him. Wow . . . that .450 just near took his head off. I killed men before; all of 'em were dark-skinned. Never had to shoot a white man before."

"Is it really that different?" I asked.

"No, 'cause we're all the same inside." His statement made me feel good about myself and my family. Whether a man was dark-skinned or light-skinned, it didn't matter a hill of beans. When would the world ever wake up and change? I wanted to imagine a world where it didn't matter.

I guess that place must be heaven. If God wanted it to be here, then he would have created it here. God made this place a testing ground for the hearts of those he chose to come here. He could have made us all the same skin color, but there would be no test in that. God wanted us not to be so darn proud of our race. Whether you are a Jew or a Gentile, black, red, yellow, white, purple, or gold, God called us to love one another. He never gave permission to any one of the races to be master to another. Seems like that gets us in trouble, thinking we are better than somebody else.

"How do you think we got here?" asked Blaney. "Weren't you a Darwinist?"

"Yeah, sorta, till Esther got a hold of me," I laughed.

"Yep . . . that girl is a heart-changer, all right," I continued. "I was a believer in Darwinism. John Rivers had a huge impact on my life. He and I spent hours and hours just talking about the theory and its importance to the world. But then I got thinking about God and who He is. If He could create this place, He could make it look like it occurred naturally."

"Sort of like He is hiding behind a curtain, don't you think?" asked Chuck.

"God is not going to show Himself to those who don't want to see Him. He is not going to make it easy to find a hidden treasure. Do you have a clue what eternal life with Him is worth? If it were something you could buy, men would be fighting over it. But since it is a gift, men don't want to have anything to do with it."

"They don't want anything to do with it because of how it changes a person," he said. "I am comfortable in my skin, and I like the person I am. I don't want to go changing into some religious fanatic."

"Is that what you think we are?" I asked. "Religious fanatics?" I tried looking at Blaney's eyes, but he wouldn't look at me.

"Well . . . maybe not *fanatics*," he muttered.

"You asked how we got here; let me tell you," I said. "From my days in college, I have retained a few things. They have been studying reproduction since the mid-1600s. The word *spérma* is Greek for 'seed.' I don't think anyone has ever counted them, but they estimate a man produces millions and maybe billions of these little guys. On the night you were conceived, your father left behind untold millions with your mother to do with them whatever she could. Do you know how much a million is, or even a billion?"

"No, not really," said Blaney, looking me in the eye.

"Ever seen a wagonload of wheat?"

"Sure, plenty of times."

"Near as I can figure, just for illustration purposes, a typical wagon can carry about a cubic yard, which is about twenty bushels. A bushel is about a million grains, so that's about twenty million grains of wheat. Nobody ever counted how many sperm a man leaves for his wife. But they estimate it could be somewhere in the neigh-borhood of a hundred million. Not that I am so good at doing this math in my head, but let's see." Blaney looked at me with a curious grin as I struggled for the number. "That's around five wagonloads if it were one hundred million."

"So what are you getting at here?" asked Blaney, trying to get me to make my point.

"Okay, so if just one of those grains of wheat that represents just one of those little sperm had been a better swimmer than you were that night and got to the egg ahead of you, you would not even exist. That egg would have developed into your brother or your sister."

"Oh, come on," said Blaney.

"That's the straight scoop," I said. "You wouldn't even be here. You would be a spirit somewhere out in the cosmos."

"What, like an angel or something floating on a cloud with a harp?" said Blaney.

"We have always been given that image, right?" I said. "But an angel is not like that. They are created beings with a purpose. They are ministering spirits specifically assigned to a person who is made in the image of God, and they follow them their whole life until that person dies. An angel is not made in the image of God." Blaney didn't speak. He just listened. "They are eternal beings who always look on the face of God. Angels can never become what we will one day become, and we can never become what they are."

"Where did you get all this?" he asked.

"Most of it from sitting around in the evening talking with my wife. Some of it is from back in the day of my medical school, and the rest is from reading the Bible." Blaney rubbed the thick gray stubble on his chin as I continued. "Think about this, my friend. Before you were born, God knew you. He chose you out of the billions of spirits waiting for a chance to be called to come here. God chose you to be made in His image. When He picked you, He had high hopes that you would one day find the truth. He has the same hope for everyone He sends here, but he lets us make our own choices. Every one of us has hit the big prize just to get here. We are not like the animals; we are something special with a huge responsibility."

"Responsibility . . . what responsibility?"

"We are not like the animals; they get a free pass into eternity. They are innocent and not held responsible for their sins. However, we are; we needed someone to save us from our sins."

"I knew this would all come back around to Jesus," he said, folding his arms across his chest.

"He is always a stumbling block, right?"

"Yep, just like you say," he answered.

"That's how He described himself nineteen hundred years ago."

"Dinner's ready!" shouted Lydia from the porch. "Time to get washed up!" I turned and waved, and she disappeared back into the house.

"Let's go get Chuck in the guest quarters; we can wash up there," I said. As Blaney followed, I wondered if anything I had said would sink in. I hoped I hadn't gone too far and felt a little guilty since Esther had said she wanted to talk with him. I didn't think anything I said would hurt any of her discussions.

CHAPTER 11

First Time, Same Time

After dinner, Blaney got a chance to hold Abigail. I knew what this meant to him, especially since he had never had children.

"You know something?" he asked, staring into Abigail's face.

"Lots of things," said Esther. "But I bet I don't know what you know right now."

"You'll be surprised at this one. You know what day Abigail was born?" A dead silence fell over the room as we waited for the answer. Blaney made a big grin as he said, "She was born on my birthday!" Esther's jaw dropped. Lydia's eyes widened, and she put her hand over her mouth.

"No," said Esther. "You have got to be kidding me. Today is your birthday?"

"That's the God's honest truth; she was born on my birthday," said Blaney, grinning ear to ear.

"Why did you wait until now to tell us?" I asked.

"Cause I just thought of it. You know, with all the commotion and all. And with all that has been going on with my work, I guess I just lost track of the calendar. I usually don't make a big deal out of my birthday. I hate counting the years; I even had to count back to remember just how old I am."

"How old are you?" I asked.

"I am thirty-eight." *Wow*, I thought, *no way; thirty-eight? How could that even be possible?* Blaney wore his age poorly, as if he were well over fifty. I scrutinized the wrinkles on his face and the graying hair in his sideburns. We were the same age, and all along, I figured Blaney to be my senior, about the same age as John Rivers, who was forty-eight. I thought about telling him gently so as not to have him take offense at me, saying he looked old. Then, I came to the realization that it wouldn't be possible.

"I never figured you to be our age," said Lydia. "You seem so mature and experienced." Blaney smiled again but didn't try to respond. I thought how masterfully Lydia had approached the subject instead of telling him the brutal truth.

So glad she said it and not me, I thought. Beautiful women have a way of getting away with murder. Sort of like Esther shooting Blackwood through the front door. Bet they don't even make her give an official statement. The whole matter will be all said and done. When they thought Chuck had pulled the trigger, the authorities were eager to make him prove his case. But now that they knew Esther did it . . . nothing.

"We could have baked a cake if we had known," said Esther. "We could have got you something."

"This little lady is a good enough birthday surprise for me," he said.

Abigail wrinkled her lip and let out a scream. Blaney held her up like an unfamiliar rifle that had just accidentally discharged, and he began struggling to locate the safety. Lydia stepped in to rescue him and cuddled her at her breast, and Abigail eased back on her roar. *Funny how women just have a special way when it comes to babies. They all seem to have the touch even if they have never been a mother.* Lydia turned and handed her off to Esther.

"I heard your first name is Arthur," I said to Blaney to see what he might say.

"That's right; Blaney is my middle name. I never cared much about the name Art when I was a kid. I was probably nine years old when I decided to go by Blaney. That was my mother's maiden name. They gave me the name after my grandpa, Arthur Blaney, who died before I came along. My mother always remembered as a kid how much he had loved her. She said that when her daddy hugged her, she could feel the adoration soaking through her skin. She said his whiskers would scratch her face, but she didn't care much."

"You ever want to have kids?" asked Lydia.

"Guess I'd have to find a wife first," he said. "I am content just to have Esther and Abigail." Esther grinned ear to ear like a beauty queen who just got her crown.

"It has been a long day," I said. "I think it's time to turn in."

"You won't get any arguments from me," said Blaney.

"At least you got a nap today," said Esther.

"It weren't worth much, that's for sure," growled Blaney. "So good night, everybody."

"Thank you so much for coming here and being with us today," said Esther, reaching out and taking his hand in both of hers. "We needed you, Blaney."

"I will always be there for you; don't forget that."

Lydia scurried around to get Abigail's bed ready in the dresser drawer for the night. "We are going to get some rest while we can," she said. "I am sure we will be up in the night several times. That is just how it goes with these little ones. They have been torn out of their safe place, the only place they have ever known, and pushed out into a world where it's cold, and for the first time in their life, they feel hunger. Then they mess in their diaper, and they have stomach cramps from drinking something. Life begins for them with all the pain and agony that goes along with it."

"You make it sound so wonderful," I said with my tongue in my cheek.

"Yeah, you know, right?" she said.

"After today, I know all too well."

* * *

I knew I would have to get to sleep quickly before Chuck. I lay in bed, and my head began to swim with all the day's events. I couldn't seem to get the image of Frank Ridley out of my mind. I supposed that would be something to deal with for the rest of my days. I tried to put my pillow over my head to erase the scene.

And then it began: Chuck's snoring. It was so loud it penetrated the goose down in my pillow; it could have taken the peel off an orange and separated the sections. It could have stopped a rhino dead in its tracks from a full-on charge. It made me fearful that the rafters in the old house might collapse. I rolled over and stared at the ceiling in the dark, then peered over at Blaney as the moonlight flickered in the window. His lights were out like a candle, with the smoke lingering on the wick. I heard it said once you could count sheep to fall asleep, but we only had six on the farm. I figured I would need about a hundred. It seemed like hours as I lay there listening to that bowstring pulled slowly across the lowest note on Chuck's oversized violin. But finally, I awoke as the light from the sunrise filtered into the room. The morning had arrived like a whole herd of sheep. *Where were they when I needed them last night?*

Something seemed different about the farm as I dressed and made the long trip to the outhouse to take care of business. Of course, it was all different: Abigail was a whole day old. Life would never be the same again for as long as I lived. How long would I have to endure Chuck's snoring? I wanted my wife back already. The rooster in the henhouse sang his familiar song as he greeted the sunrise.

"*Es-mer-elda*," the cock crowed, breaking the silence of the morning. I laughed, wondering who Esmeralda might be. It must have been one of the hens in the yard—apparently, his favorite, because I never heard him calling out to any of the others. *Esmerelda.* You would think it would be more like *cock-a-doodle-do*, but to me, it always sounded like *Esmerelda.*

Stepping up to the porch, I paused to survey the farm. The penetrating stillness from the air left me with a chill—not from the cold, but from the excellent feeling it created in my soul. I closed my eyes and let the farm soak in deep, taking a breath through my nostrils. The smell of death had vanished, now replaced with the serenity of home. The smoke from the kitchen fires drifted off the stack, lying low like early-morning fog. I didn't dare to look down at my feet and the blood stains I knew I would see. The dickey birds flitted, one here and the other there, scooting between trees as they took care of their morning business, talking one to the other in their indiscernible dialect. I called them dickey birds because the colors, shapes, patterns, and sizes were too numerous to call them by name. *At least birds don't care if you get their name wrong, unlike people who tend to carry the offense against you.* I recalled in the Bible an Old Testament prophet whose name no one seemed to remember . . . so they called him "Hey Guy." I chuckled to myself, knowing the name of the prophet and his book was Haggai.

I could hear Abigail fussing, and serenity vanished like a fish being plucked off a pond by an eagle. I could hear M'Culay tinkering with his kitchen staff, preparing for the morning meal.

* * *

I spent the morning with my girls, all three of them. A girl I once loved and put aside, a girl I had always loved and found again, and a girl I only just met but somehow had known my whole life. Chuck, Blaney, and I sat at the dining table in front of one of the few windows that hadn't been blasted out and boarded up. The girls dominated the conversation like they always did, while we men tried to get a word in edgewise.

"Lydia, shouldn't she be resting in bed?" I asked.

"I just let her get up for a bit, but yes, it's time for her to get back in bed."

"Rider," said Blaney, jumping from the table and taking the .450 off the rack.

"Get in the bedroom, girls," said Chuck, taking Esther's hand as she cradled Abigail in one arm. Blaney took the Krag off the rack and handed it to me.

"Who could it be?" asked Chuck.

"He don't look friendly," said Blaney, "that's for sure." Lydia hesitated for a minute, looking down the long driveway, then shrugged her shoulders, heading for the bedroom.

"Could be a decoy," said Blaney. "You boys watch the back." Chuck and I scurried down the hall while Chuck took up in the back room. I took the side and used the butt of my rifle to knock out a board. One end fell loose after striking it three times. The other hung tight, and I pulled it down just enough to see out. I heard the hinges on the front door squeak.

"That's far enough!" shouted Blaney. "State your business."

"Don't shoot," said the man. "I'm a *pastor*!"

"Then get off that horse, and we'll see who you are," he said. I scrambled to my feet, recognizing the voice, and ran down the hall before Blaney put a hole in the poor man.

"It's Michael Bartson . . . Reverend Bartson," I said. "Don't hurt him."

"Lance, call me Michael."

"Okay, Michael it is."

"I'm not going to shoot him, for heaven's sake," said Blaney. "I'm just defending the house."

"Chuck," I yelled. "It's okay, he's a friendly." Blaney went out the front door as I turned and saw Esther emerging from the bedroom.

"It's Michael Bartson?" she asked.

"Yes, but you have been up long enough," I said. "You need to get back in bed."

"I'm trying to convince her of that, but she ain't listening to me," said Lydia, holding the baby.

"You two are making more of a fuss over this than it needs," said Esther.

"You just had a baby; now you need to listen to someone who knows," I said. "You asked Lydia to come out and help you, so now you have to accept her help."

"All right . . . all right," she said, returning to the bedroom. As I stepped off the porch, Reverend Bartson stood by his horse.

"Sorry for the confusion," I said, trying to lighten the mood with a big smile.

"No, I guess I should have realized you might be a little jumpy out here," he said. "I heard the news late last night, so I came as quick as I could just to make sure everyone was okay."

"News travels fast," said Blaney.

"I picked up a morning paper from a carrier kid just as I was leaving town, and they already printed the story." Michael fumbled in his saddle bag and pulled out the paper. "Here's the Wednesday edition of the *Standard*, fresh with the obituaries of the men they brought back to town last night and an interview with our police chief."

"What's the mood in town?" asked Blaney.

"Near as I can tell, it's one of relief," he said. I grabbed the paper from him and began to pore over the story like syrup over warm griddle cakes. *That's a John Rivers if I ever thought of one.*

"The story is all here," I said, handing the front page to Blaney and holding the rest back. Chuck had taken a seat on the porch. I thumbed through the pages to see if I could find more interest, and my eye caught a small caption on the back page. I couldn't believe my eyes, but there it was, plain as day, right there in black and white.

"What is it?" he asked. "Did you see a ghost?"

"Right here," I said. "I can't believe it." I took the paper and pointed out a small one-paragraph article on the back page. "It says here that Harriet Tubman died on March 10 at ninety-three."

"Oh yeah," said Bartson. "She's the abolitionist, right?"

"That's right; we just gave our daughter Abigail the middle name of Harriet because of her. Esther will be shocked."

"She had the baby?" said Michael. "That didn't hit the paper, did it?"

"It should have," I said. "She will be famous soon enough in her own time. She doesn't need a newspaper to announce her arrival."

"They put all the other births in that rag from this town," said Blaney. "They may as well report on Abigail."

"They won't; you just watch," I said. "Because she has a Negro momma, the story won't be worth the trouble to typeset it."

"Where's your faith in our community?" asked Michael.

"What did the story say in the paper?" I asked. "Did they tell the whole story, or did they just make out like the men had some squabble with us they couldn't explain?"

"You read the story," he said.

"The men didn't come out here to rob us as the papers said. They came out here to kill us because I'm married to a Negro woman. They didn't report that in the newspaper, did they?"

"No, I suppose not," said Michael, kicking the ground with his foot.

"I could go in and demand they print the story correctly, but I'm pretty sure the editor doesn't want to stir that pot."

"Can I see the baby?" Michael asked, trying to change the subject—and quite skillfully, I might add. We dropped the conversation flat where Michael had made a hole in the dirt with his boot. As we took the steps, I saw him glance at the blood trail.

"Let's get Willie's men out here and clean up this porch," I said as M'Culay greeted us at the door. Michael wiped his shoes off on the wool rug just inside. Out of the corner of my eye, I saw Blaney take the empty seat on the porch next to Chuck.

"Lydia, my dear," he said with widening eyes, "so good to see you. I didn't know what to expect, but finding you here is a pleasure."

"I volunteered to be Esther's midwife two days ago, and she had the baby yesterday."

"Sounds like you had quite a day."

Quite a day indeed, I thought.

"Is Esther awake?" asked Michael.

"We can't seem to keep her down," I said. "Our little one came a month early, so I am more than a little concerned for her. She is pretty small. I got a scale out in the shop, but it has a hook for weighing sacks. Guess it's not that important to know how much she weighs."

"Can I see her?" he asked.

"Esther will be so excited to see you," said Lydia. "I'm sure she's on pins and needles right now. Come with me." Lydia poked her head into the bedroom, and Esther's eyes lit up like fireflies as she saw Michael step through the door. Lydia stepped to the dresser and pointed out Abigail to him, resting peacefully.

"She must have a full tummy and a clean diaper," he laughed. "Abigail Harriet?"

"That's the name we chose," said Esther, sitting up against the headboard, propping a pillow against her back, then straightening the blankets across her lap. Lance picked Abigail. "And it means 'a father's joy.'"

"Fitting names," he said. "A father's joy, and Harriet after the two famous Harriets who changed the world for blacks and whites. Do you know what *Harriet* means?" he asked.

"As a matter of fact, I do. But I haven't even had time to share it with Lance yet. What with all the commotion and all."

"What does it mean?" I asked, wondering why she had failed to tell me.

"It means 'ruler of the household,'" she said with a sheepish grin.

"Oh no, master of the house? What have we done, darling?"

Reverend Michael had a big smile. "You are in for it now," he said with a laugh.

"Hopefully my father's joy will outweigh any attempts for her to become master of the house."

"I would let you hold her," said Lydia, "but I think she might just go to sleep, and if she will, I want Esther to get some rest, too. I might even take a little nap myself. We were up with her at all hours and up early with the birds having breakfast. I was just getting ready to make demands on Esther to get some sleep."

"Then I showed up, right?"

"It's not a bad thing that you showed up. Believe me, we are thrilled," said Lydia. "But I have to insist that she gets her rest."

"How am I going to be able to sleep when Reverend Michael is here?" said Esther.

"You'll have to," Lydia retorted, putting her hands on her hips. "I am serious, Esther. You are way too cavalier about this whole thing."

"You are right, madam. You are trying your best. I didn't know that having a baby would take this much out of me. The thing is, I feel fine."

"You feel okay now, and that is a good thing,' continued Lydia, "but you are still bleeding inside, and your body is still fighting hard to get back to normal. You're a lucky woman, and you didn't tear up when the child came. There can be so many complications with childbirth, but right now, you appear not to have too many of them. But they can surface overnight, and bed rest is key."

"Good night, dear," said Michael. "There will be plenty of time for us later. I can't wait to watch Miss Abigail grow up." Lydia encouraged us to exit the room and closed the door behind us while she stayed inside.

CHAPTER 12

Lion Hunting

This attack on our farm makes no sense to me," I said, stepping out in the front parlor. "We're not hurting anybody by our love."

"Life never makes sense, and it ain't fair neither," said Michael.

"But kill us? I never figured that anyone would try to kill us."

"Pride, jealousy, greed, and a need for dominance are powerful emotions," he said. "I don't think we will ever understand it, but it is the cause of all wars. National pride and a desire for power and dominance all play a role. Man has been doing this since the beginning."

"Yeah, I suppose it's human nature," I said. "It's probably built into the nature of every creature. If you drop an ant into a termite hill, it won't be welcomed as a visiting distant cousin."

"Ducks like to land on a pond with other ducks of their own kind," agreed Michael. "But the fallacy here is people are people. Our diversity should not be determined by the color of our skin or the shape of our eyes. God calls us to humility, and Jesus calls us to love our neighbor. Racism is just the ugly face of pride showing itself."

"I suppose I can see it," I said. "What you are saying is that our heart and soul are things no one can see. Humans always see what's on the outside. They live in the flesh, not in the Spirit. But how can we change their attitude?"

"You think you're going to change the world?" he said.

"No, but I was hoping we could change *someone*."

"Show them your love; that will change them."

"I think you should take your conversation outside," said Lydia.

"Are you hungry, Michael?" I asked.

"I had a little something before I left home."

"You didn't answer my question. Are you hungry?"

"Oh, I'm okay," he said.

"Do you know Blaney?" I asked.

"I've met him, I know of him, I know about him, I even know others who know him. But as for me, no, I can't say I *know* him."

"You boys don't mind if I nap?" asked Lydia. "You need to have some man time, and you don't need me hanging around. Besides, I have been up and down all night with the baby, and as long as they're sleeping, I'm going to take advantage of the quiet time."

"Come on, Michael," I said. "Or do you prefer I call you Reverend Bartson?"

"Mike works for me. You can call me anything, just as long as you don't call me late for church." Lydia tried to hold back her laughter and put her hand over her mouth. Opening the front door with a squeak, I heard Abigail fuss at the noise.

The front porch chairs were empty, and I spotted the men out by the barn watching some of our boys saddle up horses. Both men had rifles slung over their shoulders. "Let's go see what's up," I said. I found myself musing, *Man time—funny how men love to kick gravel together or sit in a club and sip scotch together. Scotch—I hate scotch; it tastes like kerosene. And women love a good hen party. They are never happier than when all the men are out of their hair and they can sit around and talk about them. They talk about other stuff, too, like romance novels, babies, knitted hats, tea, scented candles, baskets, and shoes. Men, on the other hand, talk about politics, rifles, ammunition, hunting, horses, automobiles, business, farming, and war. Men love hanging out with other men, and women love being with other women. I don't see any-thing wrong with that, and I certainly would never consider it as being on the same plain as racism. What would you even call it . . . sexism? No, that would be absurd. Men have their place, and women have theirs. You would never see a woman on a battlefield or in a police uniform; that's just the way it is. It's the job of a woman to run the household, take care of the children, and take care of her husband.*

"Where you headed?" I asked as Michael and I approached.

"We're thinking about taking a ride so I can show Blaney some of the game in the north valley," answered Chuck.

"I was hoping we could spend some time together this morning so the both of you might get a chance to get to know Michael." Chuck caught my eye and wrinkled his brow.

"What did you have in mind?" asked Blaney.

"I thought maybe we could play cards," I said. Michael touched my arm and shook his head to the negative.

"You don't play cards?" asked Blaney.

"No," he responded without any further explanation. Blaney and Chuck looked at him like he had just stepped off a shooting star and arrived from another planet.

"We can't all leave the farm," said Blaney. "If we take a ride, it has to be short, and we can't all leave at the same time."

"I suppose you're right," I said.

"This thing just hit the papers this morning," said Blaney.

"You're the boss . . . so what's your plan?" asked Chuck, folding his arms across his chest. I had to think about that for a minute. Chuck had always treated me like a kid and had never acknowledged that I was the owner of the farm. Ever since he arrived, he had approached our relationship as if he had the upper hand. I had always been okay with that because of his experience and knowledge.

I felt like he had just given me a certificate of appreciation and that I had just been validated. If only he had not chosen to fold his arms across his chest at that very minute. Blaney tapped his toe in the dirt, impatient for my decision.

"I guess the prospects of us tagging along would be out of the question," I said. Chuck glared at me, waiting for my answer. I had to think briefly about the situation: Chuck and Blaney mixed with Reverend Michael. The match lit up the kerosene lamp, and the lights went on.

"Michael, you've been on your horse all morning. How about we take a ride in the Ford?" I said. Chuck put a slight grin on his face, likely relieved that I had gotten the message without it becoming awkward. I could only imagine whether Chuck had plotted the escape or if Blaney had put the plan into motion. They were like two peas nestled together in a green pod. Just then, Blaney's horse lifted his tail, and the bright green mud plopped in the dirt beside the mare's rear feet. The aroma of fermented Timothy hay filled the air and our nostrils. No one raised an eyebrow or even made a comment. *If you are going to be around horses*, I thought, *this is what you get. You better live with it. The same goes when you are with men: if you are going to hang out with them, you best put up with it. It's all the same stuff; some just smells worse than the other.*

"I'd love to," said Michael.

"Love to what?" I answered, trying to shake the image of horse manure out of my head.

"Take a ride in the Ford," he said. "Isn't that what you asked me?"

"Oh right, yes; I'll get Willie," I said.

"You can hold off on saddling those horses," said Chuck, directing his attention to our worker as he drew down the cinch strap and buckled it into place.

"*Hakuna haja ya saruji farasi,*" I said to Kimane, our horse man. He wrinkled his face as if in disbelief. "*Wanaume si kuwa na kuchukua safari.*"

"What did you say?" asked Chuck.

"And how long have you been in Africa?" I asked. Chuck shrugged his shoulders. "I told him you would not be taking a ride, so there was no need to saddle the horses. And his name is Kimane."

"I know his name," said Chuck. "It means 'big bean.' Your rifle is in the shop. I had the boys clean them from yesterday."

"Michael, do you shoot?" I asked as we walked toward the barn.

"Not for many years," he said.

"Ever killed a lion?" I asked.

"Nope . . . seen 'em from a distance, but never hunted one."

"I've got one on the farm I need to take out of his pride. He's an old bugger and sort of mean and antisocial. If I get a proper crack at him, I'll take him out before he gets in a catfight and we get stuck with a wounded lion who becomes a nuisance."

"Willie," I called as he poked his head out of the barn. "Make the Ford ready."

"Nuisance . . . I thought lions were all a nuisance?" the Reverend said.

"They mind their business most of the time. Let's go get us a couple of rifles," I said, heading for the shop. "The young ones mind their business and wait for a chance to become a pride lion. They have to challenge an old male, so they wait for their time. Finally, they make their move when they are mature enough for a challenge. If the old boy loses, he loses everything. Depending on how long he has been a pride lion, he hasn't had to hunt for several years because the women do it for him. Now, he is wounded and tossed out. You know how painful it is to lose your pride?"

Michael nodded in agreement as we walked along.

"Well, that's what it's like for him. Not only is he hungry, humiliated, and injured, but he's angry at everything and everyone. He is a danger to himself and everything around him. Then he starts trying to find an easy meal, which ends up being farm animals, old people, and children. We can't have that on our farm, so I like to take them out of the pride before it comes to any of that."

"Hunting a lion is dangerous business," he said. "You have to know what you are doing."

"I know what I am doing. Johnathan Rivers taught me everything I know, and he is the best. John was taught by men like Abel Chapman, Arthur Henry Neumann, and Frederick Selous."

"Neumann . . . didn't he commit suicide about six years ago?" asked Michael.

"I heard it said he just couldn't handle not being able to do what he loved, which was hunting elephants. At sixty, he figured he'd rather push daisies than sit around wishing he was doing something he loved. It's a shame that some men can't grow old gracefully."

"Sort of like old lions, aren't we?" said Michael. "When we lose our pride, life is over."

"I think that's what happened to Neumann," I said. "He had to leave Africa and return to England with no hope of ever returning to follow his dreams. Never did hear what was in his note, but I heard it was short."

"I also heard tell he never married," said Michael. "I did hear he had a Ndorobo girlfriend who nursed him back to health after nearly being killed by an elephant back in 1895."

"My opinion of him just jumped up about ten points," I said. Willie and his men were pushing the Ford out of the barn. "He must have been afraid to marry her. Come on, I'll get you a rifle."

This whole conversation was very interesting to me—the pride and prejudice of men, their fragile egos, and their tender heart and soul that they tried to protect at all costs with a hard shell.

"I'm excited to ride in your Ford," he said as I handed him the Lee-Enfield British .303. "That's a beautiful rifle."

"Can you handle it?" I asked.

"I'll back you up; how's that?"

"Good enough for me," I said, taking my Winchester 1895 lever-action rifle off the bench.

"Now, there's a rifle! That's quite a cartridge. What is that?" he asked, admiring the bull cartridge.

"It's a .405, just like old Teddy shot on safari. He called it his 'medicine gun for lions.'" I stuffed five cartridges into the magazine and put the extras in my pockets. This rifle had just taken a man's head nearly clean off, and now I was embracing it.

"Medicine gun for lions, huh?"

"That's what he said in his book."

CHAPTER 13

The Careful Stalk

By the time we left the shop, Willie had the Ford idling and ready to go. Chuck and Blaney were settling in on the porch, and Chuck appeared to be dealing a hand of cribbage. I didn't know why the thought had crossed my mind to leave the farm unprotected at this juncture. Yesterday's story had just come out in the papers, and God only knew how people might react to the news.

As we walked toward the Ford, Willie stood proud, waiting for us. "You can toss your rifle in the front seat; just make sure the safety is on." I placed the barrel of my Winchester on the floorboard.

"Doesn't that thing have a safety?" asked Michael as he slid in the passenger side.

"Yep, it's the half-cock position. You can let the hammer all the way down, but then it is resting on a live round. If you drop it on the hammer, the thing can discharge. It's not like the old Henry rifle that didn't have a half-cock position at all."

"The Henry?" he asked.

"That's the Civil War rifle. The Confederates said the Union soldiers loaded them on Sunday and fired them all week. They held sixteen rounds, but the load wasn't much more than a pistol round. It wasn't worth a darn out past two hundred yards. As for using it for a lion, forget it," I said, climbing behind the wheel. "Jump in, Willie;

we are just going to drive up to the upper valley and see if we can find that pride."

Willie grinned and eagerly jumped in the back. "We have everything we need in here?" I asked.

"Yes, bwana; Willie take care of everything." I didn't have to question Willie beyond that; I counted on him at every turn.

I put the Ford in gear, gave her gas, and we went off. Chuck waved from the porch, holding his cards in one hand and sitting back in the chair. I waved back, knowing what the two men were saying behind our back about Reverend Michael. Why didn't people see that the same as racism? Here were two seemingly intelligent men, quite social in their own right but unwilling to socialize with someone of the cloth.

"Do you get that often?" I asked.

"What's that?" he asked, taken aback by my question.

"People avoiding you like the plague because you are a man of faith."

"Oh yes, I'm very used to it," he said. "I just expect it now, and I don't get upset. We only get hurt in life by our failed expectations. You expect someone to act a certain way because of your values and how you think you should treat others. Then, when the people don't live up to your expectations, you get your feelings hurt. People don't want to be around me because they're afraid I am going to try to slip Jesus into the conversation and try to convert them."

"Well, aren't you?" I asked. Michael grinned, giving me the answer I knew he would give.

"We are called to be fishers of men, right?" he asked.

"That's right," I answered, swerving to miss a rock in the road. "I heard Esther say once that she never saw a fisherman yet who arrived at the riverbank and announced to all the fish that he was there to catch them." I thought Michael might be interested in the rows of coffee trees as we drove across the farm, but he said nothing about them.

"She's exactly right," he said. "Don't you suppose all the fish would just swim away?"

I laughed under my breath, thinking that Chuck and Blaney were like a couple of old fish trying to squirm out of someone's hands and make it back to the safety of the water. "I thought Chuck might be further along in finding God with his experience from the miracle he saw on safari, but he is a tough old bird."

"It's all in God's time," he said. "Tell me more about the lions. I heard that if a pride lion loses his position, the new lion king comes in and kills all the cubs from the previous ruler. Is that true?"

"Unfortunately, he will eradicate all traces of the other male. The best way to do that is to get rid of the other lion's cubs and start making his own."

"So how does that scenario play into your theory of taking out the old pride male?" he asked.

"I'm still trying to control their numbers here on the farm, and if that cuts the numbers down in the pride, I am just fine with that." Michael rubbed his chin, and I wondered how my brutally honest opinions were sitting with him. I had already established that hunting was not something in his repertoire, not an arrow in his quiver or something he indulged in, so to speak. What I had not established yet was whether or not he took a stand against it, or if he even understood the concept or the thrill of the adventure associated with it.

"How do you feel about hunting, in general?" I asked, afraid of the answer I might get in return.

"It has its place, I suppose," he answered. "Not something I would find myself doing to pass the time for sheer enjoyment."

"How do you feel about killing animals?" I asked, cringing at how I had just opened myself up.

"Never had much exposure to it; I see plenty of people doing it around here. If they're not out doing it, they are thinking about it. My passion is Jesus, and I believe men should focus on their passions."

"Hmm, I don't think hunting is my passion," I said. "Not like it is for John Rivers. I love the adventure, the challenge, the thrill of the hunt. I love being the first man ever to lay hands on a particular trophy animal without being killed or eaten. Is it a passion? Not like Esther is a passion for me, and not like Abigail is a passion for me now."

"Never having been on a hunt before," he said, "I am interested to find out what all the fuss is about. Sure seems like the poor things don't have a chance, what with modern rifles and all. What's so fun about murder?"

"It's not like that; I can't explain it. You have to experience it. It's not for some people; it might not be for you. Man has been hunting animals since God gave him the right to eat them. When you hunt, it goes way back to something in our blood."

I cut back on the throttle, as the wagon road leading down the hill had big ruts, and I tried to keep the passengers in their seats. The road flattened out, and we came through the trees leading to the north valley.

"Is this all yours?" he asked, gazing across the grasslands.

"Most of it," I answered. "There's a property line out here somewhere. If someone were to try to claim it and start a farm, I would find the line quickly. See that tree line out there about four miles ahead?"

"Way out there?" he said, pointing with his finger.

"That's about where the line is, and it runs up the valley to those hills."

"So, where are the lions?" he asked.

"We'll have to find them. We drove right up on them on Sunday, but that was a fluke. That never happens."

"How does it happen?"

"Different every time, and that's what makes it so exciting. You never know what is going to happen."

"You are going to have to tell me when we get started. Like I said, I have never been on a lion hunt."

"You are on one right now," I said.

"Where . . . do you see one?" he said nervously, scanning left and right.

"No, I don't see one," I said with a smile. *First timers,* I thought. *How funny they react when they don't know what is going on. I don't want to scare the poor man, but he seems naive about worldly things like this. I'm sure he is a very wise man when it comes to God, but farming and poking around in the wilds of Africa do not seem to be his forte.*

I drove to where the lions had been a couple of days earlier and pulled up and parked the Ford. Willie jumped out of the back and began combing the ground for fresh tracks. Setting the brake and leaving her to idle, I grabbed the Winchester, stepping out to the ground and putting a live round in the action. Then I dropped the hammer carefully with my thumb to the half cock.

"Over here is where they were on Sunday," I said, walking up on the knoll. Willie followed and examined the tracks. Michael clutched his rifle tightly, sitting tensely in the Ford, watching our every move.

"Two day old, bwana," he said, pointing to a big track in the soft dirt. I surveyed the grasslands for as far as I could see. The late morning sun shone brightly between the broken, puffy clouds, and the wind blew in my face from the west. A small group of zebra were grazing along the trees about a thousand yards away. They paid no attention to us.

"What do you think, Willie?"

"Nothing to think, bwana; the lion gone. They could be ten miles gone, or they could be right here."

I should have figured Willie would give me an answer like that. Sometimes, I think he doesn't respect me like he did John Rivers. I don't think he would have talked down to John like he just did to me. Maybe I am just oversensitive.

"You're the guide. I am asking you where you think our best bet is to find them. I don't need a commentary on the elusiveness of the lion."

"Commentary, bwana?" He asked, displaying his innocence.

"Never mind. I just need some help, that's all."

"Lion has mind of him own; they are like wind. Who know where wind blow? We find lion in place they like."

"And where might that be?" I asked.

"We cannot ride there," he said. "We must walk."

"Is it a long walk?" I asked. "I don't want this to turn into an all-day affair. We were only going to be gone for a short time this morning."

"You trust Willie. I find you lions."

"How do you feel about taking a walk?" I asked as Michael sat in the Ford clutching his rifle.

"Hey, I'm just out for the ride and following your lead. If you want me to whistle Dixie, I'll find it in the songbook."

"We are going to have to be as quiet as church mice." I glanced at his shoes to see if they were appropriate for hiking. I expected to see him in dress shoes, but to my surprise, he wore leather lace-up boots.

A man never looks at another man's shoes. That's what separates men from women. Women seem to judge another woman by her shoes, but men judge men by the choice of their rifle.

"I know about church mice," said Michael. "I have plenty of those. But I think the correct phrase is 'poor as a church mouse.'"

"What makes a church mouse so poor?" I asked.

"The pastor always cleans his plate and leaves no crumbs because every meal could be his last." Michael grinned, probably aware I hadn't put much on his collection plate last Sunday.

"Whatever. We are not going after old-world rats and mice; we are going after lions. And if we make any noise, we could get eaten."

Michael raised his eyebrows and nodded in agreement. I reached in and shut down the Ford, setting the brake. Under the seat, I found the twelve-gauge double and the survival satchel Willie had packed, and I pulled them out, handing them off to Willie. "There should be a box of buckshot under Michael's seat." Willie put the sack strap over his shoulder as Michael came around the front of the Lizzie.

"What's in the bag?" asked Michael.

"Just a few odds and ends: matches, first aid kit, some dried meat, nuts, raisins, and the sort. We just never go into the bush unprepared." I pulled three full canteens out from under the back seat and handed one to Michael.

"You *do* come prepared," he said.

"It's best to be prepared when walking into the unknown," I said.

"Sort of like being saved, right?" he said, poking me in the ribs. I flinched and then giggled at his humor, but I sobered up quickly at the reality of what I had just said. *It is best to be prepared when you are walking into the unknown. What a mouthful to ponder. Words for everyone living on the earth. Even though some of us are pretty sure we knew where we are going, I have to think that no one really knows. How true the Bible verse is . . . "no mind has conceived."*

"Lead the way, Willie," I encouraged. I knew Willie had grown up in these hills and walked every inch of the landscape from boyhood. I remembered a water hole a few miles away in our direction and figured that was where Willie would take us. I took hold of Michael's shoulder and gently nudged him up in front of me. I didn't want to put him in the point position to take the brunt of the action, but I wanted to keep a close eye on him. One never knows about another man's gun-handling skills. Also, I wanted to bring him back in one piece, so I needed to watch over and protect him. If anyone had been on safari with us, they would realize the dangers. You just never know what you might find.

We had walked about forty-five minutes when we came over a rise and saw the water hole off in the distance.

"It's deserted," I whispered, knowing this to be quite normal for this time of year when the rains came.

"Follow me. Be quiet," Willie whispered, putting his index finger on his lips. He wet his finger in his mouth and then held it up to double-check the direction of the wind. Willie moved like a leopard in the night as he made his way through the sparse gum, thorn, and acacia trees. I had to laugh at Reverend Michael as he tried to mimic Willie's movements. On his first hunt, he wanted so desperately to do everything correctly. The empty water hole could mean one of two things. Either the lions had made a kill and everything in the area had been spooked off, or it held no interest for the animals because they were getting their water from other places. I had big hopes for option one.

Willie stopped dead in his tracks and Michael bumped into him, putting his hands on his shoulders. Willie cupped his ear with the palm of his hand.

"Do you hear that?" he whispered. With all the years of shooting, my hearing had taken a real beating. Esther could hear high-pitched noises on the farm that were so inaudible to me. This was one more case of my failing ears. Maybe someday, someone would come up with a way to protect hearing besides cotton.

"What is it?" I whispered.

"Sounds like chewing," said Michael. Willie put his finger to his lips to warn Michael about his voice. I tried to cup my hand behind my ear but could hear nothing.

"Easy now," whispered Willie. He started moving again and made hand motions to follow.

"Watch your feet," I whispered in Michael's ear. "Don't step on any twigs."

"How am I supposed to watch for sticks and lions simultaneously?" he answered, gritting his teeth. I could almost feel the stress oozing out of his pores. Drops of sweat formed on his forehead. Michael eased forward behind Willie, and I took his shoulder, holding him back to take the lead. I wanted a clear shot at a lion, afraid Michael might be in the way. Regrets came over me, and I wondered why I had failed to brief Michael on exactly where the rifle was sighted in case he needed it. I had never brought a person into a situation like this without giving them the proper training. I felt stupid, as if I had betrayed myself. Amusing how if you go searching for trouble, you are more likely than not to find it.

Willie paused, listening for the sound again and trying to find an opening. He crouched low, peeking through the trees, and then attempted to stand tall on his toes. I watched intently for a glimpse of brown hair through the brush. The chewing noise had stopped, which meant only one thing: the pride knew we were there. They had spotted us or were alerted by their sense of approaching danger.

Lions are not much for worrying about danger. Hyenas are the only thing that seem to harass them, but their laughter gives them away every time. This was not a laughing matter; we were all business. I had brought a person into a dangerous situation without making him aware. If anything happened to him, I could only hope that God would not hold me personally responsible. I had to wonder what drove me to pursue an adventure such as this—could it have been a sickness? Why couldn't I just be content to sit by the fireplace and sip on a glass of wine or read a good book in the safety of my home? Why put myself in the middle of this heart-pounding adventure? I thought about the security of home and how those men had ruined the serenity for all of us—at least for now.

Willie glanced over his shoulder, and we made eye contact. He turned and began to move.

"Stay close behind me," I whispered in Michael's ear. "If they come at us, let 'em have it. Don't jerk the trigger. Just squeeze it off." Michael raised his eyebrows, and I focused my attention back on Willie. The waist-high green grass provided the perfect place for lions to hide, and I swallowed hard, trying to get rid of the lump in my throat. With every inch we moved closer, I expected to see the lions at any moment. My heart pounded like a Mandinka drum trying to free itself from my chest. I remembered the joy in those people's faces as they danced together in their tribal celebration. For me, this very moment reminded me of such a festivity. I had to control my emotions, keeping my head in the game. At any second, the scene could erupt into sheer terror.

The pounding in my ears from the Mandinka drum in my chest changed into the pounding feet of a five-hundred-pound lion at a full-on charge. Instead of it bursting through the brush before me, he arrived from the back. I turned to see him coming like a freight train, parting the grass. I lifted my Winchester and pulled the hammer back with my thumb, but Michael blocked my shot. He raised his rifle; his hands trembled, and I knew we were in trouble. The precious seconds were at a full boil, but the scene slowed to a crawl.

"SHOOT!" I yelled in panic, trying to force the outcome. I felt like the word was oozing out of my mouth like cold molasses.

My head sprang back to the moment, and I stepped shoulder to shoulder with Michael and put my rifle on the lion, which was now coming hard at forty yards. *Now or never*, I thought, and I settled in for a half second and squeezed it off.

Pow . . . it belched fire and smoke and kicked me in the shoulder like a mule. I let the rifle buck and then settle back on the target for a second shot, then jacked the empty and rammed home another round into the chamber. I saw the lion's front legs go limp; then his chin hit the dirt as he let go of a last, dying roar that sent a chill up my spine. I rolled the memory over in my head quickly, wondering if Michael had pulled his trigger. In all the commotion, there was no way to tell. I tried to see traces of lingering smoke off the end of his barrel, but it looked like it could have been mine still drifting in the wind. I turned to survey the area in all directions just to make sure of no other threats.

Michael began to jump up and down like a kid in a candy store with shiny copper-nickel.

"I got him! I got him!" he screeched.

"Hold on . . . hold on," I warned, grabbing his arm. "Sometimes these old boys travel in groups, or the lioness can charge, trying to defend the father of her cubs." Michael stopped his dance and regained his composure. Willie edged toward me so as not to cut off a second shot, holding the double barrel at the ready, and he kept his head in the moment. He and I had done this a dozen times before. We knew how the other would act in this situation, and it was like a dance for us. Willie knew he was there to back us up and take a shot if needed at the last second, but he would never claim a kill for himself.

"This is your first lion," I said, knowing we had both shot at the very same time. Michael had not even realized that I had fired, too. I figured the lion probably only had one bullet in him, and it would likely have my name on it. But if Michael thought he'd shot the lion, so be it. I had killed enough of them, and I didn't need one more. Michael stood in awe of the scene and stepped up to the beast. He picked up a paw and held it in one hand, examining the claws. Then he caressed his head.

"See here," he said, "I got him right between the eyes."

"Nice shot, man! One shot, and he was down like a ton of bricks," I said, noticing the forty-caliber bullet hole. Michael didn't have a clue about guns and ammo. He couldn't have realized his rifle would have made a smaller hole. Willie examined the lion and then looked at me with a wrinkled nose. He started to speak, but I cut him off with a frown and shook my head, knowing Michael had been distracted. He began to speak a second time.

"Michael shot the lion," I said with a firm stare. Willie pursed his lips, then nodded, knowing what I had just done. I couldn't believe we had both fired at the same time. Heck, I didn't even know if Michael had pulled the trigger. I had killed the lion with a shot right between the eyes, and that had put his lights out. If he hadn't gone down, we would have been in trouble. If it had been hit somewhere else, we would determine that later, but Michael had his first lion for now. That was good enough for me and good enough for Michael. "Do you understand me, Willie?" I whispered, and he nodded, reluctantly appreciating me. Only two people knew differently, and I felt confident our secret would remain just that.

"Understand what?" whispered Michael.

"Nothing important," I said. "Willie and I have done this many times. Here, let me hold your rifle." Michael eagerly handed me his rifle and then went back to touch the lion. I wondered how this experience might change Michael's perspective about hunting. Lion hunting was one dangerous sport, and once again, we had cheated death.

CHAPTER 14

CRACKER

We'll have our boys come get the lion," I said. "I think we should be getting back to the house."

"I stay and skin," said Willie, pulling his skinning blade out of the sheath as it glistened in the sunlight.

"Are you sure?" I said. Willie smiled and shook his head, indignant that I might be worried about his safety. "I'll send the wagon back. The native camp will be glad for the meat."

"That is why I stay, bwana. This lion's meat will sour soon."

"Do you have plenty of water?" I asked.

"Yes, bwana," he said, shaking his canteen.

"And you have everything you need in the satchel," I said. "Here, wait—one thing." I reached for the bag and searched through to the bottom. "There are some red strips of cotton in here. Yes, here they are. I'll mark the trail so the boys can find you. We're about thirty minutes from the Ford and another twenty or twenty-five from the house. Your boys will have to hitch up the wagon. It will be three hours before they get here. Are you okay with hanging around here?"

"Flag the trail?" he laughed. "Flag is for white men. You send Maitho, him no need flags. His name mean 'eyes to see with.' You remember he is tracker?"

"Okay, yeah, you're right; he'll find you." I stuffed the flags in my pocket. "Michael, you want anything out of that bag?" I asked.

"Naw, I can wait. Good thing you have a camera in that bag."

"For sure. Come on, let's get going. The sooner we get back, the sooner Willie will have company out here in the middle of nowhere." I grabbed my rifle, slinging it over my shoulder. We went over the hills and back across the flats to the Ford. Michael had a perpetual grin on his face as if he had just won at a craps table.

"Man, did you see that thing coming at us? How fast do those things run?" asked Michael.

"I don't know. Forty . . . maybe fifty miles per hour?"

"No, really?" said Michael. "That's as fast as a racehorse."

"You're not going to outrun one with one of our horses, that's for sure."

"That thing was going to get us any second. How come you didn't shoot?"

I stuttered for a second, trying to come up with a smooth answer but instead changing the subject.

"That wasn't that bad of a walk," I said, seeing the Ford in the distance through the trees. I continued to be aware of our surroundings and was watching for lions.

"Okay, let's get this thing started. Here, I'll show you how to crank it." It seemed like I had just gone through this with Dennis the other day. I went over all the steps and warned Michael about the kickback and the possibility of breaking an arm if he wasn't careful. Then we got the thing going and headed back to the farm.

When we pulled up, Chuck and Blaney were gone from the porch. I pulled my watch from my pocket and calculated we had been gone for three hours. Both men came out of the barn and started walking in our direction. The reality of my situation came flooding back into my head at the sight of the men with rifles slung over their shoulders, knowing the defense of the farm had to be of the utmost importance in our minds. A big piece of the edge had been chipped away from the joy of a successful morning lion hunt. Why couldn't people let life go on and bygones be bygones? What was done was over, and expecting someone to go back and change an outcome seemed ridiculous. Why did there have to be so much hate and discontent in the world? Why did everybody have to think they were so much better than everyone else?

"Have a good hunt?" asked Chuck. "Don't look back now, but Willie must have fallen out somewhere along the road."

"We left Willie to contend with the dead lion," I laughed.

"Nice going, chaps!" said Blaney.

"Willie wants us to send him some of his men with the cart. Let's have them hitch it and then find Maitho. Willie wants us to send his tracker."

"Tell me about the lion," said Chuck.

"It's a beautiful lion, but there will be plenty of time for story-telling later. Right now, we need to get Michael on his way back to town and get Willie some help."

"At least you can tell me who shot it," he said.

"You tell 'em, Michael," I said. Michael's ears turned pink, and he closed his eyes in an apparent attempt to avoid boasting. He wouldn't have had to worry about that if he had only known the truth.

"I got him," he said. "Just before he got us."

"How many shots?" asked Chuck.

"Chuck, let's get the wagon going," I said.

"All right . . . all right," he said, heading back for the barn and mumbling something.

"Michael, how about I run you into town in the Ford, and I'll have one of our boys ride your horse back for you?"

"No, I better take her back. She's a little particular about who she lets ride her."

"Chuck, can you get them to saddle his horse?" I said in a loud voice. Chuck never missed a step and just waved his arm above his head. "Come on, let's go check on the girls."

"I'll go help Chuck," said Blaney.

"Sure you won't stay for supper, Michael?" I said, killing the engine.

"No, I need to get back. This is Holy Week, and I still have a lot of preparation for Easter."

"What about your lion?" I asked.

"Yes?"

"You have some decisions to make. Like, do you want a full mount or a rug?"

"I am a preacher; do you know what I get paid?"

"Okay, I see what you are saying," I answered.

"Remember the church mouse? If I had any extra money, I would use it for God's service and not to display some full-mount lion. I suppose I will be content just to have the snapshot."

"Do you want the hide if I had my workers tan it for you?"

"I'd find a place for it. A lion represents good and evil in the Bible. It's like the law and the gospel. The law condemns us while the gospel saves us. One lion tries to devour us, and the other offers salvation by his grace." This preacher man had it down, all the same stuff Esther had drummed into my head from the day I met her.

"Snapshot," I said with a grin. "That is what our hunt was. We had one chance to take the snapshot. Our whole morning could have been completely different if you hadn't been successful at that snapshot."

"It's sort of like hitting a home run in a tie game in the ninth inning with two outs on a full count," said Michael.

"Just like that, except we had Willie in the dugout with a twelve-gauge loaded with double-aught buck."

"I just hope that the photograph turns out," said Michael. "That will prove I am a lion hunter. It feels good to have one under your belt."

"Yep, sitting like a good meal, right?"

"That's what I'm referring to," he chuckled.

"They should be finished with your tack here quickly. Let's have a look in on the girls."

As I stepped up on the porch, I felt a loose board under my feet. Lydia cracked the front door and poked her head out. "They are still sleeping," she whispered.

"What is with these boards?" I said, trying not to show my irritation. Lydia shrugged her shoulders.

"What do you need?" she whispered.

"Michael was just leaving and wanted to say goodbye to Esther," I said.

"Not this time," she answered. "Every minute of sleep is precious. You'll be back, won't you?"

"That is what I wanted to talk to you about," he said. Lydia eased open the door, trying not to make it squeak, and slipped out.

"Let's step off the porch," she whispered, watching for the loose board. I watched my feet; all traces of Blackwood's blood trail were erased. They had thrown fresh dirt over the stains left in the driveway.

"What is it?" she asked.

"If you know Mary," said Michael, "she is going to be chomping at the bit to get out here and see the baby. You know how she feels about Esther. You don't know her, Lance, but she knows you and Esther well.

"I don't know her," I said. "Who is she?"

"She's the wife of that professional hunter, Jack Cunningham."

"Yes, I know him. But I don't remember ever meeting her."

"She made it very clear to other church members," said Michael, "that she would put together a gathering and have a surprise luncheon on the farm when the baby came."

"Oh, Mary, that sweetheart," said Lydia. "I know what you mean. She told me the same thing on Sunday just before we left the church. That girl is cherished and well-connected in the community. If she decides to put a lunch together, then there will be no stopping her."

"So, what do you think?" he asked. "Should we just let it happen or put her off?"

"I know what she will do when she hears the news. She will rush out and invite all her friends to the farm after services on Easter Sunday."

"She might not be able to pull it off by Easter," said Michael.

"Apparently, you don't know Mary as well as I do," said Lydia. "That's just what she will do."

"If she does," said Michael, "you should be prepared for it."

"Thanks for the heads up," said Lydia. "If it happens, we are ready. I won't let Esther in on it because she will fret all week. We'll just let it be a surprise. But it's your job to get us a message as soon as you find out."

"I won't suggest it to her, but I'll have to tell her the baby came."

"That would be Abigail, of course," I said.

"I will let her know, and as soon as I hear about what is going on, I will send you a message." I peeked out the corner of my eye and saw that Michael's horse had been all tacked up.

"I'm going back in the house," said Lydia. "Thank you for coming out, Michael. That was nice." Michael smiled, and Lydia scurried back into the house.

"Looks like she's all ready," I said. We made our way toward the barn and talked as we walked.

"I'm sure I will be here on Sunday. Besides, I am anxious to have a look at the lion. Will they boil the skull?"

"When Willie gets back, we'll see what we can do." I wondered how I could make an excuse to get rid of the forty-caliber evidence between the eyes of the lion. If he wanted to display the skull, the first thing an educated rifleman would ask him would be if he shot a forty. Someone would figure out quickly that I had killed the lion and not him. *Sure,* I thought, *it is interesting how one little untruth turns into a whole lot of shoveling dirt to cover up the harmless white lie. It all starts out so innocent, like trying to make a friend feel better, and then it blossoms into outright sin.* A part of me wanted to sit him down at that very instant and tell him the truth, but I couldn't help the temptation to go with the story since it seemed to be working. I just wanted to make Michael feel good about something great he had done. Was that such a great sin?

"Better take a gun with you," I said.

"I don't need a gun; I'm a pastor."

"Isn't that what UP Gardner said?"

"Who is UP Gardner?"

"I wouldn't expect you Englishmen to know US history, but UP Gardner was a Union chaplain who rode with Captain Gross of the Thirteenth Kansas Infantry Regiment."

"Weren't those guys all issued a sword and a pistol when they signed on as chaplains for the Union?" he asked.

"That's what I'm talking about. In November 1864, he was riding with Captain Gross and thirty-two of his men along the Kansas and Missouri border when they ran into a band of twenty-seven guerrillas from Quantrill's Raiders. The Missourians were fierce fighters, and they proved it that day by shooting down twenty-nine of Gross's men. Then, a young fella named Jesse James cornered and executed Captain Gross. When James came on UP Gardner, he pleaded for mercy, stating that he was a chaplain."

"So what happened?" asked Michael, eagerly awaiting the punchline.

"According to the story, Jesse cocked his head and smiled, then cocked his pistol and shot him dead with a bullet in his brain."

"I'm glad we don't have ruthless men like that around here," he answered.

"Don't bet on it, preacher man," I said.

"Come on, I'll be fine—thanks for this history lesson, but I've been in this country a long time. We don't have wars here like they fought in America. Our wars are over land and not politics. I know the people; just don't you go worrying about me."

"The fight we had on the farm the other day," I said, pausing while Michael looked on with curiosity. "That was all the same damn stuff the Civil War was fought over." I waited for Michael to respond, and he closed his eyes and nodded.

We sent Michael on his way down the driveway and sent the workers off with the oxcart to help Willie. I stood there watching Michael's horse trot down the drive, and I couldn't help but worry about his safety. If he had only let me drive him to town. I sat on the front porch while Chuck and Blaney lit cigars. The sweet smoke of aged tobacco drifted across the porch; the afternoon sun lay heavy over the horizon perched above the white puffy clouds. I tried to keep my voice down, knowing Abigail would be awake at any moment so Esther could fill her belly with warm milk.

"The boys made short work of cleaning up the porch, hey?" I whispered.

"I put 'em to work on it just after you left for your drive," said Chuck. "Guess that wasn't such a good idea 'cause I got severely scolded by Lady Lydia." Chuck laughed under his breath as he let a puff of smoke out, and it drifted off the porch.

"Michael wouldn't take a gun with him, huh?" asked Blaney. "Ol' Michael, he is stubborn as an ox."

"I suppose," I said, thinking about the story of UP Gardner. I wondered why that hadn't seemed to matter to him. Changing the subject, I said, "We'll have to measure those windows and get some glass."

"I found some out in the barn," said Chuck. "I just need to measure it." Just then, Abigail began to stir.

"There's my wake-up call," I said.

"Won't the women take care of all that?" asked Blaney.

"Oh yeah, I just want to see my wife."

"She certainly has you whipped into shape," said Blaney.

"What do you mean?" I asked.

"You need to buck up, man. Don't let her think you will be there for her every wish and desire. She will come to expect it from you. You need to be a little slow when she asks for help."

"That's sound advice," I said. "Where did you learn that?"

"From my dad," he answered.

"Was your dad married a long time?"

"Yes, a long time and many times," he said.

"How long was he married to your mother?"

"Oh . . . maybe five years, but it wasn't his fault. She left him for another man."

I didn't want to take this conversation any further because I had a feeling where it might lead. I had an inkling of his attitude that his father might have deserved the blame because maybe he never knew how to treat a lady. My role models were my dad and my friend John Rivers, and they always treated women right. I had no intention of treating Esther any other way.

"You are a cracker, all right," laughed Chuck.

"No, Chuck, nobody on this farm is a cracker," I said, feeling like my blood was heating up.

"Sorry, I didn't think you would be so sensitive," he said, shrugging his shoulders.

"Sensitive? Don't you know about that term? I don't have to tell you it's a racial term used by Negroes in the American South toward poor whites."

"Yes, I know what a cracker is," he said. "It's a poor white man who does the dirty work for the slave owners by whipping them into shape."

"It's done here all the time in Africa," I continued, "and somehow it's accepted. I've heard it said that the natives are lazy, so you must whip them to keep them motivated. It's disgusting, and it's just awful; I can't even imagine it. Who in the hell would lay a hand on a man that works for you?" I paused for just a second to assess the mood.

"I didn't mean—" he said, stopping abruptly.

"I know you were just making a joke," I said. "But in every joke, there is a little bit of truth. You can understand why I am so sensitive, right?"

"I'm sorry," he said. "It won't happen again."

"I'm serious: have you ever seen the marks on Willie's backside?" I stepped into the house and let the door shut behind me. I could hear them mumbling on the porch as I went to the bedroom and could only imagine what they were saying once I left.

CHAPTER 15

STEALING THUNDER

Good afternoon, sunshine," I said to Esther, shaking off the load of the dull conversation and giving my wife a big smile.

"What have you done for the good of the order today?" she asked.

"I took Pastor Michael on a successful lion hunt, for one," I answered.

"That's quite an accomplishment for one day. Who killed the lion?" she asked.

"Michael claimed it; it's his lion," I said, hoping the conversation over the circumstances would end there.

"Any other important details?" she asked.

"Like what?"

"I don't know," she said with a smile. "Maybe the obvious, like how many shots you took? Was it standing, or was it on a full-out charge? Did you wound it, or did you kill it outright? Did you have to track it? Just the usual old stuff a person might tell around a campfire, that's all."

It made me think about dancing around a campfire as I tried to skirt the truth and choose my words carefully so as not to step into the pit. I described every detail, every blade of grass flattened by the charging lion, and every bit of action I could sweep off the floor of my memory, but I was careful to leave out the one remaining secret. I had to wonder: if I just left out one significant detail about the incident, was I telling a lie? The more I went down this road, the more guilt-ridden and uncomfortable I became. Esther wasn't fooled.

"What are you not telling me, Lance?"

"What do you mean? That's it—that's just like it happened."

"I can read you like a book, dear heart," she said, sitting up in the bed.

"You can close that book and put it in the bookcase because that's my story."

"Does Michael know you both shot at the same time and that you killed the lion?"

"How on earth did you know that?" I asked.

"It wasn't hard to figure out," she said. "I've been on safari; I have done my fair share of shooting, even though I never killed anything. But I know how these things go. In the heat of the action, it's impossible to say who fired."

"And it's impossible to say who missed and who hit," I insisted.

"That's right, unless one person is shooting a bigger rifle. In that case, a person like you would be able to tell in a second." I didn't know what to say. She was so smart. Nothing escaped her.

"What do we do now?" I asked.

"Tell the truth," she said.

"But Michael is back in town now, and he'll be telling his story. If I wanted to break the news, I should have told him before he left. If I tell him later, he will lose face. Is holding something in confidence a lie?"

"Let's see. A lie is a false statement that is not the whole truth. Usually, a selfish motive is behind it, but I don't see one in this case. Did Rahab lie to protect the Israelite spies in the book of Joshua?"

"We read that together," I said.

"Yes. So, my conclusion is that Rahab lied, and God spared and blessed her. But not for lying to protect the Israelites—her faith saved her. Her act was done out of faith in God; Scripture says that anything not done out of faith is a sin."

"Should we stay with the story?" I asked.

"It's a confidence at this point to protect our friend. When Jesus came off the mountain with Peter, James, and John, he told them not to tell anyone what they had seen until after his resurrection from the dead. It's not a sin to hold back information; it is only if you add falsehoods for selfish motives to put yourself in a better light. Now, if Michael had shot the lion and you were claiming that you shot it when you knew you didn't, that would be a problem. At this point, we would do more harm to Michael by telling him God's honest truth than we would be keeping silent."

"I'm going with you on this one," I said. It was like Sunday when we went to church and she wore that ridiculous-looking dress she made. Esther had thought it was beautiful. When she asked me if the dress made her look fat, I certainly wasn't going to be the one who burst her bubble by telling her the truth in her condition. Was I lying to her, or was I protecting her? *I guess there is truth, and then there is tact. Maybe tact is just a matter of being wise.*

"You finally got some rest today, didn't you?" I asked.

"You must be kidding! I listened to our farmhands on the porch, prying up boards for about an hour. Finally, Lydia put her foot down, shooing them away like crows on a cob when they started to pound nails. After that, I got some rest."

"How's our girl?"

"Hungry as a newborn lamb. She slept through all the commotion. By the way, how is that crib coming?"

"Oh no. In all the commotion, I got distracted. That should have been at the top of my list, but I was so anxious to get Michael out on the farm and get life back to normal that the whole crib thing fell off the table." I took a step back toward the bedroom door. "How's about I go out and finish up the crib right now? It's almost done."

"I would love to chat with you, but the crib has to be a priority right now," she said.

I didn't want to tell her, but I'd never had the gift of woodworking. I fiddled with it but became so easily frustrated. That is why the crib project had never come to completion. A cold sweat came over me, knowing I had already taken the crib as far as I could. I was stumped on how to finish. Gathering in my wits about me, I resolved to find a plan to get 'er done.

"I'll be out in the shop if you need me. Should I find someone to finish up the porch?" I asked.

"Now they can go ahead while the baby is awake," she said, "but tell them to get it done quickly." I scurried out of the house but Chuck and Blaney were gone. I spotted them carrying something like a crib from the barn between them.

"You finished it!" I yelled as they struggled to hold it. They had warm grins, waiting for my approval. "Aw . . . it's beautiful," I said. "You guys are too much."

"I saw you fighting this thing," said Chuck, "and I couldn't help you. I'm a worse carpenter than you are, and that's pretty bad. But I mentioned it to Blaney, who jumped in with both feet."

"Where did you learn how to woodwork?" I asked.

"Oh, I've been tinkering since I was a kid. You had it just about done. All I did was make a few adjustments and finish it for you."

"It's beautiful and turned out better than I could have done."

"We didn't know how to tell you," said Chuck. "Sort of worried you might take offense."

"Take offense?"

"Some people like to finish a project they started," said Blaney.

"Not me! You saved me a bunch of grief. Jesus was a carpenter, but he never gave me the gift." We laughed, and I felt glad about what they had done for me. They had even placed the mattress pad Esther had ordered from town. We were always trying to save money, and buying expensive furniture was not part of the budget.

"Where did the wood come from?" asked Blaney. "Looks like Muhuhu. Right?"

"Willie found it growing in a grove on the farm," I said.

"Some might call it black ironwood," said Blaney, "but it floats on water, so it really can't be classified as that. The natives use it to carve their trinkets."

"Willie found the tree and cut every slat with his crosscut," I said. "Then we had put the boards on racks to dry. That took place long before we knew about Abigail. Esther will be thrilled. I guess I am, too, even though you guys will be her heroes now."

"Sorry," said Blaney. "Didn't mean to steal your thunder, old man."

"No, you're not doing that. That's funny. Do you know where that term comes from?" I asked.

"Can't say as I do," answered Blaney, still holding the heavy bed between him and Chuck.

"It comes from the actor and playwright John Dennis, who lived in London about a hundred years ago. He invented a thunder machine that made a thunder noise to thrill the crows. He wasn't much of a playwright, so the story goes, and his play was taken off the stage, and another company came in with their own. When he attended the opening night, he became furious when they put his thunder machine on. He stood in the audience and yelled, 'That is my thunder; the villains have stolen my thunder.'" Blaney looked at Chuck, and he shrugged his shoulders.

"You are a wealth of knowledge, always some tidbit," said Blaney.

"This thing is getting heavy," said Chuck. "Where do you want it?"

* * *

I never saw Esther make such a fuss over anything like that before. Even though I said they were not going to steal my thunder, I wasn't prepared for her reaction. Steal my thunder, they did.

I convinced Blaney to take his leave because I knew he had plenty of business to get back to in town. The week went quickly. Esther, in her usual way, celebrated Holy Week every inch of the way as we moved forward to Easter Sunday morning. I had never heard tell of a woman recovering from childbirth in such a short fashion. Despite Lydia's best attempts to keep her in bed, it was as if Esther had not even had a baby.

Esther had explained to me that the Monday the men showed up to kill us was the day that Jesus had found a fig tree with no signs of coming fruit. He said to the tree, "May you never bear fruit again." Immediately, the tree withered. It was a sign for the people of Israel that they would wither because of their lack of faith. She said we had seen men like that tree with no fruit in their lives, and Jesus had made them wither. She also told me about the temple cleansing by Jesus, who threw the money changer out and tipped over the tables. She said that the arrival of Abigail would one day cleanse the temple of his church.

We celebrated Maundy Thursday and Good Friday according to Esther's lead, and finally, I awoke early on Saturday morning.

"What time is it?" whispered Esther as I pulled my pants on in the dark so as not to wake the babe, sleeping soundly in her crib.

"I don't know, but I can't sleep, so I'm going to take a walk." I knew what we were in for this weekend, figuring we would be invaded by Mary and her friends. I remembered her from church the previous week by how Michael had described her, but I still didn't remember meeting her husband. I didn't know how to prepare for a picnic if they all came. It seemed surreal, wondering if they would go or if this had all been a dream.

Isn't that what life is really like? I thought. *We have hopes and dreams, some that come to fruition, others that never materialize. The moments of reality dance on this little edge we call life, and they fade quickly into our memory and can never be changed once they have gone across the blade and fallen off the edge. How strange life is when you think of it! We are in a flickering moment for an instant, like a series of finger snaps, never knowing what twist or turn will come next. That moment happens, but then there is another just around the corner. We fret, worry, look forward with anticipation, look back with fond memories, revel, joy, cry, rest, and pray . . . then it starts all over again with a new set of problems, a new day, and anticipation. Life is like the changing of the seasons. Not here so much as we had in Upstate New York—here, it is wet and dry, but not so much real cold. Life is a whirlwind of unexpected circumstances, creating emotions that drip from our beings like droplets of morning dew.*

When I entered the main room, I saw Lydia was sitting and drinking coffee at the table with a kerosene lamp, reading by the light.

"You are up early," I whispered.

"Oh, I couldn't sleep; besides, Dennis is coming today. I feel like a teenager waiting to see her boyfriend run on the football field."

"Of course, your definition of football is much different from mine," I said.

"How so? Football is football."

"No, not so much. In America, we play with different rules, wear different uniforms, and even have different balls."

"You Americans, you always have to try to outdo somebody," she said, batting her lashes.

"I don't think we are trying to outdo anyone. We just never understood the game and wanted to make it easier for the fans to watch. Don't you think Esther has been recovering well?" I asked.

"Yes, just another example of you Americans trying to outdo us," she chuckled.

"How long should it take for a woman to recover from childbirth?" I asked.

"About eighteen years," she said. I smiled, and she put her hand over her mouth to stop herself laughing out loud. She put her coffee cup to her lips and took a sip, trying to regain her composure.

"You should have been on the stage," I whispered, trying to keep my volume down, and we smiled together. The eastern sky began to lighten behind the rolling hills as morning approached. "What time do you think Dennis will show up?"

"I'm hoping he found someone to mind the store for us."

"I can't begin to tell you what it means to us to have you come and stay."

"It's been a pleasure," she said. "I've never had a Negro for a friend before, but I like Esther very much. She is easy to talk to; it's like we have been friends forever."

"Right there, Lydia—now, that's what I'm talking about. It's so marvelous to me how you have made such an effort for the two of you to become good friends."

"It's not me; it's her. Like I said, she is so easy to talk to and pleasant to be around. She is a girl with some pluck; she has wit and faith, and she is not afraid to stand up to a man."

"Amen to that; she's not afraid of me." I heard the door open and looked over my shoulder as the morning light filtered into the room.

"What are you two gabbing about out here?" said Esther, straightening her gown and pressing it out with her palm as she cradled our precious Abigail in her other arm.

"I suppose we could have woken Blackwood from the dead," said Lydia with a smirk as Esther and I looked at each other, wondering if we were supposed to laugh and choosing to refrain. The room fell silent momentarily until Lydia realized her attempted humor had fallen flat, and she quickly changed the subject. "It's nice to have the window back."

"The boys didn't waste any time, did they?" I said. "They will have to wait on the window around the side. We only had one good piece of glass."

"You ought to get more than one," said Lydia. "I can only imagine that Abigail will probably put a baseball through one by the time she is grown."

"I suppose that girl will surprise us all," I said, thinking about my hopes and dreams for her future. I knew there would be challenges ahead, but I had to tame my imagination and excitement to avoid letting it get away from me like a herd of wild buffalo.

"I will certainly not allow her to play baseball; she will grow up like a lady, for heaven's sake," said Esther, gazing at Abigail's face and not looking up as she spoke.

"You can try, but she will have to grow up tough living on a farm. She will have to learn to entertain herself with no other neighbor kids around. Even the native village is a long way up the valley."

"I won't have her playing with native children. She will grow up knowing her place," said Esther.

"Are you listening to what you are saying?" I said, bracing myself for the consequences of running headlong into a sleeping lioness.

"What am I saying?" she said with a wrinkled brow.

"I think we need to be careful about 'knowing our place,' that's all," I said.

"Everyone has a calling and a place. I don't mean she won't play with other children. I just mean that Abigail has a calling in her life to help others, and if she becomes something other than what God has called her to become, she will not know or understand her place. I came to Africa to help the Africans, not to become a native. I can provide them much more help as a farmer's wife than I could if I married a native man and lived a tribal life. When I came here alone, I didn't know what to expect. I was following the Holy Spirit and willing to go wherever he led."

"Following the Holy Spirit is always good," said Lydia. "You can never go wrong following the Holy Spirit."

"Don't be fooled by that, my dear," said Esther, swaying Abigail in her arms to keep her from fussing. "The Holy Spirit is capable of leading you into temptation. You need to follow, but you need to always be ready."

"But I thought God would never tempt us?" asked Lydia.

"God won't tempt us, but he allows us to be tempted. The Scripture says God will not allow us to be tempted beyond what we can bear and will always provide a way out."

"But you said the Holy Spirit leads us into temptation," said Lydia.

"That's right; look at the book of Matthew where it says, 'Then was Jesus led up of the Spirit into the wilderness to be tempted of the devil.' Here, Jesus was led by the Spirit and tempted by the devil. God didn't tempt Jesus; he tested Jesus, the same way he tests our faith day in and day out."

"I will have to let that sink in," said Lydia. "All this Bible stuff is still new and difficult to understand. I'm still unsure if I understand why God would want us to be tempted."

"In the Lord's Prayer, Jesus prayed, 'and lead us not into temptation, but deliver us from evil.' Why would Jesus have prayed to his Father not to lead us into temptation if God didn't do it? He wasn't praying to the devil not to lead us into temptation."

"You make a good point," I said.

"God is constantly testing our faith. It's like making a pot of soup, and you keep dipping the spoon to take a taste every time you add more salt or other spices. That is what God does with us. He adds spice to our lives by putting us in certain situations that make us grow, and then he tests the results of his work. If he let someone else taste the soup, they wouldn't know whether it was good or bad. So he uses the devil like a fire to heat the soup and then uses circumstances in our lives to change the taste. He knows what we are supposed to taste like, so he has to keep checking along the way to see how we are progressing."

"I remember hunting wild turkey as a kid," I said. "I used a box call to make the sound of a hen turkey, and the tom would gobble back. I always wanted to hear him gobble to see how close he was, so I kept on talking to him."

"Yep, just like that. God is always checking us to see where we are."

"So are you saying the Holy Spirit led you to be tempted to marry me?" I asked.

"No, God led us together because he knew Abigail from the beginning of time," said Esther. "Think about that for a while, and that will make your head spin."

We spent a pleasant morning together, and Chuck joined us for breakfast.

And then we saw a buggy coming through the clearing about a mile down the road.

CHAPTER 16

ON YOUR NERVE

L ooks like that might be Dennis," I said.

"I wonder who is with him," mused Lydia, handing the baby back to Esther.

"Not sure," I replied.

"Guess we'll have to wait for that cat to get let out of the bag," Lydia said.

"That's a funny saying, isn't it?" said Esther. "That's the second time you have used that saying. Where'd you hear that?"

"I don't know," she said.

"I do," I said.

"Enlighten us, please," urged Chuck. "It's a great saying."

"It comes from the days when they sold piglets in bags. A piglet was worth a nickel, but cats were a dime a dozen. When a cat was in a bag, it was silent, and if you were buying several, you couldn't tell the difference between a piglet and a cat. When the buyer got home and let the cat out of the bag, he got a surprise and realized he had been swindled. The cat would meow like crazy after being let out in a pig pen, and everyone around immediately knew the whole story as well."

"I always thought it had something to do with drowning a cat off a bridge," said Lydia. "If you didn't tie the sack tight, the cat would get let out of the bag."

"I thought it came from the cat-o'-nine-tails the old ship captain kept in a bag for punishment," said Chuck. "And when he let the cat out of the bag, someone was going to get a surprise."

"I like mine the best," I said.

"Sure you would," said Esther.

As the buggy turned down our drive, I squinted my eyes to try to focus on the passenger's face. "I think that's Jack Cunningham. Do you know Jack Cunningham, Chuck?"

"Heard the name many times; I think he knows John. Isn't he a great white hunter?"

"You might be thinking of his distant cousin RJ, who led the Roosevelt safari five years ago."

"Yeah, everybody knows RJ," said Chuck. "Well, I mean, they know *of* him."

"Right," I said. "He knows John Rivers very well, and his cousin Jack does too, but neither paid much attention to me. I wonder why Jack would be coming out here."

"I don't know," said Lydia. "I just know that Dennis and Jack have known each other for many years, and he's a good guy."

I scooted out of my chair, and Chuck followed. Then, I grabbed the door handle and saw the bullet hole in the front door again. As I stepped outside, closing the squeaking door behind us, I leaned over to Chuck's ear.

"Let's have the boys cover up that bullet hole when you get a chance. I'm getting a little sick of it," I whispered. "Aren't you?" Chuck nodded and gave his approval. I heard the hinges on the door and turned to see Lydia descending the front steps behind me. The horse and buggy came down the drive to the farm, and Dennis gave a smile and a wave. I turned back to Lydia, and she had a wide grin and waved back to her husband wildly like she hadn't seen him in a year.

"How's my girl?" said Dennis, stopping the mare and waiting for one of our boys to take hold of the reins before he leaped from the buggy and hugged his wife. Dennis turned and took my hand in a firm grip. "How are you, my friend?"

"Everything is peace and quiet here," I said as Jack Cunningham stepped from behind the buckboard. "What brings you out here, Jack?" I asked, extending my hand. Jack Cunninham was a dashing sort of fellow. His hair had not been trimmed for months, but it looked good on him. His pointed nose, dark eyes, and bushy eyebrows seemed to pierce you as he spoke.

"I think we met once before," he said, taking my grip. "You were with John Rivers, weren't you?"

"Yes, that was about four years ago," I said. "How's your famous cousin?"

"Oh, who, RJ? Only he thinks he is famous."

"Well, he won a place in Old Teddy's book; I guess he is famous enough," said Chuck.

"I never see him. Besides, he's not my cousin. Everybody thinks so, but he spells his name differently. I guess we are related somehow. You know they asked me to lead the Roosevelt safari before they asked him."

"Is that so?" said Dennis. "I said I would have to think about it, and then suddenly I found out they'd picked RJ," he said with a tight lip.

"Are you going to stay for the weekend?" asked Lydia.

"Yes, we are," said Dennis. "I invited Jack out; I hope that's not an imposition."

"Imposition?" asked Esther, coming down the front steps. In all the clamor, she had escaped the front door without us noticing the sound from the annoying hinges. "There is no imposition in anyone coming out to visit this farm as long as they are friendly," she said with a smile.

"Where's the baby?" I asked.

"Oh, I put her down in the crib. She sleeps like a baby in that thing."

"Quite the farm you have here," said Jack. "I heard you killed a lion out here this week."

"Word travels fast in these parts," I said.

"My wife Mary attends church, and heard it from a person from the congregation."

"Your wife is Mary; that's where I heard the name before," said Lydia. "Mary Cunningham, of course."

"I'm between clients right now, since we are at the tail end of calving season. I don't want to get going again until June after the rains. That also gives the calves a little head start."

"How come Mary didn't come with you?" asked Esther.

"Mary would not miss church on Sunday morning, and especially tomorrow. I guess it's Easter Sunday, the day that rabbits lay their colored eggs. Oh—I'm sorry, ma'am," he stuttered. "I didn't mean colored eggs . . . well, I mean, I mean *decorated* eggs."

"What are you saying, for heaven's sake?" said Esther. "There's nothing wrong with being colored."

"Jack, this is my wife, Esther," I said, shocked that I hadn't introduced her since she came off the steps.

"I am very honored to meet you, Jack, and I am very honored to be who I am. God made me this way for his purpose. I'm certainly not ashamed of God, and I don't think he made a mistake when he made my skin this color. Do you know the real Easter story?" she asked.

"Easter story or *Esther* story?" asked Jack, showing his teeth and trying to lighten the mood. "I think I would like to hear about the Esther story—not so interested in the other one." He chuckled. "That old myth has been beaten like a dead horse."

"Are you fellas hungry?" asked Esther, skillfully changing the subject.

"We will never turn down food," said Dennis with his arm around his wife.

"You have a reputation for great coffee," said Jack. "Got any of that brewing?"

"We always have coffee on; come on in the house," said Esther as she turned and headed up the steps.

I knew Esther was likely rubbing her hands together, eager for a frank conversation about Jesus with a nonbeliever like Jack. Esther was just as excited about that as she was about spending the afternoon fly fishing on the river. She had a way about her: she spoke with authority, but she never tried to debate anyone. As she had told me many times, we couldn't argue people into the kingdom of God. *You must show them the way, not push them through the door*, I repeated to myself. *No one will come to Christ reluctantly. No one will come to Christ without the help of the Holy Spirit. It is a gift from God, not a choice of the will or an intellectual decision made with the mind. It comes from a person's soul, and it changes the heart. Then, the mind understands, and the person is changed from the inside out. It doesn't happen any other way. If it were something we could obtain by earning our way, then we could be inclined to boast of our achievement. But because it is a gift from God by his grace, we are left humbled by the experience.*

"Tell us about your work, Jack," I said as we all sat around the table in the parlor.

"Love my job," he said. "I have to pinch myself constantly and can't believe I get paid to partake in my favorite pastime."

"They say if you do what you love, you will never work a day in your life," said Chuck.

"What do you love about it?" asked Lydia.

"Everything—I love the people, the adventure, the bush life, being a teacher, and taking them through their first-time experience in this wild place. To me, it's an incredible life."

"How about Mary? What does she think of it?" she asked. The other boys around the table sat on the edge of their seats, wondering how Jack would weasel out of this one. I had heard about him and how he was gone for months, leaving his wife to fend for herself.

"Mary . . . Mary is quite . . . well, you know," he stammered. "She has her friends and her church to keep her busy."

"You never had any children, did you?" Lydia asked.

"No," he answered, squirming in his chair as he seemed uncomfortable with Lydia's interrogation.

"Why not?" she asked as now I began to feel his pain.

"She just never conceived," he said, squinting at her like an annoying gnat. I thought about those oxpeckers that live on the backs of the Cape buffalo looking for bugs. *The buff will tolerate and benefit from them, but when they become annoying, they whip their tails and shake their head to shoo them away!* I wondered how long Jack would put up with Lydia's pecking. Lydia seemed to feel the whip from his tail, and she backed off, knowing she was getting too close to his personal life for comfort. Jack gave Dennis the evil eye, and Dennis put his hand on Lydia's knee to quiet her down.

"Tell us about your last hunting trip," said Dennis, taking a turn on the road.

"We were up on the north end of Lake Turkana; I had three Dutchmen and struggled to understand their broken English." Jack smiled as he reminisced about his experience. "I had to hand it to them: two men were good sportsmen, and I greatly enjoyed their company."

"What was wrong with the third?" I asked.

"I will tell you the story, and then you will understand. If you know what I mean, I was tempted to drop the 'H' out of third." We all looked at each other briefly, and then Dennis rolled his eyes.

"Oh, I get it," laughed Lydia.

"It was early morning. The sky was pink as the sun poked over the top of the hills to the east. A chill was in the air, and a slight breeze came off the lake. The flamingos numbered in the thousands and spread across the lake's edge like a pink blanket."

"I would like to see that," said Esther. "We should go up there, Lance." I nodded, knowing we couldn't make that trip until Abigail was big enough to travel.

"We had spotted a large herd of buff grazing in the grasslands to the west and made our way through the dark to a bluff overlooking the edge of the estuary and swamps. That reed grass is as high as a man, and it is good buffalo hunting, but as you know, they will hide in that stuff like a pheasant being chased by a pointer. I told the Dutchmen to wait for the shot, but one of them was a little jumpy. I trusted the other two, but this third one had given me trouble before, and he was about to do it again."

"What were their names?" asked Lydia.

"Nicolaas was the eldest, and his brother was Smit, but the other guy was some kind of shirttail to them, and his name was Nerve— he sure got on mine sometimes." Jack sat back in his chair and looked up, squinting his eyes. "We spotted the herd, and the bull was tucked in among the cows. Other smaller bulls along the edges would have been easy targets, but this crusty old fella was nestled in with his harem. They were feeding across the short grass about two hundred yards right at the edge of where you want to take a client bullet.

"It was Smit's turn for a clean kill, and I thought I had clarified that. Like I said, this language thing was going on between us, and Nerve was the worst. Most of the time, Nicolaas had to repeat everything I said, and even then, I wasn't sure if he was making the translation correctly." Jack paused again and chuckled. "Dutchmen," he said, shaking his head. "I think they are sympathetic to the Germans, and they think we Brits and Frenchmen are greedy to be trying to colonize the world. Heck, we are just attempting to protect this land from itself. If we Brits hadn't shown up when we did to stop the slave trade, those Arabs would have ravaged her. But the Dutch—who can figure out a Dutchman?"

"You know what they say, don't you?" asked Chuck. The rest of us sat waiting for him to enlighten us. "If you ain't Dutch—you ain't much." Everyone broke out in laughter at the thought. We Americans knew we were the best country in the world, and I didn't see why the rest of the world couldn't see it. It didn't make sense why everybody thought their country was the best. *I guess that is what makes men fight to prove it. But men are just like that. They need a good fight every couple of years to keep things lively.*

"Finally, this bull came clear after the herd worked its way across the valley, and he came clear broadside at a solid hundred yards. I whispered to Smit to go ahead and take him, and I saw him release the safety on his rifle. I knew Smit had him dead to rights at this range, and he was confident in his ability to place the shot in the kill zone. Just then, a shot rang out over my shoulder from behind us, and the muzzle blast nearly took me off my feet. The explosion knocked me in the ears so hard, I thought it had broken my ear drums. I looked back, and smoke was lingering off the end of

Nerve's rifle barrel. I'm sure he could see the smoke coming from my nostrils. I stared him down briefly and then turned to watch the herd as they roared across the grass and disappeared in the reeds. I was so angry that I wanted to wrap that rifle around his neck like a bow tie. I stood up, jerked the gun from his grip, and handed it to Nicolaas, who spit Dutch at him with a red face. Winding up with a wounded bull in the reed grass was exactly what I had wanted to avoid at all costs.

"How'd you get him?" asked Lydia, perched on the edge of her seat.

"He's getting to that, honey," said Dennis, putting his arm on her shoulder as she slid back in her chair with a sheepish grin.

"This all sounds familiar," said Chuck. "I was nearly killed by a buffalo on our safari."

"It's more common than you would think," continued Jack. "There is a lot of debate over the most dangerous animal in Africa, but hands down, the wounded buff is one terrible monster to deal with. We came off the hill to the valley and searched for blood, which we found immediately. I had an uneasy feeling because of the quantity. If there is a lot, that means you have hit something vital, and the beast will die quickly. But if it's spotty, he's not hit very hard and can get you. That's when the old boy can boil out of the tall grass and make mincemeat out of you in a split second. I wanted to take the gun away from that Nerve fella, but I didn't want to leave the poor guy defenseless. Now I had to worry about him shooting one of us and getting run over by the buff." Jack paused, thinking about where he was in the story, rubbing his chin.

"Did you have to track him?" asked Esther, trying to move him ahead.

"No. I spotted where he had gone in the tall grass, and no sense in following what little blood he had spattered around. It's suicide to go into grass like that after a buff. Heck—it's a giant piece of meat with a beautiful set of horns, but it's not worth getting killed over. We stood on the edge of the short grass and tried to look through the openings to see if we could see him, but fifteen feet was the limit. I warned them to stay ready because he could come charging out any second. I kept checking on Nerve, noticing his hands were trembling. Seriously, he had no business coming out here at all. He should have stayed at camp, or better yet, back in the Netherlands."

Dennis grinned, and I chuckled to myself, knowing the nerve it took to stand one's ground in a fight. Dennis knew what it meant to face a charging lion and shoot him dead at ten yards. *This Nerve guy would have broken and tried to run; now that would have been suicide,* I thought. I looked Dennis in the eye, and we both knew what the other was thinking.

"I had just taken my focus off the reeds to look back at Nerve, and then I heard the buff snort. I looked back just in time to see the grass part and his horns coming straight at me. At that very moment, I didn't care who killed the damn thing; I just wanted him dead. I drew my rifle up, and without even taking a sight picture, I shot from the hip. Then, I pulled the double up for the second shot and fired it before Smit, just to my left, even got his rifle on target. The first shot wobbled him, and the second shot dumped him hard as if the fifty caliber had hit him right square. Smit laughed, thinking it was over, but I yelled at him to keep his head.

"As you know, the herd can gang up on you because they don't take kindly to other members of their tribe being taken out. They don't tolerate it with lions and won't stand for it with men, either. I looked over my shoulder with a stern frown, and he froze up like a novelist waiting for his following line.

"I broke my double open and replaced the empties with fresh rounds. Just then, the grass moved and another bull came bursting out of the reeds. My rifle breach was open and I snapped it shut. Thankfully, Nicolaas still had his wits about him. He had kept his head in the game; his rifle shot true and quick and the total weight of the buffalo dropped at my feet. Never before had I had such a close call in all my life! This bull was bigger than the first one, and my whole body pounded from my beating heart. I had seen one of these old boys take a three-hundred-pound lion and toss him over his back like a rag doll. They have extreme power, and a man is an annoying mosquito. They have this cap like a steel plate on their head, with those fishhook horns as sharp as daggers. They can hook you, toss you, and stomp you with their hooves, backed by their immense weight of around two thousand pounds."

We all sat in silence as we pondered the words of Jack Cunningham and his incredible story.

"What about Nerve?" I asked.

"Oh, Nerve. He never got his nerve back after that fiasco, as far as I know. I never hunted with them again, and I handed the hunting party off to one of my associates."

CHAPTER 17

PROPHESY

Esther sat glued to every word of Jack's story as if she were on the hunt herself. As I gazed at her, I realized again how much I loved her, the whole package: her nose, her smile, her little curls. Her eyes were like a cape buffalo's horns that could hook you every time. They could toss me like a rag doll or squish me like a mosquito.

I remember the day I saw her at the train stop in Nairobi. She was mesmerizing, and the moment I saw her, I knew I would spend the rest of my life with her. I had loved her all my life from boyhood, and now she was mine to watch over and protect from the lions. It had nearly been a week since the lions came to the farm looking for a fight. And now a man such as Jack Cunningham was here to offer the greatest gift of all: friendship.

"Oh my goodness, I almost forgot," said Dennis, reaching for his coat, which was on the hook by the door. "I have something for you, Esther." Dennis pulled a letter from his pocket and handed it to her. It was addressed to Esther Miles.

"It's from my dear heart!" she cried as she eagerly admired the tattered envelope.

"Who might that be?" asked Jack with wide eyes.

"My best friend in all the world, that's who—Betty Rivers."

"I did not have the pleasure of meeting her when they came to Africa last time. How long has it been since you've seen her?" he asked.

"They came two years ago now; it seems like yesterday," she said, taking a knife off the table and cutting the envelope open. She eagerly unfolded the pages, glanced at them briefly, and then folded them back, sliding them back into the envelope.

"Bad news?" asked Lydia.

"Oh heavens, no, I'm going to savor it like chocolate cake. Besides, I might cry and don't want to make a fool of myself."

"John is quite the famous person in these parts. Everybody seems to know him," said Jack.

"Oh yeah, he makes it his business to know people," I said, "and when people meet him for the first time, they like him."

"Everywhere you go, it seems like John Rivers is a household name," said Jack. "Why, he's more famous than JR Cunningham."

"What has become of Cunningham?" asked Dennis.

"He was set to lead a safari with His Royal Highness, George, Prince of Wales. But King Edward VII's untimely death in May four years ago ended that trip because George became the king of England. Guess he had other things to tend to besides taking a vacation. What about John?"

"Betty has been faithful to write," I replied, "But I'm still waiting for my first letter from John. Guess he figures his wife's pen is sufficient." I hesitated to tell him about John's conversion right at that moment. I didn't want to share something he wouldn't have appreciated.

"If you excuse me, I am going to check on the baby," said Esther, sliding her chair back and leaving the table. I knew she couldn't wait to get her eyes on that letter, and it seemed like she had smoke coming out of her pocket. I didn't have to say a word as I slid my chair back from the table and followed her. I made eye contact with Chuck, and he knew I needed to look at that letter, too. We snuck into the bedroom and as I stood just behind Esther, she rolled the blanket back off the top of the crib. Abigail's little face shone like an angel's as she continued to sleep. Esther smiled and put her index finger to her lips, sitting in the rocking chair. She unfolded the letter, and I sat in the chair next to her. Esther held the letter so I could read it along with her. I had to marvel at the longhand script, which was as beautiful as a work of art. The letter had a date of February 20. I counted the eight weeks it took to get here.

Chicago, Illinois, February 20, 1914
Lance and my dearest Esther,

Dear friends, I hope life finds you well. I am dying to hear how the pregnancy is going, and I am sure by the time you get this letter, the baby will be just weeks away. I am praying for you each day that you will have a successful delivery and a beautiful child. Sometimes, when I see the moon come up from the east, I wonder if you are still able to see it going down in the west, and then I am comforted that somehow we are still connected. Every day, it seems like John is talking about planning another trip to Africa. I know we will be coming within a year, and I imagine that by then, your little one will be walking.

So much for speculations; I am sure you would like to hear about our life, and I will wait for your letter to hear about yours.

Jason is deep in his studies and seems to be enjoying school very much. He will be eighteen this summer and enrolling in college next fall. We are so proud of him. His experience in Africa seems to have given him a boost over the other boys, and he has emerged as quite the leader. Funny how great accomplishments give a person great confidence. He often talks about returning to Africa to complete the task of taking a rhinoceros to finish out that last remaining piece of his big five. He joked that the Chicago Zoo might have an old one that needed to be put down, and he could take his rifle there and put up a painted backdrop mural of Africa so he could finish up his trophies. That boy is so full of ideas sometimes, he makes me crazy.

He is the quarterback on his football team this year and is filling out into quite a man. It has been hard for me to see how he has grown up so much in the last years. To me, he is like my son Johnny. When he died at age ten, I missed the years from ten to fifteen as if he had gone away on a long trip. So I picked up with Jason as my new son at fifteen. Jason still loves to play the piano and has had offers to attend schools of the arts, but John insists that he stay focused with his sights set on law school.

John has been discouraged at times and frustrated with his friends he thought would believe him when he told them about his faith and his experience. Many of his very good friends, whom he was just certain would find God, have turned away and now avoid John like the plague. I tried to tell him in the beginning that it wouldn't be that easy to talk to people about Jesus, but you know how hardheaded John can be. Finally, after nearly two years now, he is beginning to understand why Jesus made it plain that we were to be fishers of men.

I had to take him out to the river with me one day. I showed him again just how difficult it is to catch fish with a fly, and I told him that your bait has to be something they want to eat. I remember how, when you were with us, you never pushed your religion. You merely acted as a safari guide, showing us the track along the way and helping us to find what we didn't even know we were looking for. I had to remind John of how much *he* once avoided people who spoke of their faith and thought they were foolish.

He has been reading the Bible and studying the Scriptures like a man trying to play catch-up in a race he didn't know was being run. He has talked about going back to school and getting a degree in theology, and he has been looking into some of the finest seminaries. Now he is struggling with the different doctrines and looking for the perfect church. I told him what you said about the perfect church being the one you don't attend; the minute you attend it, you will find out it is not perfect, after all. He has met and talked with a number of prominent church leaders and has even been invited to speak at their churches. But he has not settled in on finding a doctrine that he is in total agreement with yet.

I enjoyed your last letter, which I received just before Christmas. It was the best Christmas present ever. I loved the part about how Lance was building a crib for the baby. I will continue to pray for you as you struggle to make friends in Nairobi. Sweetheart, don't get discouraged. I guess I don't have to preach to you about the difficulties and obstacles God has put in your life, but you are the most amazing person I know. Just continue to be yourself and live your faith, and God will bless you. Like I said, I almost feel silly telling you such a thing because of how you are, and how you were with me.

The only other thing to report is that Mammy May has been very sick. I am not sure if it is her age or if she has gotten a bug, but she has been down in bed for nearly a month and the doctor visits her every couple of days. We have had to hire two additional housekeepers to take up the slack, and we certainly do miss her cooking. Please pray for her because I know how faithful she is to pray for you. She asks me every day if there has been a letter. She has said that she feels like she knows you and somehow feels related. I know that if you ever decided to come visit, she would receive you like a daughter. And me? Well, I would receive you as my sister. So, until we are together again, I will pray for you every day.

One more thing . . . John told me the other day that he thinks you are having a girl. I don't know how he knows such a thing, but he said that he had a vision of her and that her name would be Abigail. How silly does that sound? No one can know such a thing as that, and you probably have a name already picked out. I just thought you needed to know.

Waiting with baited breath for your next letter, with all the love and devotion a person can muster from the depths of her soul, from me to you.

We remain indebted in life and in love to the both of you forever.

Your sister in Christ,

Betty

I looked up from the letter and could have sworn I saw Betty standing in the corner of the room. "How in the heck?" Esther said, holding the letter between her fingers with a firm grip. "That is amazing!"

I didn't know how to respond. I tried to speak, but the words wouldn't come out. I had never experienced anything like that, and I knew I had never spoken Abigail's name to John in any form or any way. "Did you tell John, pray tell?" she asked suspiciously.

"No, the name Abigail did not come to me until after you were pregnant. There is no way John would have known such a thing. I would have had to write it in a letter; I have not written him any letters. I have left all of that up to you, my dear."

"It does not surprise me, because I know how God works. He is just confirming that we picked the right name and that God has known this little person for a long time. It confirms that He has a plan for her life and that she will have incredible faith, even more than her mother."

Just then, Abigail began to stir in her crib, and Esther set the letter on the bed to tend to her.

"Come look at her, Lance," she said. "Isn't she the most beautiful thing you have ever seen?" I had to admit she was a good-looking baby, but to me, she could have been any other baby: bald-headed and red-faced. Of course, I wouldn't burst my wife's bubble and tell her what I thought. "Well, what do you say?"

"Yes, dear, she is the most beautiful baby I have ever seen."

"Look at her little nose, Lance. She has your nose, not like my nose, sweetheart."

"What is wrong with your nose? You have a beautiful nose."

"To you, maybe, but that's because your love blinds you."

"What do you mean?"

"It's pet-owner blindness. You have a dog who loves you, and you love him so much you aren't willing to see any of his faults," she said. "But look at her, Lance. There is no such thing as pet-owner blindness here. This little one is the most beautiful thing I have ever seen, and I am sure everyone who ever sees her will agree."

CHAPTER 18

Esther on Easter

The following morning, we awoke to Easter Sunday. Dennis had slept in the spare room with Lydia, Jack had spent the night in the bunkhouse, and Esther had been up early taking care of the baby and praying.

She dressed in the dark while I lay in bed, trying to get in the last few winks. I knew she would have to give a Sunday morning message before we all sat down to breakfast, so she had been strategically preparing Abigail to sleep. I dressed in my dungarees and splashed my face with the warm water, brushing my hair over to make myself presentable. I found Esther wearing her white dress, tending to Abigail. Now, the dress actually fit her.

"He is risen!" she said with a big grin.

"Yeah, I'm up—thought I would just get a little extra sleep," I said.

"Not you, silly. I am talking about Jesus. He is risen!"

"Oh, of course," I responded.

"No, you are supposed to say, 'Truly, he is risen indeed.'"

"Oh sure, you're right," I said.

"No, you have to *say* it," she insisted. "He is risen."

"Truly, he is risen indeed," I responded to make her happy. "You did some work on that dress, didn't you?"

"Do you like it?" she asked.

"Quite stunning."

"What about you?" she asked. "Is that what you are planning to wear for Easter Sunday?"

"I just figured, since we were home."

"You must have figured wrong," she snapped. "This is Easter, and even though we are home, you have to remember that we have guests here. Dressing up will show them how committed we are to our faith. Dressing up will put us in the mood and make us look smart."

"I think they know how committed we are," I said.

"They might think they know, but they don't know. This will prove it, so I need you to change as if we were going to town for Sunday morning."

This girl . . . sometimes, she makes me crazy. Sometimes, she is as hardheaded as a lead cow elephant going to a water hole. She knows how I feel, but she doesn't care much.

What to wear . . . what to wear, I thought as I went through my hanging clothes. *Not that one. That one is old.* I thumbed past the suit coat I hadn't worn in nearly six years. *Guess that one could go to someone who would wear it. How about what I wore last Sunday? I mean, I am not going to church, so no one would even know. Except Dennis and Lydia. Actually, maybe only Lydia. Funny that a man never remembers what another man wears from one day to the next. Nor does he care. I don't remember what Dennis wore to church last week, and I bet he doesn't remember what I wore either.* I grabbed the clothes off the hanger in haste and changed into them.

When I came back to the parlor, Esther rolled her eyes. "That is the same thing you wore last Sunday." I had to chuckle, knowing I would get this response.

"Isn't it good enough?" I asked.

"You have several jackets. The blue jacket will go better with those pants and that tie than the gray one."

"Okay," I said, knowing that if I had put on the blue one, she would have told me to change to the gray.

That's just how women are, Lance—get over it. Sometimes, a man just has to do what a woman says. Otherwise, he will pay for it later. You have to pick your battles, and this one doesn't matter. Give her a win and make her smile. Then you will have her eating out of your hand like a tame crow. When you are married to a beautiful woman, everything you put up with is worth the effort to make her happy. When her smile melts you and she is your best friend, you want to do everything to keep your best friend smiling. I reached for the blue jacket.

"You look quite smart in that jacket," she said.

"Thanks. Have you talked with M'Culay about breakfast?"

"Oh yes, we've planned this for weeks. Didn't know we would have an extra guest with us, but there is plenty of food. You know Easter breakfast is always a celebration, and this one will be the best."

"Why is that?" I asked. Esther looked at me and wrinkled her nose. "Maybe just because of a little girl named Abigail, silly. And because of all God has done for us. He has watched over this farm and protected us."

"It has been all God, hasn't it?" I said. "Life is so fragile, and it ain't for sissies. Life can chew you up and spit you out in a split second. Everything you are and have worked for can be taken from you in the blink of an eye. Take last week, for instance. If one of those bullets had strayed in a different direction and taken another path, one of us would be dead. Our lives would have changed in an instant. If Abigail had run into trouble by being born early, our lives would be totally different. Life is about elation and frustration. It's about living what you think you know, mixed with the hope for tomorrow. And living with the worry that pages could be torn from the book.

"When I met Betty, I could feel the heaviness in her soul," said Esther. "I thought about what it would be like to experience the loss of a child. But we can't live in fear; we must focus on God, his love, and his Spirit. We have to do what he has called us to do for the time we are given here in this life to do it. Now I understand what she has been through. When I look at Abigail and consider putting myself in Betty's shoes, it terrifies me."

"Me too—I don't even want to think about it. For now, I am hungry for breakfast," I said. "Sometimes, it's too bad that Bamira didn't agree to stay on here and cook for us. I love M'Culay, and he tries so hard to do his best, but Bamira didn't have to try."

"Ain't that the truth," she said. "Maybe we were all just so hungry on safari that the food tasted better. Still, I agree with you that Bamira was the man."

I heard the bedroom door open, and Lydia poked her head out. She wore a stylish blue dress with white lace. Her yellow hair had been braided and tied up. I caught only a peek at her high-heeled, lace-up boots as she walked because the dress flowed to the floor.

"I must have been the only one who didn't get the directive to dress up?" I said.

"There was no memo," she said. "But someone must have clued you in; otherwise, you wouldn't have worn a jacket. I know you, Lance: you live in those dungarees. If I had to guess, I bet you put those on first thing, right?"

I caught Esther making a face and then looked back at Lydia, who tried to look sober.

"You have me pegged, I guess."

Dennis emerged with a coat and a tie and came out to join us. "My goodness, you came prepared," I laughed. "There must have been a directive."

"When I left the farm last week, the last thing Lydia said to me was, 'Don't forget to bring clothes for Easter.' I guess only a fool would see that open door and not walk through it."

We heard footsteps on the porch just then, and I could hear Chuck's loud laughter. Lydia opened the door for Chuck and Jack. How silly Chuck looked dressed up in a coat and tie! And Jack Cunningham! Words cannot describe how uncomfortable he must have felt dressed in his buckskins with flowing fringe down the front of his leather jacket and knee-high boots. I remembered seeing that dress tie hanging in Chuck's closet, and that white shirt, too. At least he could wear dungarees; I had to wear these silly dress pants. I had always been able to wear my favorite pants with a coat and a tie, but since being married, that notion had gone out the window. I caught Esther's eye, and she pursed her lips. We smiled together, knowing our many mutual conversations about appropriate dress.

Our kitchen staff scurried to set the table for the six of us so we could sit down for breakfast. Willie came out of the kitchen to supervise, and Esther took him aside and had a private conversation outside of my hearing.

"You clean up pretty good for a farmer, Lance," said Jack.

"Looks like the girls orchestrated quite the event here this morning," I said. Lydia grinned, feeling quite proud of herself.

"Well, I don't know what all the fuss is about," said Jack. "I'm not even sure what Easter means." I had to hold myself back from laughing out loud because I knew what Jack would get this morning. He was about to get both barrels of Esther Miles; she had been up early on her knees, praying for what she might say—and, I was sure, praying for Jack Cunningham and his heart to receive God's words.

"Jack, do you know the story of Genesis and Exodus?" asked Esther, stepping away from her talk with Willie.

"My mother told me Bible stories when I was a boy. Her maiden name was Stein. She was a German Jew, and my old man thought she was something. My father was a Scotsman, and his family disapproved of the marriage, so in 1860, they moved here to Africa to settle. But she told me all of the stories about Abraham and Moses and how her people were God's chosen people.

"So let me ask you, sir," said Esther. "do you know how Jesus fits into the story?"

"I wouldn't have the faintest idea," he answered.

"Let me ask you this question, the most significant question in the universe." Esther paused, and Jack had a curious look in his eyes.

"What would that be?" he asked.

"Who is Jesus Christ to *you*?" she said. Jack stammered as he struggled for an answer.

"I don't know," he began. "I don't even know if the story is true or if it's just made up. So, to answer your question, this Jesus isn't anyone to me. He is not a part of my life."

"What if I told you the story is real? It happened, and many people witnessed the events of his life and reported it factually. You can't make this stuff up; their stories would have too many inconsistencies if they tried to fabricate a fairy tale. Would you like to hear the real story?" she asked.

"I think I would like that if it's not too long."

Chuck rolled his eyes, and Lydia laughed.

"I think I can accommodate that," she said with a grin, "just as long as Abigail sleeps. Shall we sit?" Lydia jumped into control mode and placed everyone around the table at their assigned seats. I offered my usual spot at the head of the table to Esther since she was about to become the center of attention. I watched her say a silent prayer before she began.

"Dear friends, you have heard the story of Abraham and about how he had a son in his old age with his wife Sarah, who was far past the years of childbirth. Abraham had a visit from three men who spoke as one, and they announced that he and his wife would have a son. The Scripture said that Sarah laughed to herself as Abraham sat at the entrance to the tent. The men questioned her as to why she would laugh. She denied that she had laughed, but these men were God in the flesh. The Bible describes them as angels, but let us not be fooled into believing they were only angels. When the Scriptures refer to 'the angel of the Lord,' they are talking about God himself. These three men were the Father, the Son, and the Holy Ghost, who appeared in the Old Testament in the flesh. They heard Sarah laugh in her soul, and she could not deny it. What is said in the soul is said to God.

"Then Abraham pleaded with God to spare the righteous in Sodom. But God told him he would go down to that place and see for himself if their sin was as great as the outcry against it. When the two men described as angels reached Sodom that evening, they met Abraham's nephew, Lot, who was living there, and he bowed low to greet them. This is where there is proof that these men were more than just angels. Lot called them his lords and bowed down to them. But in the book of Revelation, when John tried to bow down to the angel, the angel stopped him and said he should not do that because he was just a fellow servant.

"The following year, Sarah had a son at the age of ninety-one, and she named her son Isaac, which means 'laughter.' At some point, Abraham—and we can only guess because the Scriptures are unclear about Isaac's age at the time—but Abraham was told to take his son to a mountaintop and sacrifice him there. He left without consulting his wife and went on a three-day journey. He went to the place we now know is claimed by the Muslims as the place where Ishmael was taken to be sacrificed by his father, Abraham."

"That is why there is a fight," said Lydia. "Wow, that could never be settled, could it?"

"That is right, my dear, but the Bible says it was Isaac. Isaac was probably in his late teens, according to how the conversation with his father went. You can read some youth into his voice by the naivety of the questions.

"Abraham intended to follow through with what God had told him, no matter the task, to prove his obedience—even if it meant doing harm to the most precious possession he had in the entire world. The Scripture says that Isaac carried the wood, so we know he was much more than a child. So they built an altar, and Isaac demonstrated his total trust in his earthly father like Abraham had proven his complete trust in his heavenly Father. But just as Abraham was about to take the boy's life, God gave him a ram with his horns caught in a bush for the burned offering. So, God credited this act of obedience as righteousness to Abraham, and God made him a prophet.

"Isaac grew up and married Rebecca, and she gave birth to twins: Jacob and Esau. Jacob had twelve sons by various wives and concubines, and the sons became jealous of their younger brother, Joseph, because their father favored him. So, they tossed him down a well and then sold him into slavery, and he ended up in Egypt. Because of Joseph's favor with God, Joseph became the second in command to Pharaoh. There was a famine in the land, and Joseph saved Egypt because he stored up grain. His father and brothers were starving, so Jacob sent them to Egypt for food. When they arrived, Joseph recognized them, and eventually, they were reunited in Egypt. There, the Pharaoh gave them land to raise their sheep. But four hundred years later, they became enslaved. God made their life bitter, so they would want to leave the land and go to the land their father, Abraham, had been promised six hundred years before.

"So, in a series of miraculous events that included God speaking to Moses from a burning bush, Moses led the people out of Egypt. But Pharaoh had come to depend on the Israelites as his workers and refused to let them go. God then made a miracle to showcase His glory. God told Moses to tell the people to take a year-old lamb without defects to live in their home for four days and then sacrifice it. Just imagine that for a minute. You have seen lambs and how cute they are. You can cuddle them like a puppy. Imagine taking one in your home with your kids and then sacrificing and eating it. They were told to spread the blood over their doorways.

"When the Lord passed by and saw the lamb's blood, that home would be spared from the fate of death of the firstborn. When Pharaoh's own firstborn son died, he demanded the Israelites leave. There were six hundred thousand men, and with wives and children, the number would have been as high as two million. This event came to be known as the Passover. God instructed them to eat the lamb with their cloaks tucked under their belts, their sandals on, and their staffs in their hands. They were not to leave any part of the lamb uneaten in the morning but were instructed to burn all the rest. God also told them not to eat leavened bread; I believe it could be a reference to pride because of how yeast puffs up.

"When Pharaoh learned that the Israelites had encamped on the edge of the Red Sea, he had a change of heart and decided to pursue them and recapture them to bring his slaves back. The people cried out to Moses that they would all die, but the Lord told Moses to stretch out his staff, and the waters would part so the people could escape on dry ground. Then, the waters parted, and the two million people arrived safely on the other side. The Egyptians followed, but God closed the sea over them, and they all drowned."

At this point, I looked around at the faces of my friends while Esther was talking; they were glued to her every word. Jack, seated directly across from me, had a skeptical look on his face but, at times, seemed quite interested in her story.

"Fifteen hundred years later, when John the Baptist saw his cousin Jesus coming toward him, he said, 'Look, the Lamb of God who takes away the sins of the world.' John the Baptist knew the Scriptures and his role as a prophet to usher in the Messiah. Immediately, two disciples, John and Andrew, who were followers of John the Baptist, left him to follow Jesus.

"Now, Jesus knew the Scriptures and what the prophet Isaiah had said about the coming of the Son of Man seven hundred years earlier. When Jesus read from the scroll in the synagogue, from Isaiah 61, He said, 'The Spirit of the Lord is upon me, because he hath anointed me to preach the gospel to the poor; he hath sent me to heal the brokenhearted, to preach deliverance to the captives, and recovering of sight to the blind, to set at liberty them that are bruised, to preach the acceptable year of the Lord.' He would have also known about Isaiah 53, saying, 'Surely he hath borne our griefs, and carried our sorrows; yet we did esteem him not, stricken, smitten of God, and afflicted. But he was wounded for our transgressions, he was bruised for our iniquities: the chastisement of our peace was upon him, and with his stripes, we are healed.'"

"That is incredible; that was written seven hundred years before Jesus lived?" asked Dennis.

"No, what is amazing is that Esther can quote these Scriptures from memory," said Lydia.

"Do you want me to continue?" Esther asked, addressing Jack.

"Please do, ma'am: you can't leave me in suspense."

"All we like sheep have gone astray; we have turned everyone to his own way, and the Lord hath laid on him the iniquity of us all. He was oppressed, and he was afflicted, yet he opened not his mouth; he is brought as a lamb to the slaughter, and as a sheep, before her shearers are dumb, so he openeth not his mouth," she went on, continuing to quote Isaiah 53. I tried to be casual about watching Jack, but I could see in his face a reflection of Esther's words shimmering on his soul.

"When Jesus arrived in Jerusalem at the Passover, he was received as a political figure. Jesus knew that he would suffer and die on the cross. He tried to tell his disciples, but they didn't understand. They had watched Jesus do miracles, they were expecting him to drive the Romans out, and they knew he would put himself on the throne as the king of Israel. They were so at peace with him that they all fell asleep the night he was arrested, even though Jesus had asked them to stay awake with him.

"But Jesus knew his fate. In fact, he asked his Father if it were possible to take away this cup that God had called him to drink. But Jesus, just like Isaac, relented to his Father's will, was obedient unto death, and placed himself on the altar as the Lamb of God. And just as had been predicted fifteen hundred years before, they would be saved when Moses was told to sprinkle the lamb's blood over their doorways. We have the blood of Jesus that saves us."

"So, is that the story?" asked Jack. "Is that the end?"

"Not hardly—that is only the beginning. Do you know what today represents?"

"No, ma'am. Like I said, I thought it was the day that bunnies laid their eggs."

"We can save the egg story for another day. It appears that breakfast is about to be served. But this is the point of the whole thing:

Jesus died on the cross and was buried, and after three days, which is today, Jesus rose from the dead. He is the only one in the history of mankind who said he would come back from the dead and did it."

"You mean His spirit rose," said Jack.

"Not just His spirit: He rose from the dead in the flesh."

"Where is the evidence for that?" he asked.

"Because when the disciples entered the tomb, they found the burial cloth lying like someone had slipped out of it. They had wrapped the body like a mummy from His head to his feet. If someone had stolen the body like the Jewish leaders said happened, they would have taken it in haste and not taken time to unwrap it.

"There were over five hundred witnesses to the risen Jesus. In fact, the greatest skeptic of all was Thomas, one of His disciples. Thomas said he would not believe it unless he saw the nail holes for himself and could put his fingers in them and put his hand on Jesus' side. So Jesus visited again when Thomas was present and told Thomas to do just that. Thomas recognized Him and cried out, 'My Lord and my God!'

"In another instance, after Jesus' death and resurrection, the disciples decided they would go back to fishing to earn a living. They had fished all night and caught nothing, and on their way in at sunrise, they saw a man on the beach one hundred yards away. He called to them and asked if they had caught anything. They shouted, 'No,' and the man yelled, 'Cast your net on the right side of the boat.' When they did, the nets filled with fish. To the disciple Peter, this seemed all too familiar, as if it had happened before, and he realized it was Jesus. Then he jumped into the water and swam ashore. The other men struggled with the net and brought one hundred and fifty-three fish to the shore.

"You see, it is not only the death of Jesus on the cross and His blood that saves us, but His resurrection from the dead and what He did afterward that makes us believers. Jesus sat around the fire and ate with His friends; spirits don't eat fish. Our belief starts in our heads and turns our hearts and souls toward faith. And it is by our faith that we are saved by God's grace. We are all born blind to the reality of Jesus Christ."

"But how can a blind man see?" asked Jack.

"That is the question for the ages, isn't it? There is a story of a man born blind whom Jesus saw begging on the temple grounds. Jesus had just slipped away from the Pharisees, who tried to stone Him for making claims they didn't like. When He found this man, Jesus took dirt and spit in his hands, making mud. Then, He put the mud in the man's eyes and told him to wash in the Siloam Pool. When the man did, he could see. He had never seen Jesus before, so he couldn't have picked Him out of a crowd.

"Jesus said that He had come into the world for judgment so the blind might see, and those who could see would be made blind. You, Jack, were born blind, but on this Easter Sunday, you can be healed if you so desire. Jack, you could wake up like Ebenezer Scrooge and realize you did not miss Christmas. Then, you could celebrate it with Bob Cratchit and his family."

The kitchen door opened, and the parade of food carried by M'Culay's kitchen staff made its way to the table with a glorious meal of smoked ham, fried potatoes, chicken eggs, fresh milk, raised biscuits, berry jam, and butter. Everyone paused as the meal was laid out, and we waited for Esther to speak.

"Please take your seat at the head of the table, my dear husband," she said as she stood. I rose, and the rest of the men stood as Esther and I traded places and I pushed her into her seat. Then the men sat again, and I thought Esther might offer a prayer, but she sat silently.

"Will you pray for the meal, dear?" I asked.

"Yes, dear," she said, looking around at our friends and then bowing her head. "Let us pray. Almighty God, who through Your Son, Jesus Christ, overcame death on a cross and opened the gates of everlasting life for all who believe in Him, we celebrate this day of Christ's resurrection from the dead. May we be raised from eternal death and sin by Your life through the power of the Holy Spirit. We know that because of Your sacrifice, Your Spirit gave us life through Jesus Christ, our Lord. He lives and reigns with You at Your right hand, one God in three persons, Father, Son, and Holy Spirit, for now and forevermore.

"Lord, thank You for the gift of Abigail. Watch over and protect her, Lord, and make her strong. And Lord, thank You for protecting our lives last week from the enemy who desired to destroy us. Give us sight to see, hands to work, words to speak, and friends to share. Lord, grant us Your wisdom to live a life worthy of our calling. And bless this day, this farm, and all those who work it. Bless these friends, bless this food You have provided us for our bodies, and sanctify it by Your Spirit. And all this we pray in the holy and precious name of Jesus Christ our Lord. Amen."

I looked up, and Esther lifted her eyes; her face glowed like an angel.

CHAPTER 19

SPEAKING WITHOUT A VOICE

As we began to enjoy the breakfast, Jack cleared his throat loudly. "Esther, Have you ever led anyone to faith over breakfast?" he asked.

"No, I can't say as I ever have," she answered. I wondered what Jack might say next.

"I don't know what happened to me," he said. "I don't know if I can explain it, but something happened."

"What happened?" I asked.

"I don't know, but God just spoke to me."

"What did He say?" asked Esther.

"I heard a voice like a whisper that said, 'You are healed. The blind can see.' Then I felt something in my heart—like it skipped a beat—and now I feel different."

"Are you okay?" asked Lydia. "Maybe you should lie down."

"No, I'm not sick . . . I'm *healed*," said Jack. "I don't know what you said, but it was during your story. Maybe about the man born blind; I know I was blind, but now I can see. Everything my mother told me from childhood came together. All of her stories finally made sense. You told it just like her, except you finished it. I guess I was blind because the story didn't mean anything before. But now I see, from Abraham, Isaac, and Jacob all the way to Moses and the

prophets . . . it all fits with Jesus Christ and His resurrection from the dead. And now the story is finished."

"Who do you say Jesus is?" Esther asked.

"He is the Christ, the Son of the living God."

"He is who you say He is," said Esther. "We will need to talk after breakfast. I have so much that I need to tell you. You are like a child that just came into the world. Now the Scriptures will be opened up to you, and you will be able to see and understand them."

"Shall we eat before the food gets cold?" I said.

"Amen," said Chuck, reaching for the bowl of fried potatoes as the rest of us began to pass plates.

"You said you would tell me about the Easter Bunny and his eggs," said Jack, putting a slice of smoked ham on his plate.

"Yes, quite an interesting story indeed," she began. "It seems that the early church forbade eating meat, along with eggs, milk, and cheese. They were considered fruit from the animals we were to abstain from during the Lenten season. So that resulted in an abundance of eggs during Lent. The hens were safe, and no one told the birds not to lay. So, it was not until the end of Holy Week or Sunday morning that these foods could be consumed. Additionally, traditionally, eggs were colored red, likely in ancient Mesopotamia, to demonstrate the blood of Christ. When the flowers came out in spring, eggs were boiled with them to dye them.

"But here is the real reason behind the Easter egg. The shape of the egg symbolizes the rock that was rolled against the tomb, the shell symbolizes the tomb, and the egg symbolizes the resurrection of Christ bursting forth in a new life. Additionally, the egg is the perfect illustration of the triune God."

"Triune?" asked Jack.

"Yes, let me explain it to you. We have one God in three persons. Remember how I explained to you how God visited Abraham in three persons?"

"Yes, but I'm not sure exactly what you meant."

"Our God is a Father, a Son, and a Holy Spirit. Not three gods, but one God in three persons: one what and three whos. Similarly, though the egg is one thing, it has three parts: a shell, a yoke, and a white. And this egg is the life-giving model that God created to reproduce life. Even though a bird is one of the only animals to lay an egg, every animal uses this egg concept to create life. So, too, is Christ, the egg that came from heaven and broke His shell so everyone could live a new life. In John 14, Jesus said, 'I will pray to the Father, and he shall give you another comforter.' By this, he meant the Holy Spirit that will be with us forever. That is what has come on you, Jack. You said you felt different; that is the Holy Spirit."

"Is this going to change me?" asked Jack. "The last thing I want is to be some religious fanatic."

"You don't have to be a religious fanatic. That is someone who goes off the deep end by being devoted to religion. Being a Christian doesn't have to make you religious. In fact, faith in Christ does not follow the rest of the world religions. Religion is what Christ came to break with the Jewish leaders. He said there was a new way and declared *He* was the way, the truth, and the life."

"I'm not sure I follow what you are saying," said Jack, trying not to speak with his mouth full of food.

Esther finished chewing and then looked at him with her deep brown eyes. "All world religion is man's attempt to make himself acceptable to God. There are rules of conduct and rituals about worship, followed like a cookie recipe to make us into something that God will find acceptable."

"I thought that was the whole point of becoming accepted by God," said Jack.

"That is the point, but there is nothing we can do to deserve eternal life. It's a gift from God and nothing to be achieved by our own doing. We receive salvation even when we don't deserve it. When we were still sinners, God gave us His Son by His grace, and all those who believe in Him will be saved. So you see, it is not by our righteousness that we are saved, but because of His mercy and grace, which He gives to us as a free gift."

"So what now?" asked Jack.

"You will want to be baptized."

"Yeah, I've heard of that."

"It will be good; you will see. It is a public declaration that you believe, like a marriage, and then God will test you to see if your faith is real," said Esther.

"A test? What do you mean by a test?"

"I can't tell you what it is, but you will know when it happens. All I can tell you is to be ready, because it will come."

"This is certainly a lot of religion for one Sunday breakfast," said Chuck, looking around to get a laugh. I knew where Chuck was in his life. He was an aging man set in his ways, unable to walk the road to life because of all the obstacles he had put between himself and God for all these years. God could have cleared them all away instantly, but I suspected he, like many, was content to allow them to stay there. Then, he could be safe from having to change into the very thing he'd resented all his life.

"Fair enough, Chuck. What shall we talk about?" said Esther.

"How about the weather?" asked Chuck. "Do you think we have had enough rain for the crops this year?"

"Oh, there has been plenty, except today, which looks clear. What do you think, Chuck?" I asked.

"We could get a sprinkle this morning, but I bet it clears up for the afternoon," he said. I wondered if Jack or Dennis knew about the gathering that might be descending on the farm that day. I hadn't discussed it with them because it appeared Mary Cunningham might have been planning for a surprise party. *If it happens, it happens*, I thought. *It's hard to prepare for a gathering like that when you don't know if it will happen.*

"What is Mary doing the rest of her day today? We should have invited her out after church," I said, just to see how he might respond or if he would be like a cat covering up a fresh kill.

"Probably going to some social event after church," he said. I looked at Dennis to scrutinize his facial expression, but there he sat as if he were at a poker table holding a royal flush.

"We will have to have her out for a Sunday dinner soon," said Esther.

"She will be amazed at what I think happened here today," he said.

"I think a lot of people will be amazed, and many lives will change now because you have come to Christ," said Esther. Chuck rolled his eyes, likely annoyed that the conversation had turned back to religion. I could see him disengaging and hurrying to clean his plate.

"I have some work to do. I need to follow up on what we did out there on that back forty yesterday," said Chuck. "I want to ensure those coffee trees we put in are in straight rows. Besides, these clothes make me feel like I am back in Chicago, which is not a place I am longing to return to anytime soon." I didn't excuse him, Esther didn't excuse him—he didn't even ask to be excused. He simply pushed his chair away from the table and stood. "Good morning, ma'am," he said, grabbing the door handle and leaving the building. We all sat stunned, not knowing what to say. The step treads creaked under his weight, and I saw him cross the yard.

"Is he okay?" asked Esther.

"I think so," I said. "I'm not sure."

"I guess I should have been more sensitive; I should have been able to read his nonverbal language."

"You are right; you can tell what someone is saying by how they talk with their body," said Lydia."

"Sure, dogs do it all the time," I said. "Ever watch 'em talk with their tail, teeth, or ears? We are just the same way. We are submissive, angry, dominant, listening, or not listening."

"How can you tell if a person is not listening?" she asked.

"You just watch 'em; they will fold their arms across their chest every time."

"Wow, you are right," said Lydia. "I suppose if you can't tell that about a person just by watching them, then you will never be able to understand what they are saying with their words."

"I better go check on the baby," said Esther, pulling away from the table. Lydia made a move to follow her. The women stood, and then we men stood to excuse them.

"Got any more coffee?" asked Dennis once they had left the room. "I could use a warm-up." M'Culay, standing by the door, nodded and retrieved the pot in the kitchen.

"How about we get out of these clothes and take a morning drive up the valley?" I said.

"I would love to, but there is something you should know," said Jack. "I think it's supposed to be a surprise, but my wife, Mary, is coming out today with many friends for a potluck picnic luncheon. I think Reverend Michael is coming as well."

"Oh yeah! That was the last thing Michael told us when he left the farm last week. You didn't mention it when you arrived, so I figured . . ." I stopped because Jack had a big grin on his face. "Why the grin?" I asked.

"Mary," he said, shaking his head. "She is quite the girl. We have been married for ten years this year, and she is a pistol. When she gets an idea, there is no erasing it. I tried to tell her all that went on out here this week, and maybe we should give you guys a little peace and quiet, but she wouldn't hear of it. I thought it was only fair to warn you that she is coming."

"Does Lydia know?" I asked.

"I told her when I got here yesterday," said Dennis.

"So, in other words, we better get ready, right?"

"You better get ready for the likes of Mary. This old farm might never be the same after she comes." Jack's broad grin turned into full-out laughter, and Dennis and I laughed along, not knowing why we were laughing.

Epilogue

So, you have come to the end of this part of our story. There is another one coming soon, so stay tuned. I know you can't wait to meet Mary Cunningham; she is quite a girl.

I know this story was a lot to take in, with the birth of our daughter and the vicious men who attacked our farm. Blackwell wanted to kill us and burn us out just because of our mixed marriage. We developed great relationships with some new friends you likely came to love, like Dennis and Lydia Johnson, Blaney Percival, Reverend Michael Bartson, and Jack Cunningham. The part about the lion hunt—that is my secret, and I will take that one to the grave. Oh, and I hope you can also keep it a secret because Michael would be crushed if he learned the truth. Sometimes, things are just better left unsaid.

Lydia, it turned out, became a great friend of ours. She delivered our daughter with great skill and care as if she had attended nursing school, but then right in the middle of a gun battle. It was a great illustration that God brings another into the world to replace them when one person dies. My most favorite part of this story was telling you of how Jack Cunningham came to Christ. I love seeing a man raise from death to life.

World War I comes on the scene in my next book, and I join the fight as an army scout. Abigail becomes a little girl that her daddy adores, and I make a surprising friendship that no one will believe.

There is so much to tell you, and not all of it will be pleasant. But enough about that. If you have followed our story from the beginning with John and Betty Rivers, you will love the next sequel to our story. In fact, I will give you a taste by letting you read the first chapter of the next book, just to wet your whistle.

If you felt different about the life of Christ after reading any one of Mike Neil's books, I know he would love to hear from you. Please feel free to email him, or Facebook message him. I know how happy he would be.

Your Friend,

Lance Miles
Main Character
Africa Heart and Soul

A Tribute

This novel is dedicated to my wife, Susan Newschwander, who goes by Susan Neil. (I think she was relieved, when we married, to take on a shorter last name, but still, we always need to spell it.) I don't think I could have married anyone who loves me more than she does.

I was ten years old when I first met Sue. Our older sisters became best friends when we were in the seventh grade. Our mothers became friends, and then our dads became friends. I never imagined then that we would still be together all these years later. We began dating when she was sixteen and I was seventeen. Over our fireplace hangs a sign that says: "Of all the great love stories ever told, we love ours the best."

Sue and I carved out a life for each other because I loved her, and she respected me. She is still my best friend, and I tell everyone she is the girlfriend I live with, even though we have only been married since 1973—over fifty years. We have experienced the thrills of life together from the top of the roller coaster to the bottom, having lost two children together. We went on safari in 2005, and our lives were changed. Just like Johnathan Rivers discovering his wife on the plains of Africa, I think that same thing happened to me.

They say a lot of couples separate after the loss of a child. Still, for us, it made our marriage stronger knowing we had gone through the valley of the shadow of death together and survived. Adversity always makes you stronger if you let it change you. If you try to escape it, deny it, or run angry, it can harm you. If you blame others for your troubles, you will become a victim, and then there is only one person who is injured.

When you are young, you think you love your spouse, but after fifty years, you come to depend on the other, and you realize what the apostle Paul meant when he wrote about being one flesh. You know that you can live with them, but you know you could never live without them.

Susan is my wife and my best friend, my lover, the mother of my three children, and the one who made me into the man I have become. She has encouraged and shaped me by scolding me when I was off track, and telling me how proud she was to be my wife when my wheels were on the rails. Some time back, Sue said to me, "I married you all those years ago because I thought you were cute. I don't know when I realized how smart you are, but it was a long time ago." Can you even imagine what that does for a husband? She always promotes me to others and is so quick to tell people about my writing and artwork. She loves it when I write or draw, and is my greatest supporter. When I wrote my last book *Trees in the Mist*, we went on a trip to Maine and Massachusetts to do family research. At times, she seemed as excited as I was about the process, and maybe more.

That is the kind of girl I am married to, and this book is dedicated to her.

About the Author

Mike Neil is an author and artist whose first novel, the prequel to *Africa Heart and Soul*, was *The Miracle of Africa*, published in 2014. That book was followed in 2021 by *Trees in the Mist*, a historical fiction work based on Mike's research of his own family tree, going back all the way to the American Revolution.

A retired State Fish and Wildlife Officer, Mike currently serves as a national leader in the field of Police Chaplaincy, and is the founder and president of the Washington State Chaplain Foundation. Additionally, he is the founder of the National Police and Fire Chaplain Academy, and served two years as the Regional Director for Region 2 for the International Conference of Police Chaplains (six states). As the Senior Chaplain for the Washington State Patrol and the Department of Fish and Wildlife Police, Mike served for ten years helping to develop the program, leading a statewide team of professional police chaplains who support officers in various aspects and stages of their career. He is a recognized speaker and a Northwest pen and ink artist.

Mike and his wife Sue were childhood sweethearts and have been married since 1973, over fifty years. They are the parents of three children—one who lives nearby with his family, and two who have gone on to Heaven. Mike and Sue make their home in Gig Harbor, Washington.

www.mdneil.org

Coming soon! The story continues in:

The African Scout

———

CHAPTER 1

THE PISTOL

Standing on the porch of my farmhouse with my friends Dennis Johnson and Jack Cunningham, I looked up into the sky and took in the deep smell of the morning coming off the African hills. As the sun began to rise, puffy clouds played on the wind, seeming to race in a huff as if they were going somewhere important. It felt like a chapter had closed in my life, and a new day had dawned.

"Jack, how many folks will be coming to this picnic?" I asked.

"As many as my wife Mary can muster, I suppose. You know they call her a pistol," laughed Jack.

"You know I am not set up here for a large crowd. They can spread out on the grass, but it would be nice to have some tables for people to put their food on."

"Got any more of these planks?" asked Jack, looking at the new steps on the front porch.

"Yep, I have plenty of those," I said.

"You got a shop with hammer and nails and a saw?"

"I have it all," I answered.

"Then let's get building us some tables. Heck, we can even whip out some benches, so folks don't have to sit on the ground."

"I can get my workers to give a hand. Even though it's Easter Sunday, they are around, and since we are having an old-fashioned picnic, I know they will jump in."

"Let's get her done, then," said Jack, "Let's find those boys and that lumber pile."

"Okay. How about you guys take care of the tables and benches? I'll enlighten M'Culay about what is descending on us. He can get our boys on cleaning up the sheep droppings, and I will direct them in straightening up the yard. Then I can help the house crew to get the farm house presentable."

Jack and Dennis stepped off the porch and started for the barn. "Should I break the news to Esther?" I added. Just then, I heard the hinges squeak behind me and turned around to see my beautiful wife poking her head out of the door.

"News, Lance?" she asked with piercing eyes and a tight lip. I looked back at Jack and Dennis, who had stopped dead in their tracks. Esther stepped the rest of the way onto the porch, and Dennis's wife Lydia stood in the doorway behind her, holding our baby, Abigail. "What's going on, Lance?"

"I think I can explain," interjected Lydia, trying to rescue me from the fire.

"Am I the only one in the dark here; what's going on?" Esther turned to face Lydia.

"It looks like," began Lydia cheerfully, "Mary Cunningham has apparently organized a surprise picnic for you and Abigail this afternoon."

"On Easter Sunday? That's a family day, and people shouldn't be coming out to this farm. They should be staying home with their families."

"That's the point, Esther. Mary and I don't have family here in Africa, and lots of us Africans are in the same boat. We have friends, and we want to spend time with them. "

"And there will be lots of families and kids. It's going to be all church people."

"So why was I left in the dark?" asked Esther suspiciously.

"It was supposed to be a surprise picnic in honor of you and Abigail."

"Mary has worked very hard on this, and she is sure this is going to be a success for you," said Jack supportively.

"If you say so, Jack," said Esther, calming down. "Not much we can do about it now. I say let the games begin."

"That's the spirit," I said with a wink.

"You are not off the hook yet, mister," said Esther under her breath. Lydia gave me a bright smile from behind her, and I tried not to laugh.

The men turned and headed for the barn. Abigail began to fuss, and Lydia bounced her and rocked her in her arms. "Where are they going?" asked Esther.

"They are going to build some picnic tables and benches to put around the yard."

"If I had known we were having a picnic, I could have prepared for it this week."

"Yes, I know; I wanted to tell you, but I guess I just couldn't ruin the surprise."

"You know how I am about surprises; I can't believe you didn't tell me." Lydia backed away to give us privacy and went back into the house. Esther glanced over her shoulder and then reached back and closed the front door behind her, addressing me squarely. "So give it to me straight: exactly how many people are we expecting, Lance?"

"Hard to say for sure; I never got a number. Pastor Michael speculated about it when he left here last week, but he wasn't sure it would happen. I sort of forgot about it until this morning. I didn't want to you fret about it all week if there was nothing to it. I should have had a clue when Jack showed up yesterday. Apparently, he mentioned something to Lydia, but he didn't say anything to me. I only found out just a few minutes ago myself."

"It might be fun. An old-fashioned picnic on the farm for Easter Sunday dinner," Esther said with a smile. "Okay, you are off the hook, but we'd better make this place ready. Remember all the work we did when John and Betty showed up here two years ago. That took us weeks, and now we have a couple of hours. Oh well, it is what it is. These folks are going to find out who we are."

"And that is a good thing, right?" I asked.

"The problem is you never get a second chance to make a good first impression. I always like to put my best foot forward."

"Wow, that is brilliant. I never thought about it before, but you are right about the first impression. It's a lasting impression, and it's hard to change."

"That's why you always have to put your best foot forward."

"Which one is it? They both look the same to me, except this one has a scuff mark on the boot."

"It's the right foot, and not necessarily the foot on the right side of your body, but it is the right foot versus the wrong foot. If we just get off on the right foot, we will always make a great first impression."

"You are quite a girl," I said. "I am amazed every day by your wisdom. I am amazed every day at your beauty, and I am amazed every day how you love me and teach me. I am so proud to be your husband, and I am so proud of who you are." Esther tried to hide her emotions, but her cheeks flushed beneath her warm, brown skin, and then she came out like a flower in full bloom with her best Esther smile.

"But darling, you are the one who needs to be praised for all you do on this farm. Nurturing, protecting, and loving me, you are the man. We'd better get going; we have work to do," she said, throwing her arms around my neck and snuggling my cheek. "When I get fully recovered from having this baby," she whispered. "You are in trouble, mister." I laughed to myself, knowing what she meant. I kissed her on the lips and then bounded off the porch to get to my chores. If my feet touched the ground, I didn't know it because the wings of my heart gave me a lift as if I were flying. *I wonder what it's like to be in one of those flying machines. I wonder if they will ever catch on, or if it's just a passing fancy. I suppose one day they could make a machine that could take a man to the moon . . .*

For the next several hours, we did everything we could think of to get the farm ready for a church potluck picnic. I checked in on the progress in the barn and found they had built eight sturdy tables and sixteen benches.

"Are you guys expecting the whole British army?" I asked.

"Like I said before," said Jack, "you don't know Mary."

"Where do you want 'em?" asked Dennis.

"How about on the north side of the house in that long stretch of grass? I think that's the best grass for a picnic. Besides, I believe we want to avoid the south side, if you know what I mean," I said, remembering the tragedy that had befallen us just a week earlier, and the men who died there.

"Obviously, that is the best place to have a picnic, but not today. How heavy are the tables; can we carry them out to the north side?"

"You have plenty of manpower here. This will be easy," said Jack.

"But we'd better get them out quick, because I have a feeling Mary will be showing up with her friends any time now." I pulled out my watch, and the hands said one-thirty.

"We missed lunch," I noted with a smile.

"Yeah, well there will be so much food here in a little while you will be glad you didn't have lunch." I followed our boys as they lugged the heavy tables across the yard, and then I directed them to place them in rows. I thought about how I had always referred to my workers on the farm as boys and considered how that might be demeaning to them. I always called Esther my girl, and that didn't seem demeaning. Maybe I was just too sensitive?

These were boys, most of them sixteen to twenty years old. They were boys just like Jason, John and Betty Rivers' adopted son. I suppose if I referred to M'Culay or Willie as one of my boys that might be demeaning, but maybe not. That could be a term of endearment, just like I might refer to Dennis or Chuck as my boys. *Just like I thought: I guess I am just too sensitive because of my girl. But times they are a-changing. I suppose that, one day, people will be so politically correct that to refer to someone in an endearing place in your life as one of your boys will be demeaning to them. No wonder I hate politics, I never did anything in my life just to be popular. If I had done that I would never have had Abigail.*

I heard a shout from across the yard and one of my boys was pointing toward the road. I ran to see about the commotion and then saw the parade of wagons and the mass of people heading toward our driveway. *Oh Lord, what has she done? There must be eighty to a hundred people in that march.* The thought crossed my mind that I hoped it was Mary, and not some vigilante group coming out to protest the death of their family members killed last week.

"Who is it?" I yelled to Jack across the yard.

"Oh, it's Mary all right, and Pastor Michael is leading the pack. I told you there would be a mass; heck there must be fifty people there." *Fifty . . . whom is he kidding?* I quickly counted by fives the heads I could see, and there were sixty. One, two, three, four, five, six, seven wagons. One, two, three, four, five, six, seven, eight, nine, ten horses with lone riders. More heads were popping up in the wagons as they made their turn down the driveway. Kids, adults, old folks; you could hear them talking as if they were a crowd at a carnival. My stomach churned as I saw their faces, wondering how I would greet them. *I hate public speaking.* I turned and ran for the house, knowing that Esther would be my saving grace. I bounded up the steps, and the door opened as I arrived. She came out with her eyes wide and her mouth open gazing at the crowd and I stopped dead in my tracks.

"Can you believe it?" I said.

"No, I can't believe it; there must be fifty people there."

"I think it's more like sixty or seventy."

"Will you greet them, dear?" I turned and looked at the mob and could feel a pit in my stomach, and my knees were shaking."

"Oh, come on . . . this is your farm. I am just the wife; you can speak." Esther put her hand on my shoulder to strengthen me and then began to whisper. "Father, bless my husband, fill him with Your spirit and give him Your confidence and Your strength to speak to these friends. They have come out here to encourage us; Lord, give us Your words to inspire them and welcome them to our home, in the name of Jesus."

I thought the pit would do away with her prayer but at least my knees weren't knocking as the wagon pulled up to the front of the house. I put my arm around Esther, and we faced the mob. Willie stepped out to meet Pastor Michael and take the reins of his horse as he dismounted and shook Chuck's hand. People began crawling out of the wagons like an over population of lemmings ready to migrate. "Sixty-five," whispered Esther. "Looks like a solid sixty-five."

"About what I figured," I said, waiting for the people to assemble. Jack stepped in to lend a hand to a woman who his wife, Mary, to help her down from the first wagon in the line. "That must be Mary, do you remember her?"

"Oh, yes, she is a wonderful woman; so friendly, I have chatted with her at church many times. She greeted us last week; you remember."

"Yes, I do remember her," I said under my breath, following suit with Esther's tone of voice. Everyone was laughing and talking like they had just arrived at a circus, ready to see a parade of elephants. That would have been something to see in New York, but here, you might glimpse such a thing any day. But a picnic with sixty people; now *that* would surely be a sight you would not see just any day. But for an Easter Sunday, with family and friends, it was an elegant treat indeed, just as long as you didn't have to stand up in front of them and speak.

Michael waited for Jack to escort Mary through the people, and then the three of them stepped up to the porch with us to face the mass of smiling faces. Mary wore a red dress that seemed a little tight for her weight. Her cheeks were rosy and her dark curls came down on her shoulders. She had bright red lips and dark eyes. Her warm smile and engaging spirit said volumes as to why she could draw a crowd.

As I opened my mouth, my mind went blank. *Where is John Rivers when you need him,* I thought. And then the words spilled out like coffee beans from a cut in a burlap sack.

"Dear friends, we are so touched that you have come out here to be with us on this Easter Sunday. You have caught Esther and me utterly speechless. And that is a tricky thing to find Esther without words." I looked over at her smile while the crowd chuckled, and spotted Lydia standing behind us with Abigail in her arms, wrapped tightly in a blanket. "I know why you have come; believe me, we are touched. That you would take time away from what you are doing to come out and support us and to celebrate the birth of our daughter is an honor and a blessing." I could see that Mary was like popcorn in hot oil ready to explode, so I paused to see if she would pick up the ball and run with it.

"I have told you so much about this couple, everyone," she began, addressing the crowd. "I know that this day will be a blessing from God. I know that Lance and Esther will be available all day to greet us and to get to know us more.

"Lance and Esther, we have been preparing for this picnic all week and we have such a fantastic day planned for you both to enjoy on your beautiful farm. I hope we are not intruding, but we want to celebrate the birth of your daughter. We want to prove that we are sincere about embracing and accepting you as members of our community. Nearly everyone we asked accepted our invitation to come out here with us today and I know I speak for everyone in hoping this is not an imposition. I would try to make the introductions, but as you can see, that might take us well into the afternoon. We thought we would get an earlier start, but Michael went long on his sermon."

She smiled, and Pastor Michael pursed his lips and squinted his eyes at her good naturedly. Then she laughed, and the crowd roared. I could see Mary's fingers itching as she spoke, wanting to get her hands on the baby. Then she turned, stretching her arms out to Lydia, who began to hand off Abigail, checking Esther's face for the go-ahead.

"Dear friends," continued Mary, unwrapping Abigail for all her friends to see. "This is the princess of our event today, 'the belle of the ball,' as John Fletcher used it in his play, *The Beggars Bush*. Her name is Abigail, and she was born just last week, as you all know. She came early, and so she must be still quite fragile, and I am almost afraid to hold her. But you all know the issues her parents are facing and the racism that floats just under the surface of our community. Today, my dear friends, we are here to make a statement. We are here to extend our hand of love and acceptance to a dear couple who loves our God and desperately needs our support and devotion. Pastor Michael, would you lead us in prayer to start the day? Will you bless this farm and cleanse it from the evil that came here last week?" Mary cuddled Abigail in her arms as if she were holding a fragile vase.

"I would love to," Michael said, stepping front and center on the porch as if standing in his church pulpit. "Let us pray." Michael paused in silence for just a few seconds before he began. "Father, we praise you because you are the God of the universe, the God of the heavens and the earth, who is so wonderful and beautiful that we cannot even imagine who you are with our feeble minds.

"We thank you, God, for the things of this life that you have made in all your creation, from the mighty elephant to the smallest ant. We thank you for the mountains, the skies, and the prairies. And we thank you, Lord, for creating mankind, especially us, so we might experience all of your beautiful things, and might experience the things that bring us happiness, and that you would walk us through the times that bring us sorrow.

"Today, Lord, we are here to celebrate the lives of two people who are dear to us. We are here to consecrate this farm and to cleanse it from the evil that invaded here this past week. We pray for protection over these borders from the sinister forces in our world that would seek to harm such a beautiful setting and this incredible family.

"Lord, be with us today as we share our lives, love, and faith. And Lord bless this little Abagail, who has come in this world. May her life be long, healthy, and prosperous; may she grow into a person who has crossed racial lines and broken the chains of racial pride. Lord, we are entering a new millennium where race will no longer cause men to fight. And we will be able to live in a world of peace in you where all mankind will live together as one, regardless of the color of their skin.

"And now, Lord, watch over and protect us today. Bless this incredible bounty that has been so lovingly prepared. Bless this food to our bodies and bless the hands that have prepared it, carefully packed it in wagons, and brought it here today as a celebration. And all this, my dear friends, we pray in the precious and Holy name of Jesus our Lord on this wonderful day of His resurrection from the dead, Amen."

Michael looked up, wondering what to do next. Mary handed Abigail to Esther as if she might break during the exchange.

"Hey Jack," called Esther, taking the child in her arms. "Come up here." Jack's face wrinkled as he climbed the front steps, then grinned as if the lamp's light had just been lit. "I think there is something you might like to say." Mary's face went cold, and her hands fell at her side as Jack put his hands on her shoulders and faced her squarely.

"I am born again today," he said, turning around to the crowd. "Today I found faith in Christ." The people began to smile and nod, and gave up a round of applause, signaling their happiness at the news. Within a few minutes, they all returned to the loud chatter it had been when they were getting out of the wagons. At Jack's announcement, Mary threw her arms around his neck, and joy filled her face.

"How . . . what happened? You have to tell me," she squealed.

"There will be plenty of time for that," said Jack. "We don't want to delay our friends' lunch with the details. Let's have a picnic; I think everyone is hungry."

"We can talk," said Mary. Okay, everyone." Mary held her hands up and waited for just a few seconds while the crowd quieted again. "Let's unload the wagons. It looks like there are tables over there in the yard, so if you brought a basket, bring it over, and we will organize the food. Phil, you are in charge of the games, so get with Lance and explain the plan. Where would you like us to park the wagons?"

"We will take care of the wagons," I said. "You take care of the food and the people; the wagons and the horses are easy. Chuck, will you get with Phil and help him with the games?" I realized how skillful I was at weaseling out of putting myself front and center in a crowd. I knew if I partnered with Phil, I would be in danger of running the games. I didn't want to be in charge of anything. I just wanted to enjoy the day and partake in the fun as a spectator. It had been a hell of a week, and I didn't need any more stress. *Just let someone else take charge for a change.*

I glanced out at the wagons to see where I might park them as folks were unloading baskets and boxes and carrying them across the yard. They looked like porters on safari. *Oh my goodness, that brings back memories; I haven't thought about that for a while.* Just then, I spotted a horse and a lone rider making the corner at the end of the drive. I had a pit in my stomach and felt for my sidearm. I backed up and felt for the front door, then stepped back through it, not taking my eyes off the intruder. The man had a dark hat and a long coat. My gun belt was hanging on a hook just inside the door, and I grabbed it and wrapped it around my waist and cinched the buckle. I always kept it loaded, but pulled it from the holster and spun the cylinder just to make sure before putting it back in its place.

I stepped back out onto the porch for another look and the warmth of relief washed over me as I recognized the rider as Blaney. "It's Blaney," I shouted. "Blaney is here." Esther looked up from the yard, and Lydia came out of the house behind me, carrying Abigail.

"Blaney!" shouted Lydia. I jumped off the porch to greet him as he rode up in the front yard. Jack Cunningham had beaten me to his horse, and Dennis was not far behind. Willie was there to take the reigns as he dismounted and turned with a broad grin.

"I heard there was a party going on here today, and didn't want to miss it," he laughed, stretching out his hand to Jack. "How you boys doing out here?" I took his hand and gripped it like a war bunkmate.

"Thanks for coming, Blaney," I said. "The sight of you is good for sore eyes." Willie handed Blaney's horse, named Skip, to Kimane, our horseman, who led Skip toward the coral. Willie barked Swahili instructions and Kimane ran across the yard, leading the horse at a trot.

"I see you have your hog leg handy," he said. "That's a good thing; you need to keep it handy."

"What do you know?" I asked with suspicion as his comment.

"Nothing," said Blaney. "But don't forget what we did out here. Those men have friends, and people around these parts are talking and grumbling. I haven't heard anything specific, but I just know there is a lot of talk."

"Do you think they will come at us again?" I asked.

"Look, I don't mean to worry you," he continued. "But don't count nothin' down and out. These men are fueled by their hatred, and not by their love of mankind. They are not like you and me. They don't even have the same thought processes. We live in by light of day; men like this lurk in the shadows and live in the darkness. They don't even realize there might be a God. They were raised by folks who grew up in a harsh and bitter world. They only know one thing: take what you want when you can. And if someone threatens to rise above them, they will nudge them out of their place or take 'em out if they have to."

"You're right; I can't even think like that," I said.

"Just be aware of it, that's all. You have a beautiful farm here; something men would kill for. There are very few men your age who are in your station in life. They are bound to be jealous, and now they see you with your beautiful wife. If she were white, you would be very influential. But I am sorry and embarrassed to say that will likely never happen. I can't explain mankind, and why men crave power. I can only try to be wise enough to get ahead of it."

"We could talk about this stuff all day," said Jack. "But that ain't what you came out here for. There's a lot to be done to help get this party going. The rest can wait for another day . . ."

Other Books by Mike Neil

One family. One musket. Three stories across time.

Follow the tales of bravery, loss, adventure, and love across time and discover how those who came before us can teach us about who we are today.

Available on Amazon.com or wherever books are sold

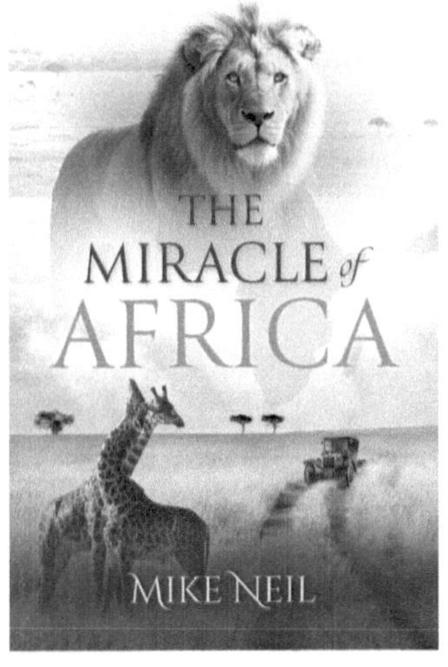

Love. Loss. Adventure. Devotion.

New hope emerges in a rekindled marriage after the loss of a child, against the backdrop of the wild African bush.

Available on Amazon.com or wherever books are sold